MAHONEY'S
CAMARO

MAHONEY'S CAMARO

A CRIME NOVEL
MICHAEL J. CLARK

Published by ECW Press
665 Gerrard Street East
Toronto, Ontario, Canada M4M 1Y2
416-694-3348 / info@ecwpress.com

This is a work of fiction. Names, charac-
ters, places, and incidents either are the
product of the author's imagination or are
used fictitiously, and any resemblance to
actual persons, living or dead, business
establishments, events, or locales is
entirely coincidental.

LIBRARY AND ARCHIVES CANADA
CATALOGUING IN PUBLICATION

Clark, Michael J., 1969–, author
    Mahoney's Camaro : a crime novel /
Michael J. Clark.

Issued in print and electronic formats.
ISBN 978-1-77041-403-7 (softcover)
ISBN 978-1-77305-294-6 (PDF)
ISBN 978-1-77305-293-9 (EPUB)

    I. Title.

PS8605.L36236M34 2019   C813'.6
C2018-905347-X   C2018-905348-8

Cover design: Michel Vrana
Author photo: Christine Bradley Portraits

The publication of *Mahoney's Camaro* has been generously supported by the Canada
Council for the Arts which last year invested $153 million to bring the arts to Canadians
throughout the country and is funded in part by the Government of Canada. *Nous
remercions le Conseil des arts du Canada de son soutien. L'an dernier, le Conseil a investi 153
millions de dollars pour mettre de l'art dans la vie des Canadiennes et des Canadiens de tout
le pays. Ce livre est financé en partie par le gouvernement du Canada.* We acknowledge the
support of the Ontario Arts Council (OAC), an agency of the Government of Ontario,
which last year funded 1,737 individual artists and 1,095 organizations in 223 communities
across Ontario for a total of $52.1 million. We also acknowledge the contribution of the
Government of Ontario through the Ontario Book Publishing Tax Credit, and through
Ontario Creates for the marketing of this book.

ONTARIO ARTS COUNCIL
CONSEIL DES ARTS DE L'ONTARIO
an Ontario government agency
un organisme du gouvernement de l'Ontario

Canada Council
for the Arts

Conseil des Arts
du Canada

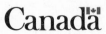

PRINTED AND BOUND IN CANADA   PRINTING: FRIESENS 5 4 3 2 1

MIX
Paper from
responsible sources
FSC® C016245

For Carol

CHAPTER ONE

JUNE 9, 1985, WINNIPEG
1:04 A.M.

Steve Mahoney didn't like the way Unit 36 was idling. Although the source of the miss could have been anyone's guess — a fouled spark plug, a gummy carburetor, maybe a cracked distributor cap — Mahoney already knew the answer: Unit 36, the '73 Chevrolet C30 chassis cab, was the oldest member of the Hook Me Up Towing company fleet, with more than 300,000 miles on the odometer and at least 150,000 up-and-down miles on the Holmes 440 wrecker boom. There was little point in trusting the readings from the instrument panel. The jumbled odometer had ceased rotations at 52,375 and six-tenths. The speedometer worked on occasion, a bouncing red needle that never went over 25 miles per hour, regardless of the actual speed. The floor-mounted stick shift was doing its best to jump out of the truck entirely. Mahoney would keep his right hand firmly on the shift knob for the first part of his tour, which started at 9 p.m. The ensuing hand cramp would set in around one in the morning. When the pain had started to creep in, Mahoney checked his digital watch: 1:07 a.m. Right on schedule.

Mahoney and Unit 36 were next in line at Boondoggles on McPhillips Street, the only drive-through burger shack north of Inkster Boulevard that kept the lights on into the wee hours. Boondoggles looked more like a 1970s' Fotomat than a mecca for the late-night munchies, strictly drive-through, with no walk-up service entrance. Patrons at this hour weren't too picky; the purpose of the greasy offerings was to act as a sponge, an attempt at soaking up the booze that had flowed so freely just hours before. Mahoney fiddled with the one interior feature of Unit 36 that still worked, the cigarette lighter. As the metal coil warmed, he looked at the car ahead of him, a rusty Country Squire station wagon. The old Ford was at capacity, with at least four drunk, stoned, or drunk and stoned teenaged girls in the rear. Mahoney settled on drunk when the tailgate swung open for a vomit volley from a skinny brunette. Their eyes met after the second coming of the pizza, Old Dutch Rip-L chips, and at least half-a-dozen Labatt Lites. Mahoney was impressed that she still had enough spunk to lob a bird in his direction. She smiled after the gesture for about five seconds, which was right about the time the third queasy wave hit her delicate constitution.

The lighter popped. Mahoney brought the red glow up to his Old Port Colt. He pulled down the cheap add-on sun-visor mirror and rubbed at his chin as he assessed his face. His three-day beard was starting to overtake his attempt at a Tom Selleck–style moustache. His shoulder-length, dirty blond mop of curls could be only partially contained by a dirty company baseball cap. The beard helped to hide the pocked landscape aftermath of adolescent acne. His best feature was his eyes, a pair of deep psychedelic blue pools that made up for his nondescript, six-foot-two frame. Mahoney was thin, but he certainly wasn't fit. The regular diet of Colts helped to keep his waist size from increasing past 32 inches, while the late-night cheeseburgers made sure that it never shrank below that measurement. He had strength, the kind you get from blue-collar lifting and stretching, without all that annoying definition.

Mahoney started to ease up on the clutch as the bags of burgers were passed into the drunk-girl station wagon. The driver seemed to be more involved with food distribution than moving ahead. At one in the morning, Mahoney knew that any revolving light in the rearview mirror was enough to get a driver's attention, especially one who had passed the designated driver threshold some four beers ago. He flipped the switch for the oversized Mars amber beacon. The driver responded with a forward throttle blip that smeared a red-head's face against the rear window. Mahoney smiled as he watched her distorted expression disappear into the night.

The attendant at the window wasn't familiar with Mahoney, though she had memorized the company greeting from the training pamphlet. "Welcome to Boondoggles, home of the Triple Cheese Yes Please, can I take your order?" The chain's signature sandwich, a double-patty greaser with heavily-processed versions of cheddar, mozzarella, and Monterey Jack. To the first-time late-night patron, it sounded like the second coming. Mahoney knew from experience that the only thing coming from it would be a phone call for a sick day.

"Gimme four single cheeseburgers and a chocolate shake, thin," he said. "Thin" was important to anyone behind the wheel, especially with a jumpy stick shift. The Boondoggles thick shake was more like the chocolate malts at the Malt Stop, cleverly hidden in the basement of the Bay downtown. Attempting to use a straw to import the contents could result in a collapsed lung, or maybe even an aneurysm.

Mahoney handed over a 10-spot to the attendant. As usual, he was quietly concerned that he received better than three dollars in change in return. The paper-wrapped cheeseburgers were already starting to turn the brown paper bag translucent in spots. "Thanks for your gobble at the Doggle," she said. Mahoney only heard about half of it clearly, as the phrase was partially swallowed by the sliding window and the crackle of the two-way radio. "Base to thirty-six, base to thirty-six. What's your twenty? Over."

Mahoney picked up the microphone and clicked. "McPhillips and Stardust, Dolores. Just grabbing the breakfast of champions. Over." The voice at the other end of the transmission laughed and coughed at the same time, a damp smoker's cough. "That cat food is gonna stop your heart cold one of these days. Over."

"And four packs a day won't? Over."

"Fig you, Baloney, and your little dog too. Over." As raw as the off-air conversation could get at the Hook Me Up office, Mahoney knew that the on-air banter for the two-way had to be kept PG, thanks to a few complaints that had made their way to the Canadian Radio-Television and Telecommunications Commission. Someone was always listening, even if it was a fat kid in a basement with a Radio-Shack scanner and virgin ears.

"Whaddya got, Dolores? It better not be some drunk rich kid's Trans Am at Night Moves, cause I'm nowhere near it. Over." Mahoney waited for the dispatcher to chastise him for his insolence with a few *figs*, maybe an offer to go multiply himself repeatedly. Instead, there was a pause. Dolores always paused when it was a bad one. Mahoney knew that the timing was right for a bad one. High school graduation season was in full swing throughout the city. Many schools were still trying to push the designated-driver concept, though the reality was that at least two teens would die that weekend in closed-casket crashes.

"It's a cop call," said Dolores. "North Main Street boat launch. Got a car in the water. Did you get that fiddling cable fixed on the fiddling winch yet? Over."

"It's as strong as your breath. Ever heard of a fiddling Tic Tac? Over."

Dolores coughed. "Ever heard of a ritual killing? Over."

"Got it, Dolores — thirty-six over and out." Mahoney hung up the mic. He steered with his knees while he ate.

It took Mahoney about 15 minutes to get to the North Main Red River boat launch. It would have taken less than 10 if it wasn't for the media blockade. Mahoney had attended to numerous bad calls where the reporters were the first on the scene, thanks to their constant monitoring of the emergency frequencies. The practice was becoming a sizable thorn in the side of the Winnipeg Police Department. Mahoney knew, like most Winnipeggers, that the force was still feeling the sting of negative publicity from a few high-profile cases in the last few years, cases that had been anything but positive in their outcome.

The third trial for Thomas Sophonow was under way, with many citizens quietly convinced that he had been railroaded into the role of the Cowboy Killer who had strangled Barbara Stoppel in the bathroom of the Ideal Donut Shop. Candace Derksen had been found in January, hog-tied and left to die in a shed within walking distance of her family home. Paul Clear had been murdered by two of Winnipeg's not-so-finest in the summer of '81. The pair was convinced that he had snitched on them for their on-duty burglary hobby. One of the cops was Clear's brother-in-law.

At the entrance to the boat launch, a skinny rookie was keeping the reporters at bay. He signalled to Mahoney to head through as the respective news outlets snapped their pictures and filled their Betacams with the barricaded scene. The CKND van tried to follow Mahoney in, stopping quickly when the driver locked eyes with the rookie's icy glare. The rookie motioned to another officer in an idling cruiser who quickly got the hint, blocking the gravel access road with two tons of black-and-white Ford LTD.

Mahoney looked ahead to the riverside activity. The road was thick with black-and-whites and unmarked detective units. An ambulance passed him on the left, looking to be in anything but a hurry, its emergency lights dark. Mahoney saw why as he started the decline to the Red River. The morgue-mobile. It was a nondescript, windowless black Ford Econoline, usually seen in the grainy pictures of the local papers. Mahoney could see the harbourmaster runabout in the water. The boat's driver was talking to a police diver, who nodded his goggled head attentively before heading back down to the watery crime scene. The stage had plenty of backlighting, thanks to the side-mounted floodlights of the *MS Paddlewheel Queen*. The riverboat had practically been at its berth near the Northgate Copa dinner hall when one of the passengers noticed the red lights in the water. The previously upbeat River East Collegiate Class of 1985 had quieted considerably. The deck was lined with boys in rented tuxedos and girls in what would most likely be the second-most expensive dress of their lives. Most watched in stunned silence. Some girls were crying. Mahoney figured there was about as good a chance of these grads going all the way tonight as there was for the waterlogged car below to start its engine and drive away.

CHAPTER TWO

Mahoney had enough room to flip Unit 36 around to reverse down the boat launch. Even with his rear spotlights on, he couldn't make out the car's shape in the dark brown water. Mahoney hated pulling cars out of the Red; the brown silt would make a mess of the cable, which would need to be uncoiled and cleaned after his shift. Most of the cars retrieved from the river were freshly stolen, though every few years the water level would drop to reveal an impressive collection of muddy cars that had been there for some time. A car retrieved quickly from its watery grave might see the road again, after a considerable amount of cleaning and tear down.

That was the story behind Jerry "Wallbanger" Waller's Corvette, a beige '75 Stingray ragtop that had been the victim of a seized parking-brake adjuster. The owner had been distracted by a working girl's services when the brake slipped, near the Alexander Docks. Legend has it that he finished during splashdown. Luckily, the top was down at the time, and both blower and blowee were able to escape. Waller saw the whole thing; his truck was Unit 32 and he'd been parked at the end of Alexander, keeping an eye on the transaction. Waller was the senior pimp and drug dealer at Hook Me Up. Mahoney would reluctantly provide transportation services for the prostitutes on occasion, leaving the job of muscle to Waller, a regular at the European Health Spa. Waller used to be as skinny as Mahoney, until he had his "Charles Atlas Moment," when a fellow spa patron turned him on to black-market steroids. When he wasn't pumping iron, Waller concentrated on the distribution of Talwin and Ritalin from his truck cab. The combo was better known to junkies as Poor Man's Heroin or Ts and Rs. Low-grade coke, shrooms, and weed rounded out the mix.

Mahoney got out of the truck and let out enough slack in the cable to toss the hook to the diver. He retrieved a small boat fender from the bed of the wrecker, attaching it with a carabiner to the cable loop at the base of the hook. This made it easier for the diver to grab the hook when it hit the water and the fender quick to remove and toss back to the shore. Mahoney grabbed his rubber boots from under the tow straps strewn across the bed. As he approached the river's edge, the diver poked his head above the water. Mahoney lobbed the cable towards him. It never went well when the police divers tried to return the boat fender, because it always fell just short of dry land. The edge of the boat launch was constructed of long concrete beams that had been secured into the riverbank with steel rebar. Mahoney knew they would be slippery, which would result in one of two things: wet pants or a full-on booter. He swore out loud when his right boot slipped, filling it to the brim and soaking most of his pant leg. Two for two.

He stood at the water's edge, balancing on one leg as he dumped out the contents of the rubber boot. He could hear the hook at the end of the cable clanging on the submerged car, an attachment that was never an easy task in the Red. Visibility below the water line was arm's length at best, by feel when the current was swift. Helping the situation was something unexpected for an underwater parking job: the lights. Mahoney squinted, trying to figure out what kind of car it was by the headlights. He was so deep in thought that he hardly noticed the veteran plainclothes detective who had ambled up next to him. "You'd think they would have shorted out by now, wouldn't they?"

The question startled Mahoney, though he felt that he had managed to conceal it, until he spoke. "Shorted? Shorted out what?" He realized what the detective meant as the words left his mouth, feeling even more foolish for saying them. "Yeah, must be one hell of a battery, I guess."

"Made the difference in finding this one fresh," said the detective. Mahoney gave him the quick once-over: mid-forties, salt-and-pepper buzz cut, probably ex-military, probably a career cop since his mid-twenties. The detective reached into his blazer for a crumpled pack of Player's. He offered the pack to Mahoney as he lit the cigarette with a swift click from a red Bic lighter. Mahoney shook his head, and the detective stowed the pack. "Trying to quit, eh? Well, good luck with that." He pointed at the water as he exhaled. "Shit like this doesn't tend to allow for the dismissal of your favourite vices. See enough of it, and you might even start some up you didn't know you had."

"What do you mean exactly, finding it *fresh*?"

"Fresh?" The detective chuckled as he rubbed his eyes. "That just means a lot less gross to look at when they come out of the water. You should see what some of the spring thaw stuff looks like. About the only way you know that it even is a body is the hair or the clothes. The rest of it just looks like a goopy mess. A big, stinky, goopy mess."

Mahoney felt the Boondoggles bounty shift to the left of his stomach as the visual possibilities of the current victim entered his mind. The detective gave him a nudge. "I think he's ready for you."

Mahoney looked at the water and saw the diver was giving him the thumbs up. He headed back to Unit 36 to winch up the submerged car. The cable spooled up lazily as Mahoney watched the swirling water. The lights of the mystery car were starting to flicker as the cable tightened. The car lurched to the left from its underwater parking spot. Mahoney knew that there was little that the police diver could do to attach the cable underwater. Judging from the lurch, the diver had decided on the lower control arm on the driver's side. The winch laboured. The car's front tires reached the first piece of submerged concrete when its lights went dead, its pedigree still hidden from view. Mahoney twisted the floodlight closest to him towards the emerging form. *What the hell is it?* he thought. The tires started to work their way up the ramp when the lights began to flicker again. They were dimmer now, though Mahoney didn't need them to know what the car was. As the rest of the car rolled onto the boat launch, his thoughts were immediately made audible.

"Holy shit, man," said an unseen teenage motorhead from the deck of the *Paddlewheel Queen*. "It's a fucking Camaro!"

1:48 a.m.

Mahoney kept his distance as the crime technicians, uniformed cops, and the salt-and-pepper detective descended upon the scene. Some of the media outlets had decided to shoot photos and reporter video commentary from the nearby North Perimeter Bridge, out of reach from the rookies who stood guard. The lights from the emergency vehicles mingled with the *Paddlewheel Queen*'s party-boat display. Some of the students were waving at the bridge, hoping that a zoom lens might pick them up for the Sunday night news broadcasts. Many of the girls were still crying. There were flashbulb bursts from the crime techs as they documented the scene. Mahoney didn't see the body inside, just the hands handcuffed to the top of the steering wheel. There was only one body he was interested in. That was the one wearing a Camaro script, dressed in a coat of factory Royal Plum. It almost looked black in the twisted sources of artificial light.

Detective Salt-And-Pepper was busy directing the team. "Okay, everybody, it looks like we got a suicide here." He motioned to a group of firefighters. "I need somebody to cut the handcuffs off her." One of the firefighters took a peek inside the car to decide on the right tool. "Hey, Whitney!" said the firefighter. "Get me the bolt cutters out of engine six!"

The bolt cutters made quick work of the handcuff chain. The body almost fell out of the vehicle when the chain snapped. The crime techs caught the corpse, quickly transferring it to a body bag that was unzipped and at the ready on a lowered gurney next to the Camaro.

Salt-And-Pepper motioned to the other firefighters. "I

need someone to punch holes in the floorboards to get the water out!"

"Why don't you just pop out the fucking drain plugs?"

Salt-And-Pepper looked in the direction of the tow truck. Mahoney stared back at him with blazing eyes. "You can get the water out without ruining the fucking car."

"*Ruin* the car?" The detective looked the Camaro over. "Looks pretty ruined to me," he said, kicking the tires for good measure.

"Let me grab my tools," said Mahoney. "It'll take me ten seconds."

The detective turned to the group and gave a why-not shrug. Mahoney retrieved a box cutter, a greasy ball-peen hammer, and a large screwdriver from the toolbox in the truck bed. The group parted like the Red Sea as he headed into the Camaro cabin. A quick slice through the carpets revealed the four drain plugs. Mahoney wondered if Chevrolet engineers thought this day would come for some Camaro owners. The plugs were at the lowest point of the floorboards. He was ready to pry up the first plug when he stopped. "Wouldn't it be a good idea to catch whatever comes out?"

The detective agreed. He motioned to the crime techs, who placed two large metal trays underneath the Camaro. Mahoney pried up the first plug, then the rest, allowing the brown water to run through. He looked underneath the car at the rushing flow from the front and rear foot wells, a gush that quickly calmed itself to a spattering trickle. The trays had a fine mesh bottom for catching larger objects as the water drained out around them. Mahoney stood back as the crime techs retrieved the trays, placing them on portable saw-horses to examine their contents. It didn't look like much: a few gum wrappers, a couple of pens, and a half-dozen sticks of Big Red that had fallen out of a larger Plen-T-Pak. There were a few cigarette butts, which received the special treatment of clear plastic evidence bags. Mahoney thought that he saw lipstick on one of them. It was red, just like the gum.

"Okay, Tow-Job, you can take it to the Plessis Road yard," said the detective.

Mahoney turned around. "Plessis? Don't you mean the traffic garage?" Mahoney didn't know its exact name, only that it was usually the first stop for a car that had very recently had a body in it. The garage for the traffic division investigations unit was in a converted power station on Princess Street, with a high brick barrier and a sliding privacy gate to keep out the eyes of the media and the car crash voyeurs. The crime techs would process the vehicle from top to bottom, then make the short walk to the offices of the robbery-homicide unit at the Public Safety Building — a journey that seldom occurred, since most Winnipeg murders involved a mix of a drinking party, an argument, and a knife.

Salt-and-Pepper didn't feel that this unfortunate event qualified for Princess Street. He made it clear to Mahoney, without all the annoying tact. "I beg your fucking pardon, Tow-Job?"

"I just thought all the body stuff goes —"

"It goes exactly where I fucking say it goes, dipshit. Hook it up and get it out of here now. This ain't an episode of *Night Heat*, it's a fucking suicide!"

"Whatever you say, Detective."

"Detective-Sergeant Milroy, Tow-Job. Now get that piece of shit out of here, if you think *your* piece of shit is up to the job." Mahoney looked over at Unit 36 as Milroy chuckled. He silently agreed with the Detective-Sergeant. Even a dirty Red

River Camaro was a step above his recovery vehicle of choice. It probably ran better.

Mahoney went about the business of cinching up the Camaro. He took longer than he normally would have for a typical river retrieval car, ensuring that no damage would occur to the front bumper and valance. Mahoney inched the sling upwards. He looked over at the scene as it started to wind down. The morgue-mobile pilots were busy loading the body. The crime-scene techs were fishing through the meagre droppings from the Camaro's floorboards, tagging and bagging. Detective Milroy continued barking orders to the rest of the police and fire personnel. *Sorry,* thought Mahoney. *Detective-Sergeant.*

The start-up of the fire engine's diesel snapped Mahoney back to reality. He confirmed the Camaro's shifter was in Neutral. He would pull the car up the hill to a level grade, then drop it down for a preferred rear-end sling attachment. All routine, but Mahoney was working slower than usual. Slow enough to document everything he needed to know. Slow enough to confirm what he already knew. It wasn't just any Camaro. It was Mahoney's next Camaro.

CHAPTER
THREE

The news vultures were waiting at the end of the service road, as expected. Mahoney knew the best way to disperse the local news media was with high beams, a touch of speed, and an air horn that sounded like an apocalyptic trumpet. The black-and-white roadblock saw him coming, backing up just in time for Unit 36 and the watery Camaro to pass. A few reporters seemed about to block the path with their microphones and cameramen, but quickly thought better of it with the first horn blast. The Camaro's lights were still doing strange things, flickering on and off as Mahoney's rig headed north on Main Street towards the North Perimeter Bridge. He pushed Unit 36 to somewhere around 50 miles an hour as he passed the reporters on the bridge, the speedometer needle still reporting a bouncing 20.

Mahoney needed about 10 minutes with the car. That would be enough to confirm what he already knew about it, perhaps a little bit more. The Camaro was a '67. He knew that because of the vent windows on the doors, a feature that was gone for the '68 model year. The car had minimal options. Mahoney had noticed that it didn't have a centre console when he first cut the carpet. There was zero evidence of a motorhead owner. It still wore factory hubcaps, the "poverty caps" expected for an entry-level car. It didn't appear that any of the newshounds were in hot pursuit, so he turned off at the service road that connected De Vries Avenue with Raleigh Street, a left at Knowles, then a right into the parking lot for the Gateway Community Club.

Mahoney grabbed the magnetic-mount flashlight off his glovebox door. There were still a few trickles of brown water under the Camaro as he lowered it to ground level. He unlatched the hood, raising it with minimal creak. *Straight six,* he thought, as he surveyed the simple in-line engine. *Hasn't had the living shit driven out of it yet.* The few options he noticed were the column-shift automatic, a push-button AM radio, power steering, and a fan-driven rear defroster on the rear parcel shelf.

The paint appeared to be original. The body was surprisingly intact, with no rust coming through the usual lower extremities. Sometimes the cheap cars had their advantages: option packages like the Rally Sport had all kinds of trim pieces that loved to trap mud and promote rust. The rear bumper had been tapped at some point in its life on the passenger side. Judging by the frost shields on the side windows, somebody's grandmother had owned it and was no doubt the one who'd backed into something. A few door dings and a slight crease in the driver's side front fender were the car's only visual scars. There were no license plates. Mahoney wondered why the detective-sergeant hadn't picked up on that.

Mahoney was checking on the VIN plate inside the driver's door when the lights started to weakly flicker again. The dashboard lights fluttered along with the overhead courtesy lamp. The odometer was highlighted in the flashes, a reading of just 77,657 and five-tenths. The reading appeared to be original; Mahoney had seen enough tampered odometers, with their telltale jumbled digits, to know that the numbers were right. That's when he noticed the keys, still stuck in the dashboard ignition switch. They seemed to be swaying more than expected, buoyed in some way by the rabbit's foot on the key ring. Mahoney grabbed them and stuffed them in his shirt pocket. The rabbit's foot was still wet and stank like the Red. He took one last look at the steering wheel. The top portion was bent forward, looking much like the steering wheels that feel the full force of a body slamming into them at life-ending speed. He raised the rear of the Camaro skyward for the journey to the Plessis Road compound. The lights flickered twice more and then went dark.

2:44 A.M.

The Manitoba Public Insurance compound was a 24-hour operation, with a security shack at the main entrance. Most people referred to it as the Autopac yard, the popular marketing name for the provincial automobile insurer. It was surprising how busy the lineup was at almost three in the morning. Mahoney waited his turn as other wreckers rolled in. Even the guard was enough of a car guy to notice what was on Mahoney's hook. "Oh, man, a submarine Camaro. What a fucking waste."

"It's just a six," said Mahoney. "Nothing special, plus it's got bad mojo."

"Mojo?"

Mahoney drew a line across his neck, enough for an indifferent wave-through. Mahoney idled lazily through the yard, past varying degrees of demise for the automotive form. He glanced at the Camaro through his rearview mirror. He couldn't tell if the taillights were still flickering or if the light was simply the ricochet from the overhead sodium fixtures. He found an oversized spot in the line reserved for fresh recoveries, easing the Camaro between a fender-bashed Ford Maverick and a late-'70s Pontiac Firebird that was in two pieces, which tended to occur when Firebirds were slammed sideways into hydro poles. BLOOD written in grease pencil on the windshield stated the obvious.

Mahoney lowered the Camaro into the parking spot. The ride had shaken out most of the river water, with drops where there were once trickles. The lights had gone dark for good. He raised his wrist, pressing the backlight on his digital watch. It was coming up on three in the morning. *Six more fucking hours,* he thought. Six more hours until the Bowman.

The rest of the morning was routine. Mahoney attended to a few lockouts in the downtown Exchange District, convincing a semi-soused permed blonde 20-something in a red leather miniskirt to take a cab instead of drive home in her equally red, late-model Ford EXP. She was planning on jamming two of her friends into the cargo area of the two-seater, a pair that were in a condition that reminded him of the Country Squire brunette at Boondoggles. One of the girls had forgotten to wipe the cocaine from under her nose, most likely a backroom bonus from the head bouncer at the Rorie Street Marble Club. She didn't pick up on her friends' over-the-top pantomime to dispose of the evidence.

Mahoney scribbled the make, model, and plate number on the invoice. He would usually scrawl *cash sale* in place of a customer name on the late-night lockouts, but Mahoney thought he saw a little more than booze in her eyes. He went with a smile. She smiled back. Mahoney felt his cheeks warm as he scribbled.

"So, I just need a name for the invoice."

"Diana McRae," said the woman. "That's with an ehm-cee."

"Ehm-cee," said Mahoney. "Got it."

"And that's *Miss* Diana McRae. Miss."

"Got it, Miss Diana McRae."

Diana dug into her purse for the cash, pulling out plenty of crumped singles and two-dollar bills to add up to the $25 fee. "I'm always doing this, locking my keys in it."

Mahoney went all in. "Then maybe I should give you my number, for when it happens again."

Diana smiled. "Yeah, that would be handy to have."

Mahoney detached the invoice. He scribbled his number on the corner of the invoice, as the Red Patch taxicab pulled up. He tipped his trucker cap as the cab pulled away.

The last calls on Sunday morning were usually from early rising apartment block managers, thinning out their parking lots of drivers who chose to ignore their No Overnight Parking signs. These were typical one-night stand cars: newer Camaros, Firebirds, Mustangs, maybe the odd import. Mahoney had to use the wheel dollies for the last pickup of his shift, a red Porsche 944 at the Parkside Plaza on Henderson Highway. He thought he heard the owner yelling at him from an upper balcony as he left the parking lot. His digital watch said 8:17 a.m. A good time to head to the Bowman.

The Bowman Industrial Park was quiet most Sundays. In addition to the Hook Me Up Towing offices and vehicle compound, the Bowman was home to a revolving door of automotive tenants, the kind that did anything but legitimate nine-to-five business. One such shop was Panhead Motors. It was listed in the Yellow Pages as a Harley-Davidson service centre, though it was best described as a satellite location for the Heaven's Rejects Motorcycle Club, better known as the HRs among Winnipeg's criminal element and the various divisions of the Winnipeg Police Department. The HRs had been increasing their presence in a variety of enterprises since the mid-'70s. Drugs, prostitution, and the theft of anything wheeled, from Cadillacs to Electra-Glides. Most of the Harleys that made their way into the motorcycle shop were freshly stolen, awaiting their turn with the cutting torch. Panhead was two doors down from Hook Me Up, which made for easy transfers of drugs and cash. They didn't have to go outside to do the exchanges, thanks to access that had been jackhammered through the cinder-block walls. The middle business was vacant, rented out as storage by an HR friendly. The holes between the businesses were each covered by a triplet of public school–style surplus lockers that swung out on hidden hinges when necessary.

Mahoney drove past the Hook Me Up office to the fenced compound at the rear of the Bowman complex. He dropped the Porsche as gingerly as he could in the rutted gravel, knowing full well that the owner would be accusing Hook Me Up of inflicting thousands of dollars in damage to his car. They always did, especially if the car was German and expensive. He figured he might as well get started on the Hook Me Up special treatment. He whistled towards a rusting Crescentwood Dairies delivery van, and three mutts with varying degrees of German shepherd scampered out. Mahoney knelt to give each a healthy ear scratch before he stood up and pointed at the Porsche. "Douchebag," he said. The dogs understood the command, taking turns relieving themselves on the tires.

CHAPTER
FOUR

The dogs continued to mark their territory on the Porsche while Mahoney hosed off the Red River sludge from the tow cable and his rubber boots. He parked Unit 36 next to the compound, making sure to grab his clipboard and money bag, a weathered night deposit satchel in another life. The newer trucks were driven by the better producers and had earned the luxury of parking in front of the office. Mahoney had tried to steer clear of becoming an outright pimp, or dealer, or both. The dream was to open his own service garage, which was something he could have easily bankrolled after two months of criminal activity. But then the Heaven's Rejects would see his business as one that they had indirectly financed, which would mean freebies for most of the upper HRs and the possibility of paying "insurance." Failure to pay protection premiums could put you out of business, with either a sign in the window or a well-timed act of arson.

He opened the front door, activating a distorted buzzer somewhere behind the ceiling tiles. The morning light accented the dust in the air and the haze of smoke coming from the dispatcher's desk. Dolores Favel was on the phone with the victim of a fresh tow. Dolores was probably around 40: an assumption based more on general condition than birth certificate. Her usual outfit was a sweatshirt and sweatpants combo. She certainly smelled the part of gym rat, though that had more to do with the occasionally washed 200 pounds that she carried on her five-foot frame. She turned to see Mahoney standing at the front counter. She muffled the handset, motioning him over with a triplet of head shakes, shaking her bleached blonde ponytail as many times in the process. "Did you pick up a red prick-mobile on Henderson?" Dolores whispered as best she could, not an easy feat with her smoker's rasp. "He's going off about his dad being some big mucky-muck."

"It's in back, getting marinated," said Mahoney. "If he wants to fuck Nor-Villa girls, he should know the risks."

"Hey! I'm a Nor-Villa girl!" Dolores let out a laboured cough. The Nor-Villa Motor Hotel was the closest watering hole to the large footprint of cheap cinder-block apartments on Henderson Highway and Valhalla Drive. "You gotta qualify to get a piece of this." She motioned over her barrel-shaped physique with the muffled handset. There was nothing to see.

Mahoney leaned over the counter, listening to the muffled tirade of the Son of Mucky-Muck. "The three D's for Delectable Dolores dates: deaf, dumb, and most definitely demented."

"You wouldn't know what to do with it if you had it," She added another swirl of her unremarkable bosom to drive the point home.

Mahoney pulled a Colt cigar out of his pocket but stopped short of putting the tip to his lips. "Well, Dolores, it's either my Colts or penicillin. I can't afford both."

"Don't smoke that shit in here. I can't stand the smell!"

Mahoney lit up anyway. "When was the last time you *could* smell?"

"I can sure as hell smell shit." Dolores picked up Mahoney's satchel, still muffling the threats coming through the handset. She inhaled deeply. "See? Shit. Must be Mahoney's Saturday night."

Mahoney exhaled. He looked at the window to the office, surrounded by cheap wooden panelling. The shutters were down. "I'm guessing Fearless Leader is in there?"

Dolores grabbed a dusty lowball glass from her work station and rolled the chair to the window with one push. She placed the glass carefully on the window and listened. "Shouldn't be long now." Mahoney didn't need the glass to hear, since he wasn't half-deaf like Dolores. He could hear the passionless grunts on the other side of the window from the front counter. Dolores rolled back to her desk. She took a satisfying drag from her cigarette before re-engaging with the customer, who was finally starting to deliver his closing arguments. Dolores composed herself before delivering her stock answer. "Sir, the compound is not open for pickups until Monday at 10 a.m. Have a nice day." She slammed the handset back into its cradle, turning towards Mahoney as she did. "You might as well go in. He's gotta be done by now."

Mahoney swung open the half-door next to the counter. As it slammed shut, he stopped. "I thought the office opened at nine."

"It does," said Dolores, as she lit up another cigarette. "I finish reading the *Sun* by ten."

Mahoney opened the door to Larry Ballendine's office, mentally preparing himself for the scene he knew was coming. The haze was as smoky as the front of the Hook Me Up office, tinged with the aroma of cheap cigars and recent sex. The woodgrain panelling was covered with yellowed pullouts of *Winnipeg Sun* girls. Ballendine was standing with his back to Mahoney, his trousers around his ankles. He was in the process of towelling off his genitals, a show that Mahoney never wanted to see. "Gimme a minute," said Ballendine. "Just gotta do some detailing."

Mahoney sat in the chair in front of the desk. He looked to his right at the bottle-dyed fire-engine-redhead hastily tying up a faded polyester kimono. She exited the scene without pleasantries, opening the bank of lockers on the wall with a knowing hand.

Ballendine grabbed a spray bottle of Drakkar Noir from the window ledge. He gave his nether regions six mists, then added two more to his posterior before hoisting up his trousers. He turned to Mahoney as he tightened up his belt on his size 44 waist. "How's the three-six running?" Ballendine still had half of a cigar in his mouth as he spoke. "Give you any trouble?"

"Nothing I can't handle," said Mahoney, as he rubbed his aching right wrist. "She hasn't let me down yet."

Ballendine settled into his well-worn Naugahyde office chair, a dark green model that had been fitted with duct-tape repairs, as needed, since the late '70s. He folded the wash towel to a possible clean spot, dabbing at his sweaty forehead. There was plenty of forehead to dab: Ballendine had started balding in his late twenties, which was roughly 20 years ago. He hadn't had a heart attack yet, as far as Mahoney knew. His desk was littered with the things that would get him there: three bottles of Pic-a-Pop Cola, spray cheese in a can, and a half-eaten double chili cheeseburger from Fat Boy Hamburgers on Henderson. He chuckled as he leaned back to put his feet on the desk. "She? She's not a she." He pointed at the bank of lockers where the hooker had made her exit. "That's a she. A hundred-bucks-a-throw-kinda she."

Mahoney glanced at the lockers. "Yeah, whatever floats your boat, Luscious."

Ballendine winced. "Don't call me that."

"What? Luscious?"

"Yeah, who fucking started that shit anyway?"

"I thought it was Wallbanger."

"Yeah, well, it stops now. And put out that Colt, that shit stinks."

"Whatever you say Lusc . . . I mean Larry."

Ballendine ignored the slip. "What did you get last night?"

Mahoney looked skyward to jog his memory as he butted out the Colt in Ballendine's overflowing ashtray. "Let's see. Four drunk tows, six lockouts, three boosts, the City yank out of the Red, and a D-bag with a Porsche."

"Not bad," said Ballendine. "Be a lot better if you dealt like Wallbanger."

"That's not my style, Larry. We've been over this."

"Yeah, yeah, No-Baloney Mahoney. Squeaky clean, never pissed anybody off. Except for the service manager over at Terry Fucking Balkan."

Mahoney didn't care for that dig. "Fuck you, Larry. I didn't steal those tools from the shop. They went out the back door like that Corvette did. The whole place was dirty as fuck."

Ballendine remembered the story. "Yeah, some guy took that Vette for a test drive and never came back. Probably be fishing it out of the river when the water goes down enough. In the meantime, you can't get a legit wrench gig in this town. Best you can hope for is changing spark plugs for the rest of the Elmwood grandmothers. What they pay you with? Pie?"

"I do all right."

"Bullshit," said Ballendine. "You work here nights six days a week for ten bucks an hour. You want to get your own shop on that? Yeah, I know about that. Good luck getting a bond or credit with a jobber with a thieving rap, even if it's trumped up. Indie shop. What a fucking waste of time. The only thing you can afford is a caved-in ex-Gulf in the ghetto that's on fire. You'd be better off putting on a wig and sucking dicks. Maybe Wallbanger can set you up."

"Are we done here?"

"Yeah, we're done here. Speaking of wrenching, when are you gonna fix three-six?"

"When you give me two bills for parts."

"Two bills? What are you tuning it up with, baby seal pelts?" Ballendine threw five twenties at Mahoney. "Here's a hundred. Plugs, cap, rotor, and wires. The rest you can get from Merv's."

"Oh, goody," said Mahoney, as he scooped up the cash. "I guess I'll just find a slightly less fucked-up carburetor."

"Why don't you take the one off that hot-rod Camaro of yours? You're never gonna drive that thing again."

Mahoney looked straight at Ballendine, hard. "It's not for sale. And I'm fixing it."

Ballendine couldn't contain his laughter. "Fixing it? What, you got a steel mill in your garage?"

"Whatever," said Mahoney. He was about to open the door when Jerry Waller opened it for him. He was wearing a black T-shirt that was at least two sizes too small, showing off his drug-fed muscular physique. Waller hoisted his white Vuarnet sunglasses on top of his permed black locks. The hairdo looked ridiculous, though no one in his right mind would point it out. One of the side effects of Waller's steroid use was a hair-trigger temper. He smirked at Mahoney as he passed, throwing a much fatter satchel at Ballendine. "Cleaned up last night, boss-man. Must be all the grad boys who went stag."

Ballendine unzipped the satchel. He looked at the wad of bills, easily in the realm of three thousand dollars. "That's a lotta horny blue balls," he said. "Probably the shortest work the girls have had this month."

"Eight seconds to love," said Waller. "I love grad season." He turned to Mahoney. "How about thirty-six? Not too many dead-battery calls in June, eh Steve-Oh?"

"More than you'd think," said Mahoney. He faked a yawn, turning to Ballendine. "I'll pick up the parts. Thirty-Six will be ready for the Monday night shift."

Ballendine waved him off. "Sounds good. And Steve-Oh?"

Mahoney turned to hear him. "What?"

"I'll give you fifty bucks for the carb off your schlock rod."

Mahoney rolled his eyes. He could hear Waller and Ballendine laughing as he closed the office door.

CHAPTER
FIVE

Mahoney eased behind the wheel of his powder blue Plymouth Gran Fury. The mid-'70s model looked like a retired police unit. It had started life as a supervisor's car for the Winnipeg transit department. The shape of the City of Winnipeg crest was still evident on the front doors where the stickers had been removed. Everyone at the auction thought it was a police car, putting in low bids. Mahoney made it his for six hundred. Not bad for a beater that wasn't too beat. He prodded the gas three times for ignition. Two was never enough. Four would flood it for sure.

Mahoney fished the five twenties out of his pocket. The one good thing about Luscious Larry Ballendine was that he never asked for a receipt for any of the parts that were needed to keep the Hook Me Up fleet mobile. In his previous life as a Chevrolet technician, Mahoney knew how to spot the best of the used parts on a wreck. He checked his watch: 9:38 a.m. Merv's Auto Parts would be opening in 22 minutes.

Merv's was a favourite hunting ground among the motoring poor and the outright cheap. It was one of the few businesses that opened on a Sunday in Winnipeg, located east of Highway 59 on Springfield Road. During the week, the operation would stay open till dusk. On Sundays, the "We're Closing" buzzer would sound at 10 to four in the afternoon. The business model was best described as self-serve auto parts, with an *Enter at Your Own Risk* sign as the only safety warning. Mahoney knew the drill. A customer would enter the cashier shack and open his tool box. The cashier would nod, then re-inspect the tool box to make sure that no free parts were leaving the premises. Mahoney had been a regular long enough that no one checked his tool box. They knew he paid for far more than he stole.

A thief. That's what they tried to call him, back when he worked at Terry Balkan Chevrolet Oldsmobile on Main Street, across from the CN Rail station, in the summer of '81. The cops searched his garage, unable to find the set of impact sockets that the service manager had accused him of stealing. They fired him anyway, making a point of letting every General Motors dealer in town know about his sticky fingers. The actual reason for dismissal was something more biblical. Mahoney had been having an ongoing affair with the service manager's wife, which had started with an impressive standing cloakroom fuck in the Marlborough Hotel, at the staff Christmas party in '79.

The next few years were thin for work. The private garages knew he came with baggage. Most tried to take advantage of it, paying less for his skill-set than most shops would pay for apprentices. He had been driving Unit 36 for about a year and a half. Ballendine had been correct about Mahoney's back-lane business. The work was simple fare, usually light tune-ups and maintenance in the customer's driveway or garage, carrying most of his tools in the ample trunk of the Plymouth. It was a good cash business, with plenty of referrals from grateful grandmothers and stingy pensioners. Mahoney would draw up simple ads with a Sharpie and place them on the bulletin boards of the neighbourhood supermarkets. He would write his phone number vertically along the bottom of the ad about 15 times and use scissors to turn the phone numbers into detachable business cards.

Mahoney lucked out at Merv's. A recent train derailment had pummelled a baker's dozen of new General Motors products. A Chevy Suburban with a 454 cubic-inch big-block V8 engine gave up its spark plugs, along with their wires, and the complete distributor. This would be a major upgrade for Unit 36, since the new electronic unit had done away with the mechanical breaker points system. Someone had already made off with the Chevy's carburetor. Mahoney hoped that a can of carb cleaner would do the trick on Unit 36. He stowed the spark plugs in the tool box as the freebie. Sixty dollars in cash bought the rest.

The night was starting to catch up with Mahoney. He stopped at the Mac's store at Springfield and Rothesay for breakfast: a Pepsi and a Schneiders Hot Rod meat stick. The Sunday drive home was light. He had missed the morning church traffic, most of which was parked in front of the various denominations on Watt Street. The smell hit him like it always did, usually a block before Mission Street. It was the kind of smell that would make most men check their shorts. The stench was as much a part of the St. Boniface neighbourhood as the bilingual stop signs. Loveday Mushroom Farms had been around since 1932, and business was still booming, along with a compost scent that no scratch-and-sniff sticker could do justice. If you ate a mushroom in Winnipeg, chances are it was a Loveday. No one in their right mind would want to live next door.

McTavish Street always seemed to be in the proverbial downwind draft of the mushroom farm. The houses were located on the east side, with the west side devoted to the rail siding for the Central Grain elevator. If the smell didn't get you, the rumble of slow-moving trains would. With all these things going for it, McTavish Street was one of the better bargains in the city for single-family dwellings, without having a ghetto postal code. Mahoney had purchased his one-bedroom bungalow in 1980 for just over 15 grand. That price included the oversized double garage.

Mahoney pulled the Plymouth up to the garage door. He held the meat stick in his mouth as he fumbled for the keys to the industrial padlocks on the sliding barrel bolts. He opened the door to the darkened garage, hitting the four wall-mounted switches with a knowing hand. The fluorescent tubes flickered at first, then started to build with illumination. Mahoney looked at the prize they had revealed: an Ermine White 1967 Chevrolet Camaro SS 350 coupe. His Hot Rod. Mahoney had purchased it off the Terry Balkan lot in the spring of '79, a fresh trade-in from a weekend sale. The story went that the 60-something owner had found the Camaro's non-assisted drum brakes to be hard to actuate with his age-related foot issues. On paper, the dealership showed a trade-in value of $1,350 for the Camaro, on a new Monza 2+2 hatchback. Mahoney picked up his prize for just $725.

The Camaro was half-covered with an old paint tarp. Mahoney pulled the cover off the car, revealing the reason why. The entire roof was caved in, thanks to a lazy summer Sunday at Kildonan Park in '83. Mahoney had been parked across from the green space on Peguis Drive, the unofficial stretch for cool cars to park. He was checking out a yellow '71 Ford Mustang Mach 1 parked in front of him when the branch from a hundred-year-old elm broke free from its trunk, landing on the Camaro's roof. The thin pillars and sail panels did little to soften the blow. Neither did the picture of the car that appeared on the front page of the *Winnipeg Sun*, thanks to a freelancer shooting summer-themed background shots at the park. The headline didn't help: CAMAR-OW!!! The insurance payout was painfully low. The Autopac coverage was cheap for the Camaro, though there were no extension policies in place for a car that wasn't old enough to be considered an antique. The only plus was the ability to buy back his crushed Camaro for a minimal subtraction on the insurance payout. The adjuster looked at Mahoney strangely when he opted not to cancel his plates. "Maybe I'll turn it into a convertible," he said, as he exited the office with the cheque for $1,300. He had at least that much in the Camaro's engine rebuild, and he'd be damned if he let some vulture pick the carcass clean for cheap at the salvage auction.

The car still ran, and Mahoney made sure by starting it once a month, though the collapsed roof made it tricky to reach in for the key. The pummelled roof skin had stopped three inches short of crunching the blue bucket seats. Mahoney knew the blue interior was going to look a little off with a purple paint job, if he could even get the Red

River suicide car at the salvage auction. Manitoba Public Insurance auctioned off the cars deemed as total losses every Wednesday. It was a popular sale for the backyard mechanics, usually in search of lightly damaged cars that needed a fender, or maybe a door or two, to look whole again for an easy curbside flip. It was anyone's guess as to when the Camaro would hit the auction list. Mahoney figured it would take at least a couple of weeks. He also knew that someone else could want it more than him. The tales of cars missed haunted his garage, as well as the garages of his friends, the way that fishing stories haunted the docks of a Manitoba lake.

Mahoney walked to the front of the car. He let his right hand fall knowingly to the hood release. He raised the hood to reveal the Hot Rod's heart, an energized chrome-laden re-interpretation of the original 350 cubic-inch V8. Mahoney figured the rebuilt powerplant was putting out close to 400 horsepower by now. At least, that's what it felt like when the car finally found traction. He had added as many of the pieces that he could find that had started life on the big-block Camaros, like stiffer springs, front disc brakes, a beefier rear axle, and a Turbo 400 transmission in place of the original Powerglide. All of it would fit in any '67 Camaro with minimal fuss, even a water-logged one.

Mahoney took a chomp of his meat stick as he checked his watch: 11:07 a.m. Sunday night was his day off, which meant he could grab a few winks, then start dismantling the Hot Rod in the late afternoon. A hard wake-up for 4 p.m., some cold pizza, and he'd be ready to start. All he had to do now was call the crew.

CHAPTER
SIX

Mahoney didn't hear the clock radio buzzer, the one he had set for 4 p.m. He did hear the hammering on the screen door. He checked the time: 3:37 p.m. That could only mean Rick Scheer. He was always early.

"It's open, Rickles," Mahoney said groggily, as he rolled off the couch and knocked the Gondola Pizza box and the leftover crusts to the floor. The screen door creaked open. Rick Scheer gave a knowing kick to the bottom of the swollen door, the easiest way to pop it open. Scheer was in his early 30s, about five-foot-six, bald as a cue ball, and maybe 140 pounds soaking wet. He was a handy mechanic to have in tight places. Mahoney had met Scheer during his Terry Balkan days. The dealership had gone into receivership by 1982, the year Scheer jumped ship to Garden Gate Pontiac on McPhillips Street.

"Phew," said Scheer, fanning his hand at his nose. "Smells like a ten-dollar hooker convention in here. Seven dollars after taxes!" Scheer was living up to his Don Rickles nickname the best he could. He wouldn't be showcasing in Vegas anytime soon.

"It's the shrooms factory," said Mahoney, reaching for his boots. "After a few hours, you won't even notice."

"Or I'll cut my nose off, one or the other." Scheer plopped himself into the well-worn Barca Lounger in front of the console TV, then instantly realized he should have gone to the kitchen first. "Got any beer?"

"Stocked," said Mahoney. "Even sprung for your favourite."

"Old Vagrant?"

"I thought you called it Old Vagina."

Scheer had already popped open the fridge. "Vagrant, Vadge, Vienna, or just plain OV. As long as it's Carlings, and as long as it's cold." He flipped the cap off with a mag-mount opener he had discovered on the fridge door. "You want one?"

"Naw, gotta keep my head. Tag and bag all the important stuff."

"So, we're actually doing it?"

"We're actually doing it."

"You found a car?"

"Looks like."

Scheer peeled back the curtain to look outside. "Where is it? With the SS?"

Mahoney had just gone to the fridge himself for a swig

from the milk carton. He wiped the dribbles off his face. "I haven't got it yet."

Scheer looked at him. "Well, you always were a bit of an optimist. Hope it's not a fucking rust-bucket."

"It's not. Straight-six with a glide. Granny wagon for sure. Autopac write-off."

"Oh, shit," said Scheer. "You better have a lot of money in the coffee can for that one. Every idiot with a hard-on is going to be fender-humping that thing."

Mahoney shook his head. "No one wants this thing. Came out of the river."

Scheer winced. "A gumbo-wagon? Count me the fuck out."

Mahoney explained. "I mean it came out yesterday, right after it went in."

Scheer scratched his forehead. "It's still going to be a disgusting mess. We gotta pull everything out of it. I'll bet it's still got at least three catfish in it. Hey! Maybe I can sell 'em to the Filipinos in the wash bay at work!"

Mahoney winced. "Why do they eat that shit anyway? Go to a lake, get some pickerel!"

"I dunno. Must remind 'em of some slimy weirdo fish from back home or something." Scheer reached down for one of the loose crusts. As he chewed, he punctuated his concerns with the rest of the crust. "We gotta pull the wiring, the heater box, and anything soft goes straight in the dumpster."

"Right," said Mahoney. "And, remember, I got everything here that we need. We're only taking the good stuff. The rest gets trashed."

Scheer's eyes lit up. "Or clean up the old stuff and put it in the *Buy & Sell*!" The *Buy & Sell* tabloid was a hotbed for used cars and parts.

Mahoney wasn't convinced. "Rickles, you're nuts. Everything will smell like ass!"

"Not if they come here! The whole *street* smells like ass! 1967 Camaro buckets seats, seventy-five dollars for the pair!" Scheer firmly believed that everything had a value and someone was sure to pay it eventually.

"If you want 'em, be my guest," said Mahoney. "But I'm not taking the calls."

"You won't have to," said Scheer. "The machine will."

"The *what* will?"

"The answering machine will."

"What answering machine?"

"The one I won at the wedding social for my cousin's kid sister. I'll go get it."

Scheer returned with the box. It was a Panasonic dual-tape set-up. Mahoney figured it had to be high-end, judging by the woodgrain finish. He read the instructions as Scheer was setting it up. "Why does it have two tapes?"

Scheer rolled his eyes. "Cassettes, Steve-Oh. They're called cassettes."

"Okay, Rickles, why does it have two *cassettes*?"

"Easy. One is for the outgoing message, the other one records the incoming message."

"But what if I don't want to be outgoing?"

Scheer stopped uncoiling the cords. "What are you talking about?"

"Well, what if I don't feel like being all cheerful while I record the message?"

Scheer blinked hard. "Who gives a shit what you sound like? You just record the message, like this." Scheer put the cassettes into the machine. He hit the record button and spoke as close as he could to the little hole that said MIC.

"Hi, you've reached Steve at 668-4922. I can't get to the phone right now, cause I'm probably jacking off in the corner to a very sticky *Hustler* magazine."

"Hey, fuck you, Rickles."

"Shush! It's still recording!"

"Then do it over," Mahoney grumbled.

"Gimme the book, I don't know how." Scheer started to flip through the instructions, only to be interrupted by a loud beep. He threw the booklet on the coffee table and returned to his Old Vienna. "I'll do it later. Need more lubrication."

Mahoney grabbed the instruction book. He'd flipped to the message page when the siren started to wail from outside. "Oh, shit," he said.

"What?" said Scheer. "What is it?"

"It's the answering-machine police. You can't fuck around with this shit. Federal rap, straight to Stony Mountain."

"Bullshit!"

"You'd be married inside of a week."

Scheer was warming up his retort when they heard the siren start up again. There was something weird about it. It didn't sound like most current Winnipeg emergency vehicles. Mahoney opened the curtains a crack to check. He smiled, then looked at Scheer. "False alarm, Rickles. They sent an ambulance instead to take you to the nuthouse. Must be your Chevette."

Scheer grabbed his beer and yanked open the door. He started to laugh when he saw the source of the song, a red-and-white 1962 Cadillac Miller-Meteor ambulance with WINNIPEG SPEEDWAY painted on the sides. "Awesome!" said Scheer, as he headed outside to greet the driver and passenger. "Fiddy brought the Jaws!"

Fiddy was Evan Fiddler, another former member of the Terry Balkan crew. He was a beefy six-footer, the kind of mechanic that every shop needed, especially when something heavy had to be held in place or removed. He grew up on the Peguis First Nation, beginning his mechanic career like most youngsters born on a reserve, handing wrenches to his father as he fixed the very tired family car. A snowmobile accident in '71 had taken his dad when Fiddler was 17. His mother and grandmother kept him from getting into the usual troubles that most of his friends were getting into on the reserve, keeping his nose in the textbooks and his hands dirty fixing neighbours' cars. He secured a spot in the auto mechanic program at Red River Community College, then cut his teeth and his knuckles on Ford products for his apprentice levels. He had just started up with some Korean car company that had come to Canada the previous year by the name of Hyundai, at a dealership called Bridgeway on Nairn Avenue. Like most of the dealership staff, he still wasn't sure how to pronounce Hyundai correctly.

The ambulance was the ride for his part-time gig, as a volunteer at the Winnipeg Speedway. The dirt oval coupled with varying degrees of driver skills meant that Fiddler didn't have to wait too long to swing the ambulance out onto the track. He hated the sight of blood, but he loved the sound of the siren. "Give us a hand, Dickles," said Fiddler, adjusting Scheer's nickname for comedic effect. "This thing is almost as fat as your mom!"

"Now that's what I call fat," said a disembodied voice. Howard Petkau was already at the back of the ambulance, bringing out as many pieces of the Jaws of Life as he could handle on his own. Petkau had worked on an impressive selection of the motoring weird in his 12 years holding a wrench: the oil-and-gas-sucking Mazdas of the early '70s, then a stint with Motor Sales on Main Street, with the constant tuning and re-tuning of Jaguars, MGs, and other pieces of British Leyland crap. When the Russian-built Lada showed up at Motor Sales, Petkau left to try his hand at Subarus. Fiddler had told Petkau about the Hyundai gig. He was looking for someone he could get along with, since there would only be two technicians in the shop. Petkau was a thin-but-toned six-footer and an avid jogger, usually swapping out his safety boots for his colourful Nikes after hours. They went well with his shock of curly red hair. "Hey, Fiddy," said Petkau. "Grab the other end of this pump. It's stupid heavy."

"Takes one to know one, I guess," said Fiddler. The hydraulic pump unit was the heaviest piece of the Jaws of Life, since it was also attached to a welded cage that carried its power source, a six-horsepower, pull-start engine that allowed the Jaws to be used anywhere on the track. "This should slice through the Camaro like that sharp-cut knife on TV."

"I want the one that makes those spring potatoes," said Petkau.

Scheer stood with his arms crossed, still managing to hang onto his Old Vienna bottle. He didn't look pleased, though even that look seemed contrived. "Hey, Pet-a-cow, don't talk that way about my mom. I mean, c'mon, that's my mom!"

Petkau continued the heavy lifting with Fiddler and the digs at Scheer. "Pet-a-cow. Is that what your dad calls it when he finger-bangs her?"

"HEYYYYYYY!" Scheer raised his hand in protest, half-chuckling. Mahoney slapped a freshly opened beer into it.

Scheer took a swig of Old Vienna, then put his attention back to the Camaro carving. "Hey, I could sell the fenders, the doors, maybe . . ."

"And maybe I could use some spare parts, Rickles. I can't exactly buy that shit from Lars at Pro Car." Mahoney looked at the garage. Fiddler and Petkau had already opened the overhead door. They were laying out the key Jaw pieces on the hood of the Plymouth. Mahoney didn't mind, but he still felt the need to say something as the faded blue paint was scratched away. "Hey, Fiddy!"

"What?"

"Make sure you cut through the right car!"

Fiddler waved away the concern. "No problem." He pointed at the Plymouth. "We're gonna practise on this piece of shit first!"

JUNE 10, 1985
1:52 A.M.

It was getting late. Mahoney didn't need his watch to tell him that. He hadn't got around to asking the crew if they had to work on Monday or if they had to leave by a certain time. For whatever reason, they wanted to get the job done just as badly.

The Jaws of Life had made quick work of cutting through the battered roof. The crew had placed as many old blankets as possible inside the Camaro to catch the bits of glass and metal, though Mahoney knew it would take a few swipes of the Shop-Vac before the carpet went into the new car. The Hot Rod came apart easily, thanks to the penetrating fluids that Mahoney had been squirting on the undercarriage for the last two years, whenever a potential donor car presented itself. *The car*, thought Mahoney. *What if I don't get the stupid car?* He put the idea to the back of his mind, a smart place to put it, as the hoist raised the powertrain out of the engine bay.

Mahoney finally checked his watch as the crew was backing out of the driveway: 2:30 a.m. He closed the garage door from the inside, then turned towards the Camaro to survey the teardown. The roof had been completely removed and was now just another piece of scrap metal leaning up against the rear of the garage. The interior had been completely stripped, right down to the drain plugs that would need to be reinserted into the Red River Camaro's floorboards. The engine and transmission were resting on a purpose-built pallet in the corner, next to the complete front subframe and the rear axle. Aside from some coolant and brake-fluid spills, now sprinkled with kitty litter, the dismantle had gone much cleaner than expected. Mahoney's Hot Rod didn't look like much of a car anymore. The crew had rested the remaining hulk on a homemade dolly, built from Hook Me Up tow-truck parts that Larry Ballendine didn't know were missing. The shell would eventually go to General Scrap on Springfield Road. Even in its current state, the Camaro would still be sure to draw a few groans of disappointment from car guys, on the way to its shredded metal grave. He looked at the Hot Rod's parts a long time before he killed the lights.

Dick Loeb sat at his oak desk, in the oak-
panelled president's office of Commonwealth
Motors on Portage Avenue. He looked up at the
clock on the wall, a vintage "It's Nash Time" piece
that pre-dated the American Motors signage on
the front of the dealership. The electric clock
made a faint buzzing sound, as the second hand
clicked its clockwise course. He stared at the
Nash logo, the car brand that his father had sold
at various Winnipeg locations before settling
on the current Portage and Simcoe Street digs
in '53. Next to the clock was a picture of Loeb

and his father, Dick Sr. The junior Loeb's black hair was in full Brylcreem pompadour. He was smiling with his trophy for winning a mechanics' troubleshooting competition. Dick Sr. didn't seem so happy about the contest's sponsor, as evidenced by the indifferent way he was looking at the Plymouth pennant that Loeb was holding with his trophy.

Loeb wondered how happy dear old dad would be with him right now. He twisted to his right to allow access to his desk drawer, not an easy feat for someone who clocked in at six feet and 340 in such a tight space. He reached inside the drawer, removing a half-used tube of Brylcreem. He applied the pomade to the remaining hair he had, about half since when the picture of father and son was taken in 1957. He twisted his chair to the left to exit the cramped confines of his father's former office. Dad had died in the same chair and the same office, in 1967. Loeb had gone from a preferred existence as a mechanic into a starched shirt and a half-Windsor noose. He had doubled in size from his days in the shop. The longer hours had become even longer. He was still married, though the only evidence of a wife was the new shopping bags littering the foyer of his father's former house on Wellington Crescent, on the nights that he chose to go home at all. He would usually fall asleep in his chair at work, and clean up in the mechanic's locker room in the morning. It had become such a routine that his dry cleaner would drop his clothes off at the dealership.

Loeb walked to the open door of the president's office. He surveyed the empty showroom: the salesmen were still finishing up their Monday morning sales meeting. There would always be a couple of lookers wandering through, service department customers who had grown tired of watching the morning news on the console TV in the customer lounge. One was checking out a deeply discounted 1984 AMC Eagle sedan, a four-wheel-drive model that had been sliding in sales since the introduction of the new Jeep Cherokee that same year. The new Jeep had been a major sales boost for Commonwealth, so much so that Loeb had pushed the problem-prone Renault inventory out of the showroom, much to the chagrin of the prairie zone office. He had just received his plane ticket to a dealer event in Las Vegas in August. Loeb figured that it was probably the unveil for the new Comanche pickup truck.

Loeb wasn't up for a chat with a customer. He headed through the showroom, past the cashier, the service lounge, and the reception desk. The receptionist smiled. Loeb knew what would happen next. As he headed towards the shop, he heard the announcement come through the overhead speakers. "Service, call holding on line six. Service, line six." There was no line six, as any of the phones in the dealership would show. The announcement was a head's up to the rest of the dealership that the boss was on the move.

Loeb pushed through the door to the shop. All the bays were full, with varying degrees of work under way. The used car department had purchased most of the retired gas-meter-reader cars from the Greater Winnipeg Gas Company. The robin's-egg blue paintwork on the well-used AMC Concords had been covered with various hues of fresh paint in the body shop. Equally fresh was the mileage on the cars. Loeb watched as two technicians spun back the odometers to figures that would be more pleasing to his buyers. Another used Concord was being fitted with a vinyl roof for an upscale look. Blemished whitewalls were being installed on a fresh trade-in, a Pinto Squire wagon. The tires were Uniroyal, but the only letters left on the sidewall were NIRO.

Loeb walked to the rear of the shop, through the open overhead door that was inviting in the morning warmth. He walked towards the back row, where the weekend trade-ins that weren't getting the deluxe makeover treatment were stored. Most of the cars were destined for the wholesalers, the kind of cars that would be priced right for the North End dirt lots. Some would be heading straight for the scrapyard, early-'70s trade-ins that started rusting while sitting in their respective showrooms. Loeb kicked at the crumbling rear quarter panel of a dark green Laurentian wagon. His foot went right through. He was leaning against the car, shaking the rust flakes out of his loafer, when he saw the orange '74 Bricklin pull in. He watched as the driver struggled with the gull-wing door, which didn't seem to be benefitting from any additional assist mechanism. It had been that way since the car had been traded in by a transplanted American. He walked over to help.

The additional leverage that Loeb provided to the gull-wing revealed a mop of freshly permed blond hair, attached to the head of Peter Scrapneck. "Attached" was the best way to describe the hairdo, since Scrapneck was a regular customer of the El Coredo hairpiece studio. This week, he was a blond. Next week, it could be wavy brown. It was a little confusing for the customers who would come into the dealership, look at Scrapneck's picture on the wall with the rest of the staff eight-by-tens, and then be greeted by someone with a completely different hair colour. But Loeb didn't care if Scrapneck wore an oversized rainbow wig. Scrapneck sold cars, and a lot of them. He carried two Motorola Optrx alphanumeric pagers, fed messages by a local answering service. One was for the morning. He'd put it back on the charger when it died around 11, and it would be ready when the second one died around 3. His official title was general sales manager. It wasn't the only business he managed for Loeb. He smiled as he exited the Bricklin.

"Thanks, boss-man. I'd get some parts to fix it, if they actually still made parts for this piece of shit."

"At least the mill is American Motors," said Loeb, as he lowered the door as gingerly as he could. "I'd get you into a new Wagoneer, if I could keep them on the lot for more than an hour and a half."

"Yap, they're pretty hot right now. Just like that beater Camaro I'm about to report as stolen."

Loeb looked around with concern. "Jesus, Scrap. Keep your fucking voice down!"

"No worries, boss-man. Cops already found it. Looks exactly like I said it would look."

"Did they figure out who it is yet?"

"Don't know, don't care," said Scrapneck. "And if they even bother to look, what are they gonna find? A divorced thirty-something bookkeeper, lived alone, needle marks from a habit. She's yesterday's trash."

"And the note?"

"Yeah, got this week's old lady to write it out. Goodbye cruel world, that sort of shit. They'll find it when they search her place, thanks to her SIN card I put in her pocket. She won't be missed."

Loeb breathed a sigh of relief. "So, where's the car now?"

"At the salvage yard," said Scrapneck. "I spiffed my guy at Autopac a couple of hun to get it added to the auction this week. Our guy will buy it, then straight to the shredder."

Loeb reached into his front pocket. He pulled out a roll of $50 bills. "How much does he need?"

"For that thing? I dunno. Three, four hundred?"

Loeb started counting, then thought better of it. He handed the wad of bills to Scrapneck. "Give him a grand. We gotta be absolutely sure we get this thing and get it gone. I want nothing coming back on us."

Scrapneck looked somewhat perplexed at the wad of bills. He transferred them to his front pocket. "Okay, boss-man. Doesn't get much more sure than a G-note for a submarine with wheels."

"We have to be sure of everything right now," said Loeb. "You of all people know what we've got riding on this."

Scrapneck chuckled. "You still think this phone thing is gonna fly?"

"*Cellular* phone thing," said Loeb. "It's called cellular."

"What does that mean anyway? Cellar-lar?"

Loeb rolled his eyes. He pointed at the two pagers on Scrapneck's belt. "In a couple of years, you won't be able to sell those things for doorstop money. They're launching cellular service in T.O. and Montreal on Canada Day. It's coming here soon enough."

Scrapneck rolled his eyes. "Okay, maybe this portable phone shit will fly in Hogtown and Frogtown, but here? We've got maybe six or seven assholes in this shithole who could even afford it!"

"It won't be just fat cats," said Loeb. "Think about all the road warriors, the guys on the construction sites. Commodities, bankers, doctors, lawyers. Everybody who's somebody is going to want one, and everybody who *dreams* of being somebody will want one."

"Whatever you say, boss-man. It just seems like an awful lot of grown-up trouble we're going through to get people to stop using a pay phone."

Loeb decided to use simple sales logic on the Scrapneck objections. "Okay, Scrap. Let's walk through a typical beep-beep on those pagers of yours. Customer calls the service.

They don't get you, just some hag with a three-packs-a-day habit coming through loud and clear. She says you're not in, which is bullshit. They ask if they can hold, they say they can't, it's an answering service. Some leave a message, some don't. How many do you think don't?"

"How the fuck should I know?" said Scrapneck. "I sold forty-six cars last month. That's one of the best numbers in town for sure."

"I checked for you," said Loeb. "Told the head hag at the answering service that we were thinking about getting all the salesmen on pagers. You sold forty-six cars? You missed out on sixty-five other calls! That's uh, let's see. That's a hunnert-and-eleven cars. *That's* what a cellular phone could do for you! That makes all the money we're going to need to do the side deals legit, instead of that snap-crackle-pop garbage you've got us into."

"You mean crack," said Scrapneck. "You say cell-it-lar is the next big thing for phones? Well, crack is the next big thing for coke."

"That may be," said Loeb. "But that attracts all the wrong kinds of people. Junkies, bikers, and cops."

"We can do both," said Scrapneck. "Fuck 'em with cars, and fuck 'em with crack. Then we fuck 'em with these phones that you think are going to be the cat's ass. Just a good old-fashioned fuck-fest."

"Just keep that shit out of the dealership. I don't need Sandra Lewis from *24*-Fucking-*Hours* doing the news out front with a dozen narcs leading us out in cuffs."

"Don't worry," said Scrapneck. "I got a guy. He's already dealing. The crack gets cooked up local. I've got a kilo coming up from Minneapolis this week. That should pay for all that cellphone shit you want."

"Cell-you-lurr," said Loeb. "It's cell-you-lurr."

CHAPTER
EIGHT

Steve Mahoney was rolling into his driveway a little sooner than he had on Sunday morning, thanks to an absence of river retrieval calls for the Tuesday night shift. There was no reason to hose down the tow cable. The Hot Rod's tear-down had taken a toll on his muscles and his sleep. He parked the Plymouth in the usual spot and was making a beeline for the couch when he saw the flashing red light on the answering machine. Mahoney had already received three messages since Rick Scheer had installed the machine. The first was for an overdue gas bill.

The second was a call from the City Inspections Branch about cleaning up the metal behind his garage. *That old bat Wilson two doors down must have complained again.* The third was from the drunk girl he had convinced to take a cab home from the Marble Club on Sunday morning. He vaguely remembered writing his home number on the invoice for the lockout. He wasn't exactly sure when he was going to have time for her, even if it was just casual.

Today's first message was from the video store on Provencher. "Hello, this is Video Stop calling, just a reminder that your ten videos for ten days for ten dollars will expire today at five o'clock. Please return your videos during normal business hours. A late charge of one dollar per day per video will occur if videos are not returned. Thank you for choosing Video Stop on Provencher."

Mahoney rubbed his eyes as the next message played. "Hi, Steve, this is Diana calling. Don't know if you got my call the other day, but I was thinking that maybe we could get together one of these days, you know? Maybe watch a video or something at your place? Anyway, gimme a call when you got time. Oh, that's right, you work nights. Well, I'm off on Thursday, so maybe we could do breakfast or something? I wanted to thank you for the other night. Oh god, I was so drunk. I really don't get drunk like that all the time. I . . ."

The message clicked. She'd talked too long for the tape. Another message: she called back to apologize and then hung up. Yet another message: an apology for being so spastic, and finally, her phone number.

Mahoney lay back on the couch to listen to the rest of the messages, half-expecting another Diana explanation message or another late utility bill. But this call was coming from someplace noisy. It was Rick Scheer. He must have been calling from a phone in the shop at work.

"Hey, Steve, Rickles. Just got a call from Tim at Dr. Hook, said there's a sixty-something purple Camaro going up at Plessis today. I didn't see one on the list. Is that *the* Camaro? Last-minute add with some other shit. I guess you're not home yet. Anyway, auction starts at ten, like always. Better put on a fresh bra and check it out. I gotta pull a tranny out of a Skylark. Fuck me. Later!"

Mahoney was on the move the moment he heard "purple Camaro." Scheer hadn't mentioned the auction number for the Camaro or where it was in the list. Last-minute additions to the Wednesday auctions were fairly common. It could have been added to the bottom of the list. It could also have been added near the top. Mahoney checked his watch: 9:33 a.m. The auction would start in 27 minutes. He grabbed an entire stack of bills from a Tupperware container in the fridge icebox. He hoped it was enough.

The Plymouth was still warm. Mahoney spat plenty of gravel as he reversed out of the driveway. There were no stops and no cops on Mission Street East. As bumpy as it was, he was still able to manage about 60 miles per hour on the stretch. He knew there'd be no parking at the salvage yard by now, so he pulled into Team Auto Parts on Plessis, an import wrecking yard that was just north of the salvage yard. He banged the office door open. The counter staff were busy handling various parts inquiries. He got the attention of Vic, the owner. If Vic knew you, and knew that you were parking in the lot for the sale, he would point you through to the other entrance to the salvage yard: a ladder against the fence. Mahoney nodded his thanks as he headed through the yard. Three of the guard dogs followed along, as Mahoney zig-zagged around the half-dismantled inventory. The last user had propped the ladder against an orange Volkswagen van. Mahoney took four steps to the top, then over the barbed wire. He twisted his left ankle a bit on landing, though he still managed a good trot towards the auction hall. He heard the announcement over the loudspeakers: five minutes to the sale. Just enough time to get his bid number.

The auction hall was a windowless, prefabricated metal building. There was a counter to get your bid number, a counter for payment, and the lunch counter, where the coffee and the French fry gravy duked it out for the thickness win on a weekly basis. He wrote his name next to bid number 867, printed in large red letters on a piece of heavy paper stock. He grabbed the best position he could, in line with the auctioneer's one good eye. The auction microphone looked like it came out of a 1940s' boxing match. The auctioneer was heavy-set, with a thick shock of white hair, sideburns to match, and tinted bargain glasses. Mahoney had never bothered to find out his name. The only sure thing was that if he hadn't seen you, you hadn't placed a bid. The arguments from losing bidders added at least a half hour to every auction. He was readying himself with the auction list. An Autopac employee was nudging him to start, pointing at his watch. The auctioneer looked annoyed but took the hint. He leaned in close to the microphone.

"All right, gentlemen, welcome to Manitoba Public Insurance salvage auction number one-three-four-seven, over three hundred items up for bid today, let's start at item number one, four Firestone 721 radial tires, size two thirty-five, seventy-five fifteens. Who'll give me two hundred dollars *WHERE?*"

Mahoney breathed. He figured that the Camaro would occur further in, since it wasn't on his list. If there was an updated list, he hadn't seen it, the counter bare of the extra lists printed for the auction. He thought about the gravy and the coffee for a moment. He decided against both.

The auctioneer continued. "Two-two-two-two, now one hundred, who'll give me one hundred, hundred-hundred-hundred annnd now fifty, now fifty, fifty-fifty-fifty *I HAVE FIFTY!*"

Mahoney continued to consult the list, somehow believing that the Camaro would magically jump off the page in front of him. He didn't notice Freddie Rondeau from Grosvenor Towing until he spoke into Mahoney's left ear. "What're you bidding on, Mahoney? Better not be the parts car for my Magnum."

Mahoney shook Rondeau's hand. "Hey, Ronco! Haven't seen you for a while. You still souping up that ugly Cordoba?"

Rondeau looked annoyed. "Why does everyone think it's a Cordoba?"

"Because it is a Cordoba. And a Fury and a Chrysler 300."

"And it's also fast as fuck," said Rondeau. "I put that 440 in from that RCMP highway car. It's fucking scary."

"Now it's as scary as it looks. Nightmare scary. Shit the bed scary."

"Well, if you ever fix that Camaro of yours, we might have to find out."

Mahoney nodded. "It's a date. That's why I'm here."

"For what?" said Rondeau. "There's no Camaro today."

The auctioneer corrected Rondeau. "And now we've got a last-minute addition for today, item number one-b, a 1967 Chevrolet Camaro two-door coupe, water damage, no keys. Who'll give me a thousand dollars *WHERE?*"

"Well," said Rondeau. "I stand fucking corrected."

Mahoney had tuned out Rondeau. He got his bidding card ready. The auctioneer would always start high, then drop to a sensible number to bring in multiple bidders. He had already dropped from a thousand dollars to two hundred. Six hands shot up. The auctioneer played his bidders. At three hundred, two hands dropped out. At four hundred, two more. Things started to stall at $450. The auctioneer felt it too. "Four fifty going once. Four fifty . . .."

"Six hundred!" Mahoney shouted. He felt the eyes of the hall upon him. Four fifty was nuts, but someone went to six? Now they all shook their heads and rolled their eyes. Even the auctioneer perked up. "All right, whoever wants it is gonna get it, I have six hundred, who'll gimme six-fifty, six-fifty, six fifty, *I HAVE SIX-FIFTY!*"

Mahoney looked for the competing bidder. He couldn't see him, just an arm that went up as quickly as Mahoney's counterbids. Six-fifty became $700, $750 became $800. At nine hundred, the counter staff left their posts, eager to see the contest. The auctioneer kept poking the bear. "All right folks, we have nine hundred, nine hundred, can I get nine-fifty-fifty-fifty-fifty-fifty, *I HAVE NINE-FIFTY!*"

"Twelve hundred!" Mahoney heard the number without realizing he'd said it. The audience let out a gasp, peppered with holy versions of shit and fuck. Mahoney looked for his opponent, but the hand was gone.

The auctioneer brought the drama to a close. "Twelve hundred once, twelve hundred *TWICE!*" The well-worn gavel hit the podium with a crack. "*SOLD!* Item number one-b to bidder number eight, eight. Just a minute here, folks. *CAN THE BIDDER PLEASE SHOW HIS NUMBER?*"

Mahoney was riding the winning bid high, so high that he didn't realize his hand had obscured his bid number. He adjusted his grip. Most of the people around him were still shaking their heads, including Rondeau. "And you think my

Dodge is a joke? Why don't you just go buy a decent Camaro for four grand?"

"Simple," said Mahoney. "I don't have four grand." He smiled as he headed over to the counter to pay for his purchase. There was enough change left over from his stack of twenties and fifties for gravy and coffee. Mahoney decided against both.

The arm that had tried to outbid Mahoney was now in use outside the auction hall, dialling on one of two pay phones mounted on the exterior wall, near the entrance.

"Commonwealth Motors Jeep Renault AMC, how may I direct your call?"

"Gimme Scrapneck," said the arm's voice.

"Surely. May I tell him who's calling?"

"No."

The receptionist didn't know how to answer that, though the tone told her not to question it. "One moment, please." The arm tapped its fingers on the phone as the call rang through. Scrapneck answered on the third ring. "Commonwealth Motors, Peter Scrapneck speaking."

"Pete, it's Guy. We got a problem."

CHAPTER NINE

Mahoney headed over to the Hook Me Up office. He fed Larry Ballendine a story about taking Unit 36 home to check its timing. By 11:30, he was back at the salvage compound, hooking up the car that had become the overpriced talk of the Wednesday auction. By noon, he was easing the Camaro into the coin-operated car wash on Rothesay, next to Wiebe's Foods. He had 12 dollars' worth of quarters in his pocket, and he planned to use every one of them. He also knew that this coin-op had the longest cycles in the neighbourhood.

It didn't take long until a few curious pensioners stopped by to watch the strangest of car washes. He had torn open the rest of the carpet, slicing off large chunks to get the water out faster. He laid down across the buckets seats, shooting water up behind the dashboard. He hosed down the entire engine bay, paying no attention to how the water was saturating the inline six. Wherever he saw brown water, Mahoney sprayed until it flowed clear. The adhesive holding the trunk pan drains was brittle enough to open with a screwdriver, just like the floorpan plugs. Mahoney raised the car as high as Unit 36 would let him in the wash bay, rinsing the undercarriage clean. He took special care with the headliner, using a sponge soaked with healthy squirts of dishwashing liquid to clean it. It was black and would look a little strange with his blue interior, but it was intact. So were the metal bows behind it. The ones on his Hot Rod had been mangled by the Kildonan Park elm.

Mahoney felt the sleep coming back hard. He grabbed a Pepsi Big Gulp at a 7-Eleven but passed on the meat stick. He brought the Camaro back to his garage, easing it past the hulk that remained of his Hot Rod on the driveway. He gazed at the purple car and its soon-to-be-attached parts for longer than he should have. He locked up the garage and headed for the couch. He checked his watch: almost half-past three. Enough time for some shut-eye before the evening shift.

JUNE 12, 1985
3:33 P.M.

Guy Clairmont was checking his notes. He had followed Steve Mahoney from the salvage yard to Hook Me Up Towing, back to the salvage yard, the car wash, the 7-Eleven on Edison, and the bungalow on McTavish Street. Clairmont had flipped the A/C to the recirculating function on his black Merkur XR4Ti. It helped to slightly reduce the effects of the mushroom farm, though the smell was still making him queasy. He was parked beneath the CN Rail line. The train rattling overhead and the heavy trucks passing by him on the gravel industrial street did little to distract him. It did knock his Carrera sunglasses off the dashboard and into the passenger-side footwell. Clairmont didn't flinch. He gave his green eyes a rub with his left hand, then a pass with the same hand through his wavy brown hair. He continued by grooming his bushy moustache before flipping to the next page of his notes.

The pay-phone call with Scrapneck hadn't gone well, as expected. Clairmont had been authorized for a grand on the Camaro. He had three hundred of his own on him, and it would stay on him. He'd been burned before in similar deals, topping up a difference that he would be questioned about, and, just as likely, never see again. Scrapneck had demanded to know why he didn't up the ante to secure the car. Clairmont was blunt: "I don't spend what I don't have."

There was another reason for not dipping into his own personal kitty: maximizing profit. The job was simple: make the Camaro go away, by any means necessary. The longer that took, the more he could potentially make, even with the failed Autopac bid. Making wheeled things go away had been Clairmont's specialty since the mid-'70s. He wasn't a big guy, but what he lacked in height, he made up for in skills. He had familiarized himself with the latest car-alarm wiring schematics, the mechanical parts of the locking systems, and the electrical systems of numerous vehicles. He took offense to being called a common car thief. Clairmont had made far more through legitimate repossession work than the days of the Bowman chop shops. Nowadays, dealerships and finance companies were his biggest clients. On occasion, a client would request a special service, a cash-money, no-questions-asked situation. The Camaro was one of those cars.

Clairmont glanced at the digital clock on the dashboard: 3:37 p.m. He checked it against his dress watch, an Omega Seamaster Classic. The hands were parked at 3:39. He corrected the car display. A beeping from his sports jacket on the passenger seat didn't startle him, a beeping that he had thought he heard *before* it happened, like the way that "Radar" O'Reilly heard approaching choppers on the reruns of *M*A*S*H*. Clairmont reached over to the jacket without looking, retrieving a Motorola numeric pager from the inside pocket. The number was the Commonwealth Motors main line, with Scrapneck's extension and "911" next to it. Clairmont tossed the pager onto the seat. It fell to the floor beside the sunglasses.

Peter Scrapneck slammed the receiver down, hard enough for the receptionist and three of the salesmen in their offices to notice. He was starting to sweat, which was never good for the adhesive strips gripping his hairpiece. He opened his bottom desk drawer, revealing a mirror, and leaned down out of sight of the rest of the show- room staff. Once his hairpiece was adjusted, he could think clearly. He looked up at the AMC clock in the showroom; he was late for his pager swap and coke bump. He slid the dead unit into the charger, then headed for the men's.

He was leaving the washroom when he saw the car hauler pull in. It wore Minnesota plates. Scrapneck smiled. He met the driver at the cab, directing him to unload the truck at the rear of the dealership. Twenty minutes later, Scrapneck was surveying the latest additions to the used car department; an Oldsmobile Cutlass, an Impala Sport Coupe, two Ford Granadas, a Chevette, and a Dodge St. Regis sedan. They were all 1979s, easy to import into Canada. All the cars were in good shape, except for the Dodge, which had had something large and heavy recently dropped on its trunk lid. Scrapneck drove it over to the body shop. A replacement trunk lid had already arrived from the wrecking yard, having been re-sprayed in the correct colour. The dented trunk lid eventually made its way to the back of the lot, with the rest of the scrap sheet metal.

The remainder of the evening was typical Wednesday dealership fare. Scrapneck sold two Cherokee Chiefs that had just arrived on the lot on Tuesday. There was a deposit on the Eagle in the showroom, but it didn't look good on the financing side. The used car department sold the American Chevette before it had a proper cleanup and took a deposit on one of the former gas company cars. The grease pencil teaser on its windshield was truthful enough: ONE OWNER.

It was almost 9:45 p.m. when the last customer left the main building. Scrapneck exited through the shop, making sure the man door was locked behind him. As he was securing the door, a pair of headlights swung into the lot. They were attached to an old Ford half-ton. The magnetic signs on the doors said "Free Scrap Metal Removal," with a phone number under it that had to be a pager. The driver gave a quick horn hit, even though it was obvious Scrapneck had seen him. "Hey there," the driver said. "Got any scrap I can take off your hands?"

"Help yourself," said Scrapneck. "It's over there, by the garbage bins." The truck driver nodded his thanks. Scrapneck watched as he went through the panels one by one. He hoisted the Dodge trunk lid into the box, leaving the rest of the panels behind. Before he left, he removed the magnetic signs from his truck and threw them in the open garbage bin. The doors now stated that the truck was in the painting business, with a new pager number. Scrapneck watched as his crack cook drove off the lot, with a kilogram of 90 percent pure cocaine stashed inside the Dodge trunk lid.

Scrapneck wrestled open the driver's gull-wing of his Bricklin. He held the door as high as he could, fishing out a thick manila envelope behind the driver's seat. He locked the Bricklin and headed over to a nondescript Dodge Aspen with his spare dealer plate. The cold Dodge protested, but finally started. Scrapneck headed towards the lab.

The lab space was about 10 minutes from the dealership, in a cinder-block industrial building off Wellington Avenue. Scrapneck gave a quick horn chirp at the rear of the building to open the overhead door. He pulled in quickly when he thought the door was high enough, forgetting the antenna, which was still flailing madly as he exited the car.

The building was a former upholstery shop. Most of the space on the ancient workbenches had been taken over by various chemicals and lab equipment. The damaged trunk lid from the scrap pile was on a folding metal sawhorse, and the crack cook was using an air chisel to separate the exterior panel from the inner structure. The vibration was walking the lid off the sawhorse. Scrapneck caught it. The cook nodded his thanks. Five minutes later, the trunk lid was on the floor. Scrapneck and the cook separated the two pieces with a pair of pry bars.

The cocaine was stowed near the lock mechanism. Scrapneck's connection in Minneapolis had disconnected the mechanism after the drugs had been stashed. The damage, and the fact that the trunk lid couldn't be opened at the Emerson crossing, was of little concern to the border guards. Commonwealth had been buying used and lightly damaged cars at various American dealer auctions for years. The paperwork was always in order. The transport drivers never seemed jumpy during the inspections. It also helped that the dealership had recently sold a large fleet of Cherokees to the local federal government office. Commonwealth was a trusted vendor, properly vetted. Nobody ever strip-searched its cars.

The Dodge was the first car to make a smuggling trip. Scrapneck knew he could probably get away with three or four more shipments until he had to shut things down. Once the crack hit the streets in Winnipeg, the local police and the RCMP would watch the border more closely. Eventually, known criminals like the Heaven's Rejects would move in and probably use their preferred channels from Montreal for the coke base. The window of opportunity was small, but the payoff would put Dick Loeb into the cellular phone business and Scrapneck into the president's chair at Commonwealth, if he wanted it.

Once the cocaine was out, Scrapneck tossed the envelope to the cook. The cook rifled through it. He gave an approving nod for the five grand, then hit the garage door opener for Scrapneck to exit. He felt his throat constricting as he approached the Silver Heights apartments, better known to current and former residents as the Silverfish. Once a pinnacle of 1950s apartment living, the Silverfish needed both a serious makeover and regular visits from an exterminator.

Scrapneck wanted to see if there was any police activity at the apartment block. Judging by the black-and-white, the unmarked Ford LTD, and the Crime Scene Investigations van parked in front of the Silverfish, the police had found the home of the woman in the Camaro. It was apartment 207. It had chocolate-brown appliances and green drapes. It had a bubble-gum pink bathroom, with a toilet handle that needed an extra jiggle to keep it from running after a flush. Scrapneck knew the apartment. He knew the woman who lived there.

The one he had agreed to handcuff to the steering wheel.

CHAPTER
ELEVEN

JUNE 16, 1985
8:24 A.M.

Steve Mahoney decided on a proper breakfast at the
end of his shift. He eased the Plymouth through
the McDonald's drive-through on Henderson
Highway, opting for two Egg McMuffins, hash
browns, and a large coffee. He had succeeded in
taking a few catnaps during his Saturday night
shift in Unit 36. It had been slow, allowing him
to duck out early. Larry Ballendine had told him
on Friday that he would be switching Mahoney's
shifts to days. He gave him the opportunity to join
in with the illegal shenanigans of the night crew
one last time, but Mahoney refused. "Then days

you fucking get," said Ballendine, as he slammed the door to his office, shaking the venetian blinds on his window. Mahoney had made the decision that today would be a full garage day and had already stocked the fridge accordingly: Old Vienna for Scheer, Black Label for Petkau, and Club for himself and Fiddler. Two extra-large Gondola pizzas chilling in the fridge would supply the fuel.

The Camaro had dried out sufficiently from Wednesday's coin wash, aided by a couple of dehumidifiers in the garage. Since the auction win, Mahoney had done as many of the one-man jobs that he could, saving the major mechanicals for the crew. Scheer was sent in for the under-dash wiring harness work, the usual task assigned to the most compact of mechanics. Mahoney had made a cardboard template from the Hot Rod's floorpan to make sure the hole would be cut in the right spot for the floor shifter. The consensus on the donor platform was that it hadn't seen many winters, if at all. Things that should have been seized by rust came off easily. By 7 p.m., the team had assembled around the pizzas on the Plymouth's hood. The faded blue steel also served as the coaster for their respective beers.

Mahoney gave the toast. "Here's to probably the easiest buildup of any piece-of-shit car that any of us has ever owned." The bottles clinked, along with boisterous approval from the rest of the crew. Scheer took a swig of OV, then went back to examining his hands, flipping them back and forth. "What's the matter, Rickles? Did you get a sliver?" Mahoney asked.

"Look at my hands," said Scheer. "What's wrong with this picture?"

Petkau glanced over. "Well, they do look a little like ladies' hands."

Fiddler agreed. "Yeah, when you use that Palmolive to jack off with, that's what happens."

"Fuck you, Fiddy," said Scheer. "Look at them, they're not cut up!"

Mahoney looked at Scheer's hands, then his own. "He's right. What about the rest of you guys?"

Fiddler checked both sides of his hands, while Petkau did the same. They looked at each other, and Mahoney started laughing as they played Patty Cake. "Patty cake, patty cake, baker's man. Fix this car as fast as you can. Wash it, clean it, rub-a-dub-dub. Fuck this shit and give me a Club!" Fiddler sang.

Mahoney was still laughing as he grabbed another Club out of the cooler. As he came back up to the Plymouth table, he noticed that Scheer was still looking at his hands intently. He wasn't laughing. Mahoney popped his cap with his Bic lighter and took a large swig. "Okay, Rickles, so you're not as cut up as a typical day with Ponchos and old-fart Buicks. What's so weird about that?"

Scheer looked at Mahoney, a look that was far more serious than one would expect for anything car-related. "*I always* get cut when I'm working on anything. Whether it's my truck, the day job, or that Shit-Vette behind me, I always nick something." He turned to Fiddler and Petkau. "C'mon, guys, help me out here."

"He's got a point," said Fiddler, checking his left hand with a beer in his right. "I mean, I don't get as cut as much as I used to. Everything we're working on is new at the dealer."

"Fiddy's right," said Petkau. "The used cars'll bite yah. Look at what this fucking Malibu did to me on Friday." A deep slice on his thumb was only starting to heal. "Stupid Iraqi taxi. Had a burr on the shifter linkage. Who the fuck orders a three-speed stick on the floor anyway?"

"I heard it's all those guys know how to fix," said Fiddler. "The automatic is too complicated."

"There's something else," said Scheer. "How much shit got broken?"

Mahoney thought about it. He looked at the Camaro in the garage. The open hood showed off the gleaming chrome of the transplanted engine. "Nothing I can remember. Fiddy? Pet?"

"Nothing from me boss," said Fiddler. "Howie?"

"Not even a stripped bolt," said Petkau. "I mean shit, we got it done in *one day!* This thing went perfect."

"Well, that's what we hope," said Mahoney. "I guess we better make sure." Mahoney put his beer down and went to inspect the engine bay. Everything had been tightened and torqued to specification. The radiator cap was off, a funnel inserted in the hole, ready to add additional water when the thermostat opened. The engine bay wiring harness from his Hot Rod had been fastened to its factory-approved routing. The Cragar Screamer wheels needed a little more spit and polish, but they still looked respectable, especially with the fresh set of Radial T/As that Mahoney had installed on the Hot Rod a week before the tree branch came down. A newish battery was ready to supply the starter drive. Mahoney headed for the driver's seat.

The rest of the crew had moved to the front fenders as Mahoney slid behind the wheel. He had convinced himself that the blue upholstery was working. The black headliner was the only piece of soft trim retained from the Camaro's river plunge. Mahoney took a deep breath. Any Red River funk left behind was barely noticeable. He looked over at the keys, the set he had pocketed when he had first pulled the car out of the river. He brushed against the rabbit's foot, and it swung back and forth. He turned the key to the ON position.

The various idiot lights came on in the gauge cluster. The heater fan motor started to hum. The Pioneer Supertuner II transplanted from the Hot Rod started up into a promo for the Lamont Hollywood afternoon show on 92 CITI FM, with Streetheart's "Hollywood" as the music bed. Mahoney turned the key. Nothing. He poked his head out the window. "Hey, Rickles!"

Scheer looked up from the engine bay. "Hey what?"

"Did you tighten up the battery?"

"Uh, maybe." Scheer checked the connections. He grabbed a wrench from the tool stand to snug up the nuts. "Try it now!"

The engine cranked without issue. Mahoney turned the key back, gave the gas four solid pumps, then cranked again. The Hot Rod's heart roared to life. He prodded the accelerator to get past a momentary fuel delivery stumble. The engine found the fast idle it needed and stayed there until Mahoney kicked it down. The crew hooted their approval but stayed attentive for any gushing fluids. Scheer added water to the radiator when the thermostat opened. Fiddler checked underneath the car for exhaust leaks and main seal drips. Petkau moved the Plymouth patio table back, allowing the Camaro to roll out into the last of the day's sun. The car wore the Hot Rod's old plates. As far as Autopac was concerned they were still valid. There was a bit of a loophole to allow the plate transfer, even if the paper trail was an outright forgery. Mahoney had stated on a hand-drawn bill of sale that he had sold what was left of the Hot Rod to Scheer on the 15th of June. That meant that the Hot Rod's plates could be transferred to another car for a one-week grace period, with insurance. That also meant that the Camaro was headed out for a Sunday-night cruise.

"Shotgun!" Fiddler shouted. Scheer and Petkau didn't argue the request. Fiddler was the beefiest of the crew, the best fit for the front seat. Scheer pushed the rear folding seat back up into position. Mahoney was doing lock-up duties: house, garage, Plymouth. He returned with a cheap pair of aviators perched atop his head and his acid-washed jean jacket in hand for when the sun went down. He closed the driver's door firmly, throwing the jacket in the back seat onto Petkau and Scheer. "Try not to fart too much on it while you're back there, ladies." He put the Camaro in drive and headed north to Mission.

"No farts," said Petkau. "I'll just wipe the sleeves on my nut sack."

"Fuck, that's gross," said Fiddler. "Like those mushroom farts on the corner."

Scheer agreed. "At least you're not back here smelling it." He poked Mahoney in the left shoulder. "Hey, your Steve-ness. Turn on the fan, get some air moving back here."

Mahoney turned to look at the rear seat crew, then at Fiddler. "You boys want some air moving back there?"

The crew caught the tell. Scheer and Petkau frantically scrambled for their lap belts. Fiddler had done the same, smacking the door lock knob down for good measure. The memo about the Hot Rod's return must have made it to 92 CITI FM. The opening gallop of Aerosmith's "Back in the Saddle" filled the cabin. Fiddler turned the volume up to 11. Mahoney saw the hole in traffic. He took it, with about three-quarters of the throttle pedal, as Steven Tyler announced at full volume that Mahoney, the crew, and the Hot Rod were finally back. The shrieking tires were almost drowned out by the approval of the Camaro's occupants. Mahoney let the car's rear slide out just enough to the right, then backed off the throttle to straighten it out. He then gave the throttle a floor-stomping push. The Hot Rod's heart tried to push the Camaro sideways again. Mahoney knew exactly where to compensate. He wasn't as aggressive for the yield onto Provencher Boulevard.

Sunday night was the official car cruising night in Winnipeg. Mahoney had seen the odd black-and-white rolling down the main drag of the French Quarter on previous Sundays. He would have to keep things tame on Portage Avenue, on his way to the Polo Park Shopping Centre. The deserted parking lot made for a popular destination for the car-crazy, in addition to other closed businesses along the Portage strip. The parking lots would become impromptu car shows of varying sizes and makes, if enough cars from a club showed up together. Shop would be talked. Brags would be made. If enough bravado presented itself, drag races would be organized. The Brady Road landfill access was a popular spot, but it was a dead-end street. Park Lane Avenue had better escape opportunities, as did many of the city's industrial areas. But Mahoney wasn't here to race. He was here to re-introduce his Hot Rod.

The crew was sitting at a red light at Portage and Broadway when they heard the rumble coming up on the passenger side. A black '64 Rambler American sedan was doing its best to keep idling, with a supercharged Chevy 427 Big-Block hanging out of the hood. The driver shouted to Scheer with a familiar handle. "Hey, Rickles! Is that you?"

Scheer returned a friendly wave. "Hey, Jamie! How's the Rumbler?" Jamie Johnston's Rambler was something of a local legend, with a nickname to match. It was hard to miss the car, in visual and in tone. The Rumbler was a Pro-Street build, a street-legal drag racer, with more tire than axle visible at the rear. The entire car shook, something that most 500-plus horsepower cars will tend to do. Johnston said what most men do while behind the wheel of a roll-barred monster. *"What?"*

Scheer stepped up the volume. *"How's the Rumbler?"*

"The Rumbler? She's fucking awesome! Hey, is that the U-boat Camaro?"

Word had got around regarding the Autopac salvage Camaro. The car, and Unit 36, had been splashed across the front pages of the *Sun*, the *Free Press*, and the *Winnipeg Sentinel* earlier in the week. The *Sentinel* picture had a pretty clear shot of Mahoney. The flashbulb had hit him just right as he crossed the North Perimeter Bridge.

"It's a lot better now," said Scheer. *"It's got the guts from Mahoney's Super Sport!"*

"Sweet!" said Johnston. *"See you at Polo!"*

The light went green. The pair kept their speed respectable, as they drove past the flapping streamers strung atop the new Jeeps at Commonwealth Motors.

CHAPTER
TWELVE

Dick Loeb heard the rumble. He knew of
such things better than most. Sitting in his
Commonwealth office, he looked up at a black-
and-white picture of his own Hot Rod, taken
around 1956. It was a 1940 Ford coupe, fitted
with a Cadillac V8 that he had pulled out of a
wrecked hearse. Part of him wanted to open the
lot on Sunday nights, clear the front row, and
spend some time just hanging out with the gearheads. Two wood-panelled Grand Wagoneers
stood sentry over the dealership's Portage
Avenue access points. It was Scrapneck's idea,

keeping out the riff-raff, minimizing the litter. Loeb looked at the keys to the Wagoneers, keys that Scrapneck had thrown on his desk before he left. If only he had the time.

The white noise from the cruise night cars and the Nash clock helped him concentrate, as he looked over the plan that could get him out of the car business for good. The stack of news clippings told the story of the new portable phone service known as cellular. Cantel had been granted a national license for cellular service in Canada, while the Manitoba Telephone System would surely transition from its current mobile operator phone system to the new cellular technology in short order. Loeb felt that Cantel was too "Toronto" to make it on the prairies. He cringed every time he went to dealer meetings and his plane started its bumpy descent into Toronto's Pearson airport. Most Easterners still viewed Winnipeg as a hick town, especially after former Blue Bomber's quarterback Dieter Brock had dubbed the local zoo the only attraction worth visiting. Loeb knew that view could work to his advantage. No one would expect a car dealer from Winnipeg to become a major player in the uncharted world of portable telephony in Canada. Loeb was betting on it, big time.

He flipped through the feasibility reports, prepared by a cellular provider out of Los Angeles. Putting up towers in the rural areas wouldn't be a problem. Most farmers would welcome the extra dollars to lease a site on their land, especially when the footprint would take little away from their canola crop or grazing plots. Downtown was the challenge. The only way to ensure calls wouldn't drop was to place multiple antennas. Loeb looked through his folder of lease agreements for downtown rooftops in Winnipeg. The property management companies had looked at him sideways when he had made the arrangements in the spring of '84, paying for space on top of buildings where he didn't even have a key for access. That didn't stop them from sending their monthly invoices. Loeb did the math on what was outstanding for June. It came close to the price that was scrawled across the windshield of the Eagle that nobody wanted in the showroom. What Loeb wanted and what the property management companies saw little concern in providing was exclusivity for that rooftop space. He had secured the best possible antenna placement points in the downtown area for the next five years. The only way any cellular provider could secure the site leases would be to buy him out, and that wasn't going to come cheap. Loeb figured that the payout would be enough for him to retire comfortably and even afford a messy divorce.

There were other messes that were more pressing. Loeb picked up the Monday edition of the *Sentinel*. The front-page image was split in two. One half was a picture of a car being pulled out of the Red River, taken from the North Perimeter Bridge. On the other side was a graduation picture from the University of Manitoba, of a red-headed woman by the name of Heather Price. The story, entitled "Watery Grave," delivered the basic facts: 33 years old, divorced, no children, parents were dead, lived at the Silver Heights apartments, worked as a freelance bookkeeper for multiple clients. Foul play was not suspected, according to Detective-Sergeant Patrick Milroy, the lead investigator. Commonwealth Motors did get a mention of sorts, the nameless Portage Avenue car dealership that had reported the car stolen from its used inventory.

There was a secondary story at the bottom of the page. The police department's auto theft unit commented on the rash of thefts of pre-1969 cars in the city, which pre-dated locking steering columns. Loeb knew that auto-theft was

a problem at most dealerships, when lot boys more concerned about their hot dates forgot their jobs and left keys
in unlocked cars. Commonwealth lost some four cars a year
because of it, along with four lazy lot boys. The possibility
was plausible. That was all that mattered.

Loeb put down the newspaper, returning to the rest of
the files. He came across one entitled *Ventura Communications*.
The folder had additional invoices for rooftop leases in
Regina, Saskatoon, Calgary, Edmonton, and Vancouver, plus
details of money transfers from Commonwealth Motors
(1967) Incorporated to Ventura. There were two files sand-
wiched into the folder. The first file had the word *Real* written
in red Sharpie across the top. The second file said *Inflated*.
Loeb had explained to the now-late Heather Price that he had
been receiving cash payments from a few select customers.
He needed a way to make the numbers jibe with what was in
the accounts. Price had found a way. The actual source of the
cash was from a second mortgage that Loeb had taken out on
the Wellington Crescent house, forging his wife's signature
to get the funds. Price did her magic, adjusting all manner of
accounts payable and receivable to present two business ventures that, on paper, looked as solid as a new Jeep. Loeb figured he could keep making the payments on the leases until
September with the current kitty. Scrapneck had assured
him that the cocaine venture would stretch that buffer to the
spring of '86. Loeb figured that Cantel and the provincial telecommunications companies would have realized what he had
done by late August, as they prepared for their expected roll-
outs. That's when the phone would start ringing, along with
the cash register in his head.

Loeb stopped sifting. He went back to the front page of
the *Sentinel*. Scrapneck had told him it had to be done, an

unfortunate turn of events that no one could have predicted, that there wasn't any other choice. Loeb wondered if there was anything more to that story.

He only wondered for a moment.

Steve Mahoney and his crew pulled into his driveway just after 11 p.m. The inside of the Camaro had been getting a little rank, thanks to the after-effects of the beers and pizza. At least there weren't any strange smells from the car itself. It wasn't pulling to the left or to the right. The brakes felt firm. Nothing was leaking from underneath. There wasn't even the expected dieseling event when the engine was finally turned off. For a Chevy, Mahoney thought, it was about as perfect as it could get.

Mahoney gave the crew a prolonged, oversized wave as they backed out of the driveway. Mahoney rolled down the garage door to encase the warmth of the Camaro's engine. He switched on the fluorescent tubes overhead. It made for a weird effect on the Camaro's hood, as though the car was still moving under the street lamps of Portage Avenue. Mahoney opened the driver's door and stretched out in the seat. He turned the key to the accessory position. The radio fired up halfway into "Bust the TV" by The Pumps on 92 CITI FM. He turned the tuner dial to the right. KISS FM was playing something by some guy named Gowan, who was quite concerned about strange animals. Mahoney thought the song sounded more AM than FM. He checked the AM band. Sure enough, KY-58 was playing the same song. On 13 CFRW, it was Corey Hart's "Sunglasses at Night." *Ugh, Corey Hart.* He pulled out the mix tape from his jacket pocket, the one that had appeared in his mailbox from the spastic Diana, the leaver of voice messages. *She must have dropped it off tonight.* They had finally connected by phone on Saturday, before he left for his last night shift. He had given her his address while making plans for Monday night, after her suggestion of cooking up some hamburgers on his barbecue. When he mentioned that he didn't have hamburgers or a barbecue, she offered to bring both. He listened as the first song kicked in. It was Foreigner, though not the "Dirty White Boy" cruncher that Mahoney preferred. Lou Gramm wanted to know what this thing called love was all about, and that it would be nice if the girl in question could show him. After a few bars, he hit fast-forward. More Corey Hart, needing more time than Mister Hart had allotted for, in his pursuit of true love. *Ugh.*

Mahoney hit the fast-forward button, hard. He landed on a blank spot in the tape. Perhaps this was Diana's first mix tape. Mahoney doubted that, judging by the expert spacing of Diana's lettering on the cassette tape's liner. He listened as the next song started up. There was something that sounded like a synthesized organ. Then, a strong guitar riff. Substantial bass. Mahoney played around with the tone dial to get the sound right. There was a lot of talk about pain as the song began, pain that the female antagonist couldn't ease. A lot of infidelity going on, even less truth. The guy was pretty broken up about the whole thing. According to the cassette liner, his name was either Godley or Creme. *Maybe Godley Creme?* A single word comprised the title. Mahoney heard the word leave his lips.

"Cry."

He liked what he was hearing, something that seldom happened when the Rolling Stones were excluded from the Supertuner. He turned up the volume to the edge of distortion. He leaned back in the bucket seat. He rested the back of his neck on the top of the seat. He stared at the backlit courtesy light on the roof as his reference point. He closed his eyes as the Godley, or possibly the Creme, spoke of the action that occurred when water filled theirs.

Mahoney held the top of his steering wheel as he listened to the lyric fade into the music. That's when the tape died, but it wasn't the only thing that went dark. The fluorescent tubes overhead flickered out as well. The only light in the entire garage was the courtesy lamp directly above Mahoney's head. That went out too, slowly, the way the tube on a TV set dies out when it's turned off in a dark room.

Mahoney sat up. There was a strange hum coming from behind the dashboard. The dial on the Supertuner started to flicker. Then it started to move. The car's exterior lights started to flicker as well. The radio dial stopped on 680 CJOB, on the AM dial. The radio transmission was cutting in and out. Then it tuned in.

"It's 8 a.m., and it's time for the news on 680 CJOB. I'm George McCloy. Winnipeg Police are investigating the discovery of a vehicle in the early morning hours yesterday . . ."

Yesterday?

". . . submerged at the boat launch near the North Perimeter Highway. The body of a woman found inside the vehicle appeared to have drowned. Winnipeg Police are not revealing any additional details at this time but are appealing to the public for any information. The vehicle is described as a dark-coloured, older model Chevrolet Camaro two-door coupe . . ."

Mahoney watched wide-eyed, as the radio self-tuned again, this time to Information Radio 990 AM, the CBC. Mahoney heard the date come in for the newscast during the tuning. It was for June 11th. Five days ago.

". . . the woman found in a vehicle in the Red River early Sunday morning has been identified as Heather Price, a thirty-three-year-old St. James resident. Price was last seen by neighbours at her residence at the Silver Heights apartment complex around six o'clock Saturday evening . . ."

Mahoney didn't know what to do. His mind was telling him to run, while his body was fused to the bucket seat. The random tuning continued, returning to Information Radio. He thought he heard the date as June 14th. The story wasn't fractured like the other transmissions. It came through loud and clear. No hiss. No pops.

Bad mojo. That's what he himself had said about the car.

"Winnipeg Police announced today that the cause of death for Heather Price, a St. James woman found in a stolen car in the Red River on June ninth, has been officially ruled a suicide. Detective-Sergeant Patrick Milroy of the robbery-homicide division made the announcement at an early morning press conference at the Public Safety Building . . ."

Mahoney listened to the detective tell the official police version of events. *Oops*, he thought. *Detective-Sergeant.*

"We believe there is no reason to suspect foul play. Investigators recovered a note from the victim's apartment, speaking to her intentions. There was also evidence of drug use that was discovered at the apartment and during the autopsy."

Mahoney's legs were starting to cramp up. The CBC announcer continued with the story.

"The vehicle was discovered during the early morning hours on June ninth, after passengers on the *MS Paddlewheel Queen* noticed lights shining underwater at the North Main Street boat launch. In Sports, the Winnipeg Blue Bombers will host the Calgary Stampeders for the second game of the pre-season this Sunday at the Winnipeg Stadium. Head coach and general manager Cal Murphy said the loss to the Saskatchewan Roughriders on Monday . . ."

The radio dial went dead. The lights came back on in the shop. The radio went back to playing the tape. Bruce Springsteen was apparently on fire. Just like Mahoney's brain.

Mahoney hit the eject button, hard. He pulled the key out of the ignition, and finally found the strength to spring from the driver's seat.

CHAPTER
THIRTEEN

It was coming up on midnight. Steve Mahoney
had momentarily forgotten where to knock
his foot to open the bungalow's sticky door.
Truth be told, he had almost taken the door
off its hinges with his body weight. He was
trying to catch his breath from the garage-to-
house sprint. It wasn't the Colts, the pizza, or
the four-ish bottles of Club that needed to be
drained. It was the car. Or maybe it was the
garage, and that stupid ballast resistor messing
with his eyes. Maybe Loveday Mushroom Farms
had mixed in a batch of shrooms by mistake

into their fresh manure base, which had somehow made their way south onto the Mahoney property and into his olfactory receptors. Whatever it was, the experience felt very real. *Not even a skunky Club could do this*, Mahoney thought. Black Label maybe, but not a Club.

He turned on every light in the bungalow. He checked under the bed, in the closet, and under the kitchen cupboards, somehow convinced this was all part of an elaborate prank by the crew. There were no tape recorders, no electrical connections, no snickering friends in any hiding places that could have concealed them. He peeked through the curtains at the front of the house. None of the crew's cars were in the driveway or on the street. The only sounds were from the nearby rail line, an oversized freight, heading east.

There was one tape recorder that had been working throughout the evening. Mahoney walked over to the flashing red light of the answering machine. He pressed play.

"Hello, this is Video Stop on Provencher calling about your late videos . . ."

Mahoney looked at the top of the TV. The videos were right where he had left them. He hit the fast-forward button.

"This message is from the Winnipeg Water and Waste Department. We have been unable to obtain a meter reading from your residence for . . ."

Mahoney hit the fast-forward button. The machine beeped with the next message start. It was Diana.

"Hi, Steve, it's Diana. I hope you don't mind, but I dropped off a mix tape. It's in the mailbox. Maybe we could, uhm, listen to it together tomorrow? I could bring some candles I got from Avon. What is it with the stink in Saint Bee anyway? I'll give you my pager number just in case. It's . . ."

The message had gone too long, again. Diana called back,

apologized, then somehow managed to squeak the pager number in within the allotted time. It did cut off all her additional ramble. The last message was from the manager at Video Stop. He sounded pissed. A robotic voice announced that there were no new messages. Mahoney rubbed his eyes. The switch to days would take some adjustment. He changed the alarm clock on his digital watch. He doubted that sleep would come as he curled up on the couch. One thought filled his mind. *What the fuck was that all about?* The rumbling of the eastbound freight helped silence it.

JUNE 17, 1985

The new Monday day shift was routine. Mahoney had a few calls to pick up cars from garages where customers had failed to pay their repair bills, part of the provincial protection under the Garage Keepers Act. The cars went to the Autopac compound for auction. A few downtown lockouts, a mid-'70s Malibu Classic with a popped radiator hose, and a three-car pileup at Broadway and Maryland rounded out the day. All the while, Mahoney was thinking about the strange events inside the new iteration of his Hot Rod. He had called Scheer from a pay phone, asking if he remembered anything strange about the wiring harness installation underneath the dashboard. "It all plugged in sweet and tight!" yelled Scheer, over the din of a grinder in the stall next to him at the dealership. "It was a little cramped, but if there's a problem with the radio cutting in and out, I'd say it's the radio."

As Mahoney pulled into his driveway just after 5:30, he noticed a familiar car parked in his usual Plymouth spot, a red Ford EXP with the rear hatch open. His house door was still closed. There was something in the air mixed with the usual St. Boniface aroma. Mahoney followed his nose to the backyard. Diana was making the most of the surroundings. A vinyl red-and-white tablecloth meant for a square table had been placed on top of the wooden cable spool that Mahoney had re-purposed as his patio table. She had stacked a few of the loose cinder blocks on the lopsided patio into a platform for the barbecue, a Hibachi that she had just purchased, judging from the open box next to the bag of Kingsford briquettes. She had obviously been there a while, as the briquettes had burned from black to white. She wore cut-off jean shorts and an oversized white T-shirt that read FRANKIE SAY RELAX DON'T DO IT. Her permed blonde hair was pulled back, contained in some form of clip or hair band he couldn't see, keeping it clear of the sizzling burgers. The shirt was loose enough that he could see the top of her breasts, as she leaned over the Hibachi with an equally new spatula. A red slim-line Sanyo boombox on the cable spool table was cranking out what had to be another Diana mix-tape. It was a Cyndi Lauper standard. Diana sang along, badly.

Mahoney couldn't resist. "So, is that all you really want?"

Diana looked up. She smiled, turning as red as her boombox. She put her arm in front of her eyes. "Don't look at me! Don't listen to me! I know I suck!"

Mahoney smiled back. "You need some help with that?"

Diana looked down at the flaming burgers, a combination of regular ground beef and minimal charcoal experience. "Uh, no, I think we're okay." Diana checked the rest of the bags. She frowned. "Uh, you don't have any buns, do you?"

"I'll check the freezer," said Mahoney. "You want a beer?"

"Sure thing. This is thirsty work!" Diana continued with the Hibachi, bending over farther than she needed to, for

Mahoney's benefit. At least, that's what he told himself. He went inside to check on the meagre foodstuffs in his bachelor fridge. No hamburger buns, though he had a half-dozen hot dog buns with minimal freezer burn. He defrosted them in the microwave as he checked on the condition of the condiments. After a gagging fit from opening a jar of putrid Miracle Whip, he settled on the fast-food ketchup, mustard, and relish in the junk drawer. He grabbed the two lawn chairs that were set up in the living room for the crew, then headed to the patio with the condiment packets, the buns, two Clubs, and some paper plates.

The burgers were very well done, probably a good thing, when Diana mentioned that the meat was half price at Penner Foods. Mahoney was as chivalrous as possible as he set up the bistro space and cut the burgers to fit the hot dog buns. He helped squeeze out the toppings from the packets onto Diana's burger dog while she told him about her day. She worked for a company by the name of Maclean-Hunter Paging. She showed Mahoney her pager, a Motorola numeric model, explaining how she could be reached. "So all you do is call the number, wait for the message to end, then punch in your number."

Mahoney held the pager in his hand, then smirked. "I guess I better upgrade my rotary phone."

Diana almost launched her beer onto him. "Better get with the times, old timer. Actually, I'm one to talk."

"What do you mean?"

"They keep talking about these cellular phones in the States," said Diana. "It's starting up at the end of the month out east. Then I guess it'll head this way and then I'm out of a job."

"Or you could sell those phones instead. Looks like you got some experience."

Diana looked at him, suddenly serious. "I beg your pardon?"

Mahoney stumbled. "Uh, what I meant was, I mean . . ."

"Just kidding, *Steven*." Diana took another swig from her Club before continuing. "I've been looking into what it's all about. The shit is expensive! I saw an ad in the States for one for like four grand! That's almost half what I paid for my car! And that's just for the phone! Then they charge you for the minutes. You gotta be a rich asshole to even think about it."

"Yeah, that's a real problem around here." Mahoney pointed to his next-door neighbours. "I'm surrounded by millionaires."

Diana hurried to finish a bite, motioning with her finger that she was about to speak. "Yeah, the whole street smells of money. I can't believe the city allows that place to be there."

"Keeps out the riff-raff." Mahoney figured it was time to dig for some more personal information. "So what end of town do you live in?"

"West K, on Jefferson," said Diana. *Bit of a haul,* Mahoney thought. He wasn't quite sure if she was worth the mileage, yet. He thought of a way to find out. "So, you want to watch a video or something?"

"Sure!" Diana reached into her oversized purse, producing the Avon candles promised in her message. "We can try these out, see if they take away the smell of all that money."

The two finished their dinner before heading in. Mahoney checked in on the Camaro, telling Diana that he needed to retrieve her mix tape from it. She wasn't into cars, but she did like the colour. The ballast resistor issue had calmed itself, as had the other lighting issues of car and garage.

Mahoney made the usual apologies for the state of his place. Diana didn't seem to be bothered. She went through the videos on top of the VCR as Mahoney changed into a less-greasy shirt, one that still had some remnants of cologne in the fabric. He doubted she would find anything in the selection. The crew had spent a night comparing car chases from various car classics. It came down to a tie between *Bullitt* and *The Seven-Ups*, with an honourable mention for Burt Reynolds as Gator McKlusky in *White Lightning*. She stopped on the one title that Mahoney hadn't got around to viewing. "What about this one?"

Mahoney looked at the Video Stop box. Like most video stores, the Video Stop outlet had switched out the flimsy consumer packaging with something more durable. The only identification for the movie was the title, in black script on a bright yellow background with the Video Stop logo. "Yeah, we could watch that if you want. I hear it's kinda scary, though."

Diana didn't look too concerned. "I don't mind. As long as you don't mind if I freak out a bit."

"I'll protect you." Mahoney took the video box from her. He fast-forwarded the movie while she lit her Avon candles and retrieved two more bottles of Club from the fridge. He adjusted the tracking on the movie as the screen displayed the warning about video piracy and explained that Interpol had agreed to start doing something about it in September of 1977. Mahoney sat down on the couch. Diana moved in close. He hit Play on the remote. The sound of something old and carbureted growled through the speakers. A gold vee emblem appeared out of the darkness. The first line of script mentioned that the movie was one of John Carpenter's. The engine revved. The title appeared in red. The movie was also a Richard Kobritz Production. Diana addressed the elephant in the room. "So, is Christine, like, a person or a car?"

Mahoney thought about it for a moment. "I guess she's kinda both."

Steve Mahoney had a feeling he would only be seeing bits and pieces of John Carpenter's *Christine*.
By the time the smouldering Plymouth had pulled
into Darnell's Do It Yourself Garage, Mahoney's
face was firmly planted between Diana's legs,
his pants bunched around his ankles, in return
for Diana's introductory blow job. He'd caught
glimpses of what Christine had done to a similar '67 Camaro Hot Rod, and Buddy Repperton,
while he was removing Diana's RELAX T-shirt.
Now wasn't the time to offer a running commentary on the issues of car continuity for the film,

like the fact that the Camaro that Christine had smashed at the gas station didn't have an engine under its hood. He concentrated on the slippery matter at hand. *Hand*, thought Mahoney. He inserted two fingers inside Diana, pushing her over the edge.

He lifted her up from the couch, planting himself firmly inside for the short trip to the bedroom. He could still hear the movie playing in the background during their romp. After the third coming of both parties, Mahoney excused himself for a glass of water. Christine was being pummelled, doggy-style, by a bulldozer in Darnell's Garage, as Mahoney strolled naked past the television. He watched the climax as he sipped from his *Return of the Jedi* Slurpee cup, the one with the Ewoks on it. The punishment on the small screen truly fit the crime, as far as any Chevy lover was concerned.

Mahoney felt Diana's arms around his waist. "That's what I should have done to my last car."

"Really? What was it?"

"Pinto."

Mahoney took another swig of water, then offered the cup to Diana. "I thought those things destroyed themselves."

"Pretty much." She took a drink, then handed back the cup. She let her hands wander south. "Speaking of destroying things . . ."

Mahoney got the hint. "They're going to have to call a tow truck for my dick after this crash."

Diana smiled, leading him back to the bedroom. "I hope your Autopac is all paid up." She laughed as she jumped on the bed, swinging the door closed for round four.

Guy Clairmont had made a few passes down McTavish Street that night, before heading over to the Robin's Donuts on

Provencher to consult his notes. He had seen the permed blonde arrive with her hamburger and cooking gear. He had seen the pair go into the house. He had seen the lights go out inside, except for what must have been a RadioShack strobe light in the bedroom. The pair had used that freaky light show for about an hour before turning it off. He had also seen how the man who had outbid him at the Autopac auction had locked up the garage with the Camaro on his current Get List: tight, with an EXP and a Plymouth shitbox blocking the door.

Clairmont wasn't thrilled about what it would take to get the car out of the garage. He had been successful in obtaining cars from darkened driveways and back lanes when the conditions were beyond perfect before. The best driveways for a boost had the steepest inclines. He could glide a vehicle out of a driveway in Neutral, usually landing it a house or two away if the roll speed was right. If the coast was clear, the start-up on the freshly moved car would be far enough away that its owner wouldn't even roll over in bed. That wasn't going to happen on McTavish Street. The garage was set too far back on the property, with zero incline. Even if he could make his way down the driveway without a nosy neighbour seeing him, he still had to break into the garage side door before that. Clairmont had no idea how the roll-up door was secured. He could be staring at a separate pair of padlocks for all he knew. That would probably be the moment when the owner would burst into the garage. Judging from the man's size, Clairmont figured his ass would promptly be handed to him.

Clairmont doodled for a moment. *The girl*, Clairmont thought. She would be the key. He didn't know how much of a player Mahoney was, only that the property had anything but an ongoing woman's touch. Even if the current relationship was destined to crash and burn in a couple of weeks, there would at least be something resembling a proper date within that time. Clairmont figured that it would be soon, probably a dinner date, maybe a stroll down Corydon Avenue. The Italian Quarter would be a good spot for a first summer date in Winnipeg, and a good place to boost the car for Scrapneck. It didn't seem to matter what day a couple chose for lasagna and garlic bread; the parking always sucked on Corydon. The chances of parking at or near the establishment of choice were slim to none. That meant the lovebirds would have to settle on one of the surrounding side streets. They were well-treed, with minimal opportunity for the street lights to shine through. The Camaro would be beyond simple to lift. Mahoney didn't look like the kind of guy to spend large on car alarms or defeat systems. If the tits on the permed blonde were as perky as Clairmont suspected, Mahoney would have other things on his mind.

Clairmont had noted that the work shift for his mark had changed from evenings to days. He checked his Omega. Almost Tuesday morning. If the sex was good, Clairmont figured that Thursday would be date night, Wednesday if it was great. Then he could stop avoiding the pages from Scrapneck. He thought about making a few reservations for the lovebirds, just in case.

CHAPTER
FIFTEEN

JUNE 19, 1985
5:46 P.M.

Steve Mahoney checked what remained of his cologne collection. There were a few department store samples of Drakkar Noir left in his sock drawer, each with at least a nano-drop of fragrance left to extract. He poked a Q-Tip into three of the miniature test tubes until it was soaked, then dabbed. He had found his dressiest black T-shirt, a half-wrinkled pair of tan chinos, and a dark blue houndstooth sports jacket from Jack Fraser that he had last worn while screwing over his career at the Marlborough Hotel. He hadn't decided on whether he wanted to goop up his hair; he didn't want to throw a wrench into getting another proper thrashing by Diana. This run-of-the-mill Wednesday would make it three nights in a row, if he could seal the deal. He didn't know where this was going. He decided not to worry about it.

Tuesday night at Diana's apartment had confirmed one thing: the uninhibited sex would be occurring at his McTavish Street address. Diana had a roommate taking summer courses at the U of W. The couple tried to subdue their passionate volume, though not quite enough for the roommate. The summer student protested by stomping up and down the hallway and banging the doors on various cupboards and closets.

Dinner was set for eight, giving Mahoney plenty of time for the three Ss: shit, shower, shave. It also meant that he could do some light detailing on the Hot Rod. He made sure to pop the Diana mix tape into the deck. *Every point matters*, he thought. He even sprang for a new Royal Pine air freshener. The Camaro was date-ready. Mahoney had made reservations at Colosseo Ristorante on Corydon, even though it was a little on the pricey side. He hoped that Diana liked chicken.

Guy Clairmont was giving his Merkur a much-needed spritz at the Mohawk car wash on Archibald. He had driven past the Mahoney bungalow around 6 p.m., and noticed that the Camaro was getting a detail. *Date night tonight*, he thought. The Merkur needed to be clean, as a grubby car would attract the wrong kind of attention in the city's various date zones. He could leave the car overnight on a side street, if the boost went off as planned. He didn't see how it couldn't. The Slim

Jim door-lock pop would take seconds. So would the dash-mounted ignition switch on a '67 Camaro. *No locking column, no fucking problem.* He drove over to Provencher and waited.

At about a quarter to seven, Mahoney's Camaro rumbled past, heading west. Clairmont kept a reasonable distance, though he realized that Mahoney probably wouldn't be looking for such a concern in his rearview. Mahoney opened the throttle as he entered the CP Rail underpass at Main and Higgins. Even Clairmont was guilty of the throttle push on that stretch of Main, as was any driver with something potent under the hood and something to prove. The underpass made for impressive amplification of the mechanical music. It made a crap car sound good. It made a good car sound *great*.

Clairmont drove past the Garden Towers apartment block, while Mahoney walked up the sidewalk to pick up his date. Clairmont had done a check on the EXP plate through a cop connection at the district three station. The title had come back to a Diana McRae, 23 years old, apartment 509. Clairmont watched as Ms. McRae walked hand-in-hand with her beau. She wore the quintessential little black dress, dangerously close to falling out of it. Mahoney opened the passenger-side door for her.

Corydon Avenue was packed for a Wednesday. Clairmont checked his Omega: 7:52. He corrected the clock on his Merkur, slow by three minutes. Clairmont figured he had at least a two-hour window, maybe longer if the date included the usual Corydon dessert stroll to Nucci's Gelati shop. It would be dark enough by 9:30 to boost the Camaro. He parked the Merkur in a visitor's stall at a nearby high-rise condo. He waited.

The light was changing to Clairmont's advantage around 9:15. He'd lost his sports jacket and Carrera shades, opting for a pair of well-worn Ray-Ban Wayfarers perched atop his head, with a navy-blue zip-up hoodie. His shoes had gone the way of Reebok trainers. He walked towards the Camaro with an Adidas gym bag. He wanted to look the part of the Camaro's owner as best he could. For a BMW, Porsche, or Mercedes, he would have kept the sports coat, the Carreras, and he'd have a leather briefcase to tie it all together. If a black-and-white rolled past, it would keep rolling, as long as Clairmont wasn't smashing the side window with a brick.

There was plenty of age-related gap between the window glass and the shrivelled weather seal, shaving off a solid second for Clairmont to open the Camaro with the Slim Jim. He stowed it in the Adidas bag, throwing it in the back seat. He pulled out his lock-pick tools from a thin case in the hoodie's front pocket. Clairmont had boosted enough cars to know that most dash-mounted ignition switches were easier to pick than resorting to splicing wires. The Camaro switch was well worn, which would help. In eight seconds, he was able to turn the lock cylinder to the on position, illuminating the idiot lights. Clairmont smiled. He turned it to the start position. Nothing. He tried again. Still nothing. *Shit*. He had a few basic tools for such a scenario, but so many things could cause a no-start on an 18-year-old, piece-of-shit Chevrolet. He gave the cylinder a third turn. The Camaro cranked and caught, and Clairmont gave a sigh of relief. No need to tear the damn thing apart this time.

He put his foot on the brake to move the shifter, but that's when his luck ended. It wouldn't come out of park. *Double fucking shit*. He jiggled with the shifter as much as he could, worried he might break it. When the car stalled, Clairmont reinserted the lock picks into the cylinder. The assembly turned, but the idiot lights didn't come on. The car was dead.

Clairmont was debating on how much time he had left to try again. That's when the door lock buttons clicked downward, the driver's side that he had just opened first and the passenger side second, since Diana had forgotten to push in the button on the exterior door handle when she closed the door. Clairmont couldn't believe that he had forgot to try it. He checked for a power lock switch on the door panels and on the centre console. There was none to be found. *How could they work without power? Did a '67 Camaro even HAVE power locks?*

Clairmont pulled out the lock button. He watched wide-eyed as it locked back into place. He did the same to the passenger-side door, with the same result. The door release handles wouldn't budge. The windows wouldn't roll down. Clairmont was trapped. And then brown water started rising up from the floorboards. The water was cold. It stank like hot-buttered assholes. And it kept rising. Clairmont struggled with the door handles. He hammered on the side glass. There was no one to help. The water was up to his mouth. He went under. He closed his eyes and waited for both the inevitable and the unbelievable: an inland drowning in a car parked off of Corydon Avenue.

A second later, he opened his eyes. The car was full of water, but it was clear, not brown. He could see outside. He was still parked on Hugo Street. He could breathe. There were bubbles, like he was attached to unseen scuba gear. And he wasn't alone. There was a woman in the passenger seat — at least, he *thought* it was a woman. There was a certain ethereal quality to her features. Her red hair floated lazily in the liquid. Her dress wasn't like anything from off the rack at Clifford's. It was moving, shimmering, just like the hair.

She looked at Clairmont, her green eyes backlit by some unknown source. She moved towards him in the mystical

Camaro water. She was almost close enough to kiss. She closed her eyes. Clairmont closed his. He didn't feel anything on his lips, but he did on his wrists. He opened his eyes. He was securely locked to the steering wheel with handcuffs. He screamed, and the water that he'd been able to breathe in before now flowed into his open mouth. He knew he was drowning. The woman wasn't shimmering anymore. She was covered in brown silt. She opened her eyes, and they were just milky-white orbs. She grabbed him, pulling him close. He heard her words clearly.

"I think you're in the wrong car."

Clairmont let out a flurry of screaming bubbles. The cuffs were gone. He grabbed the handle and opened the door. He fell out of the car and slammed the door to keep whatever it was trapped inside. He ran in a panic and didn't stop until he reached the intersection. He was still backing up from whatever was in the Camaro as he tried to catch his breath.

He never saw the Route 68 bus.

CHAPTER
SIXTEEN

Jerry Waller checked the time on his digital Seiko Pulsemeter as he sat in the cab of Unit 32 at Higgins and Meade. It was coming up on 10 p.m. He held his finger on the watch's touch sensor to check his pulse. The watch warbled for a successful recording. He tapped the backlight to read it. He wasn't sure if 90 beats-per-minute was a good or bad thing. All he knew for sure was that the mirrors at the European Health Spa were filling up with his chiseled physique. One of the regulars had even suggested he try out for an upcoming amateur bodybuilding competition. He had regretfully declined. He was far too busy for any additional extracurricular pursuits.

The night was slow for tricks, which was to be expected for a run-of-the-mill Wednesday. Waller kept his eye on two of the Hook Me Up girls across the street. One was talking to the driver of a silver '70s Trans Am. Waller had checked his plate log to confirm that the Trans Am driver was a regular, and a fan of the number three. The two girls got into the car. Waller would follow to confirm the destination, which according to his plate log would be the La Salle Hotel, just over the Louise Bridge. Mr. Trans Am would usually take a two-hour block of time and had no issues with pre-payment at the Unit 32 cab. Waller stuffed the four fifties into his shirt pocket. He watched as the john took the girls into the hotel. Waller wondered if the john's feet were even touching the ground.

The two-way crackled to life. Dolores Favel's voice crackled as well. "Base to thirty-two, base to thirty-two, what's your twenty? Over."

Waller picked up the microphone and clicked to talk. "Lockout at the La Salle on Nairn. Just finished, over." Waller would always throw in a plausible deflection for his location.

"Got an abandoned over on Union west of Roch," said Favel. "Prepaid, customer wants it dropped at General Scrap. No plates, busted side window, '66 Strato Chief, dark red."

"Got it, '66 Ponti-crap, over and out."

As promised, a tired red Pontiac sedan presented itself, with a flat tire on the rear driver's side, a dented driver's door, a pushed-in rear bumper, and the trunk lid held down by a piece of nylon rope. Waller hooked up the Pontiac from the rear, locking the steering wheel into place with the lap belt to keep the wheels more-or-less straight for the tow. He stopped at a closed gas station to retrieve the crack pellets from under the spare tire, which was slashed to deter the neighbourhood delinquents from stealing it. Peter Scrapneck had dropped the car on Union Avenue. Waller was his guy.

Waller knew he was playing with fire, or at least hot coals. Perhaps the steroids had started to instill a feeling of invincibility, a bravado to match his bulky biceps. The nightly hits of dashboard coke probably helped. He was still selling the regular Heaven's Rejects drug selection. The HRs didn't know about the steroid sales, which was still at a volume that wouldn't be of interest to manage, let alone discipline. Ballendine made sure that anyone dealing the HR's drugs was on the up-and-up. The drug accounting records were tighter than that for the Hook Me Up day-to-day. The HR's accounts would sometimes be settled before the outstanding Hook Me Up bills for tires, fuel, and hydro at the office. The same practices were used for the prostitutes. At best, Hook Me Up was little more than a franchisee for the Heaven's Rejects' street operations. Waller wanted to be much more than that.

A few chance meetings with Scrapneck in the Rear Row of Rust at Commonwealth Motors had got the ball rolling. Scrapneck had been buying his pharmaceuticals from Waller for about a year, usually delivered when Waller picked up a car on its way to the shredder. Scrapneck would throw news magazines in the front seats of the crusher wagons for Waller to mull over, with stories about the rise of crack cocaine in the United States. Waller wondered if all the cocaine that Scrapneck was snorting helped his attention to detail. The articles were often modified by Scrapneck for easy reading, with many of the points on the financials of the crack-cocaine business treated to the neon yellow glow of a highlighter marker. Being much more was looking achievable.

All that was needed was a serious infusion of capital. That's where an unwitting Dick Loeb came in.

Waller knew as much as Scrapneck had told him about Loeb's idea for the cellular phone business. Judging from Scrapneck's exuberant updates, Waller figured that he had told him just about everything. As far as Loeb knew, the money funnelled into the shell companies had gone towards securing the downtown antenna sites. What Loeb didn't know was that a quarter of the sites had been cancelled for about eight months, allowing for the capital needed to buy the cocaine from Scrapneck's connection, a wholesaler that he had met at a stateside auction. The cocaine had tested at 90 percent pure in the Twin Cities. It had been separated into two shipments. The first had just arrived in the battered Dodge trunk lid, its potency confirmed by Scrapneck's cook. The second shipment would be on the next trailer load of used cars, which would arrive on the 24th. Loeb had been led to believe that the investment into the narcotics side of his portfolio was 20 grand. It was actually closer to 60.

Waller remembered how Scrapneck explained it after taking a coke bump off the roof of a rusty Mercury Capri that Waller was hooking up. "He's not even going to know that the money is missing. The coke gets cooked into crack, hits the street, hits the right people, and then we jack up the price. We'll have him paid back in a week, get back the cancelled leases on his pipe dream, plus put some serious cash in his pocket to keep his rooftop bullshit going."

Waller needed a little more convincing. "And you're absolutely sure that this book-fudger isn't going to hamstring you? It's an awful lot of money. People get ideas when there's an awful lot of money."

"That's where I've got an ace up my sleeve," said Scrapneck. "Actually, it's up *her* sleeve."

Waller remembered how Scrapneck had tapped his arm a few times to drive home the fact that the bookkeeper used. Waller wasn't sure if the bookkeeper was shooting heroin, Ts and Rs, or a combination of the two. The whole thing felt dangerous. The whole thing started feeling *very* dangerous on the evening of June eighth. Waller had been keeping an eye on one of the girls in a suburbs-friendly station wagon, who was with one of the eight-seconds-to-love high school grads that he would joke about with Larry Ballendine, in his Hook Me Up office the next morning. His Motorola numeric pager started to beep as the wagon pulled away. He checked the number. It was Commonwealth Motors, with Scrapneck's extension and a "911" next to it. He dropped the girl off at the Mount Royal Hotel for a regular customer and then went to the pay phone in the lobby. Scrapneck answered on the first half-ring. That couldn't be good, especially at 10:30 on a Saturday night.

"Wallbanger! Where are you?" Scrapneck sounded like his brain was on fire.

"Working the day job," said Waller. "What's the problem?"

"Come to the dealership. I got . . . just . . . FUCK!"

"What the fuck is it?"

"I think she OD'd."

"Who OD'd?"

"The bookkeeper. She's in the back. Jesus, man, I need your fucking help!"

"Gimme ten." Waller hung up the pay phone. As promised, Waller and Unit 32 arrived at the rear of the dealership at 10:40. Scrapneck was peeking from behind the rear man-door when Waller pulled in. Even in the minimal light, Waller could see Scrapneck was in bad shape. His hairpiece had slid halfway off his head. He was sweating bullets. His eyes were darting around frantically. "Quick!" he yelled, pulling Waller inside with coke-laced strength.

Waller squinted in the near-darkness. An older purple Camaro was parked in the middle of the shop. Waller could see that someone was in the passenger seat. A redhead, out cold, crumpled against the door. Scrapneck was pacing back and forth. "Jesus fucking Christ. Sweet Jesus motherfucking tap-dancing Christ."

Waller looked through the open driver's door. He didn't know if the woman was alive or dead. Scrapneck was still doing panic laps next to the car. "Is she still alive?" Waller asked him.

Scrapneck hit the brakes. "How the fuck should I know? This is a car dealership, not the Health fucking Sciences Centre!"

Waller figured he should check to be sure. He slid behind the wheel. The woman had not appeared to have moved since he arrived. He pushed up each eyelid, although he wasn't quite sure what he was looking for. Nothing appeared to be looking back at him. Waller remembered his Seiko. He placed the woman's index finger on the touch sensor and waited for the warble. It didn't come. He tried again. This time, he got a sound he hadn't heard before. He hit the backlight to check. The screen said ERROR. Waller had hoped that it would simply say DEAD or ALIVE. He figured that ERROR was close enough.

Scrapneck finally came over. "So, is she, is she . . ."

"I think so. Either that or she's really, really close."

"Then we gotta get rid of her!"

Waller put the woman's hand back. He turned to Scrapneck. "What the fuck do you mean by *we?*"

"Jesus, Wallbanger, *she's the bookkeeper!*" said Scrapneck.

"She's got all the records on the money that old man Loeb doesn't know about!"

"And she's also dead. Who the fuck is she gonna tell?"

Scrapneck pointed over to a Dodge Aspen; its trunk was filled with file boxes. "I've got all the paper I could find at her place. I don't know if there's any more. I gotta get rid of it. We gotta get rid of her."

"How the fuck did she get here?"

"I went to her place to pay for the accounting," said Scrapneck. "I found her on the floor with a needle in her arm!"

"Did anyone see you?"

"How the fuck should I know? I threw her in the Aspen and grabbed all the files."

"So why is she in the Camaro?"

Scrapneck blinked. "Because we only put a hundred bucks into it on the trade-in! I'll get at least fifteen hundred on the insurance claim when I report it stolen!"

Waller was starting to realize how much of an amateur Scrapneck was. *The fucking idiot could have just left her there!* Waller knew what he was dealing with: too much coke and not enough brain. He could understand the file grab, but why all of them? After a few days, the smell would have attracted the landlord. *It could have been so easy!* And now, he was smack dab in the middle of Scrapneck's fuck-up. The realization cocked his anger. He leaped out of the driver's seat and grabbed Scrapneck by his jacket. He walked him quickly backwards, slamming him against the back of the Aspen, knocking his head against the open trunk lid. "Are you completely fucking mental? *All* her files? Do you think the cops might notice that when they search the place?"

"Why would they search it?" said Scrapneck. "There's no body in there. It won't smell up the place."

Waller tightened his grip, giving Scrapneck another head whack before he continued. "All you had to do was grab what pointed to us, but you couldn't even keep your fucking head straight for five minutes to figure that out." Waller looked at the woman in the Camaro. He turned back to Scrapneck. "So, what's your genius plan to get rid of her?"

"*That's why she's in the fucking car!*" Scrapneck yelled. "We can dump it in the river, make it look like a suicide! Then report it stolen."

Waller released his grip on Scrapneck's lapels, but only by half. "How the fuck does she drive the car into the river from the passenger seat? That's not a suicide. That's a fucking murder."

Scrapneck didn't have an answer. Waller did. He let go of the sales manager and headed out the man door. He returned with a small nylon duffle bag, small enough to stow behind the seatback of a truck like Unit 32. He opened it on the hood of the Camaro. He fished around inside it, removing a few items as Scrapneck cautiously approached. A handful of sex toys hit the surface of the hood one by one. Scrapneck blinked. "What are you gonna do, stick a dildo up her ass?"

Waller picked up the largest dildo, a Day-Glo orange model more horse than human. He turned to Scrapneck. "I'm gonna stick this up your ass for being such a fucking moron." Waller finally found what he was looking for: a pair of handcuffs covered with pink fake fur. "Find me an X-acto knife," said Waller. "I gotta cut this shit off first."

Scrapneck wouldn't be much help for what was going to happen next. Waller knew that going in. The good news was that the Camaro was a runner. The bad news was that it had no plates. A dealer plate would stick out like a sore thumb. Waller decided on borrowing a set from an engine-less Matador parked in the service lot. He moved the woman to the back seat while Scrapneck swapped the plates with shaking hands.

This old Chevy runs pretty good, Waller thought, as he headed east on Portage to Main Street. He told Scrapneck to follow as close behind as possible to hide the rear plate from a cursory check by a black-and-white. Waller knew he was taking a chance on Scrapneck rear-ending him. He came close a couple of times.

Waller had told Scrapneck to circle though the cloverleaf system on the Perimeter Highway for a few minutes before picking him up at the exit to the North Perimeter Bridge. He killed the lights on the Camaro before he headed down the darkened service road to the boat launch. The car's dark colour would help hide it from anyone passing over the bridge.

Waller decided to let the car roll backwards into the river, hoping that an air bubble in the trunk might carry it farther into the water to submerge the car. He moved the redhead to the driver's seat, securing her to the steering wheel with the fuzzyless handcuffs. He had seen it done before, at a water recovery he had been called to near Selkirk three years earlier. Some bigwig from the financial district had decided to check out from his charges of embezzlement the old-fashioned suicidal way. There had been rumours that the waterlogged owner of the Mercedes-Benz might not have had the final say in his demise. He had been linked to a few of the HR's business fronts. Whether it was his decision or not, the silt of the Red River erased any of the forensic evidence that could have proved otherwise. Waller rolled up the windows. He removed the license plates. He made a final check under the woman's eyelids. Nothing indicated that she was still alive. He shifted the Camaro into neutral.

The car rolled backwards into the water. It floated for a moment, as though equipped with some amphibious option that wasn't standard equipment. The momentum of the car carried it about 15 feet from the shore. The weight of the engine started to pull the front end below the water. That's when Waller saw it, and his blood went cold. The woman was alive. She was awake. Her head thrashed madly. He heard her muffled screams. The headlights came on. Then the Camaro slipped below the surface, and everything was quiet.

Waller ran as fast as he could to the North Perimeter exit.

Mahoney thought the dinner had gone well.
Diana had earned a fiscal assist for ordering the
chicken parmigiana, which just happened to be
on special. They left the restaurant a little after
10 and a little too full for afters in the neighbourhood. Mahoney noticed the commotion
on Wellington Crescent. It looked like a jaywalk gone bad, judging by the bus, the cops, the
ambulance, and the sheet-covered body in the
street. Diana thought it strange that whoever
was under that sheet hadn't used the nearby
crosswalk. Mahoney helped himself to a pair of

Ray-Bans that were lying in the street. He had just missed stepping on them.

Hump Day would have to wait. Diana had an early morning meeting at her office, something to do with a competitive advertising push from the paging company she worked for. The panic regarding cellular and its first-of-July launch date seemed very real, even if radio silence for such telephony in Manitoba would be the norm for the foreseeable future. She explained the nuances on the drive home, how the pager made more sense for business professionals. "You get to decide when you want to call them back instead of having to answer and deal with it right away. I mean, what if you don't have all your notes and stuff with you when they call?"

Mahoney addressed the obvious. "What if you just turn the thing off?"

Diana smiled. "Yeah, I guess you could do that too."

Mahoney dropped off Diana at her apartment after two solid minutes of grope and tongue at the curbside. He pushed the throttle as expected, as he headed south on Main Street through the CP Rail underpass. The Hot Rod sounded even better than the last three times that evening, a sound that had elicited a "give'r" from Diana on the way back to her apartment. Mahoney figured it was the two glasses of red wine. He took the car back through the downtown, mirroring his route through the French Quarter. There was one thing that seemed out of place as he rolled into his driveway. The Saint Bee stink appeared to have the night off.

Mahoney backed the Camaro into the garage. He was about to lock up for the night when he noticed something in the back seat. *Shit. Probably forgot her purse.* He opened the passenger door and pushed the seatback forward. But it wasn't a purse. It was a two-toned Adidas gym bag, sky-blue with white handles and accents. He retrieved it and waited for the fluorescent fixture above the workbench to come to life before he unzipped the bag.

The first thing he noticed was the item on top, an item that any tow-truck driver would be familiar with. The Slim Jim lockout tool was modified, cut down as a custom build for a locksmith or a well-heeled thief. It had obviously never been part of a tow-truck driver's gear. The metal had minimal scratches. The rubber handle wasn't stained with grease. Someone had loved this Slim Jim. Someone knew how to use it.

The next item was a summer weight leather coat, rich brown in colour, with just the right amount of wear. Mahoney checked the tag: size 36. It would never fit him. He checked the pockets. A pair of Carrera shades in a soft sleeve, a chrome Cross pen and pencil. A small coiled notebook had been jammed into a high-end leather boat shoe. Mahoney opened the book and was shocked. It was all about him: what he did, the Hot Rod, Diana. *Diana McRae.* Fuck, he hadn't even gotten around to asking her last name, and here it was, in a book, in a bag, *in his car.*

The fluorescent light over the workbench started to flicker, quickly joined by the rest of the fixtures. Mahoney turned slowly towards the Camaro. The Supertuner radio dial was flickering and self-tuning again. He wanted to run, but his legs hardly held him up. He gripped the workbench, wondering which news story from the recent past would be first up on tonight's broadcast. And then: *what if the radio can tune into the future too?*

The broadcast started in the past. Way in the past. At least eight different voices came in and out, all saying, "We interrupt this program for a special news bulletin." Mahoney released his choke hold on the workbench and moved closer.

The flickering of the dial stopped. A voice came from the speakers. "Are you sitting comfortably?"

Mahoney blinked. It sounded like the intro to that Platinum Blonde song — the one that didn't suck.

The voice repeated. "Are you sitting comfortably?"

Mahoney opened the passenger door of the Camaro. He lowered himself into the passenger seat, slowly, cautiously. He didn't feel he had a choice in the matter. He stretched his legs into the footwell.

The voice asked a third time. "Are you sitting comfortably?"

Mahoney tilted his head back to answer. He wasn't enthusiastic. "Yes."

The passenger door slammed shut. "Then we'll begin."

Mahoney was truly hoping for Platinum Blonde at this point. The fluorescent tubes started to swirl overhead. Different colours started to pulse through the tubes. Mahoney thought it looked like a low-rent version of the crazy light show in *2001: A Space Odyssey*. The entire garage was humming. The overhead door was vibrating. Tools fell off the workbench onto the floor. Mahoney closed his eyes tight. Then it stopped. The garage went as dark as a moonless night. That's when Mahoney heard a new voice. "You can open your eyes now."

Mahoney resisted at first, then slowly opened his eyelids. The Hot Rod was filling with small nodules of soft light, some swirling, some floating, some blinking like summer fireflies. The light was everywhere, not resembling a shape or trying to become one. Mahoney watched in awe as the lights started to move towards the driver's seat, the swirling becoming more intense. The swirling arrived at its crescendo, with a blinding burst of light that made Mahoney look away, hoping that the flash wouldn't consume him. He closed his eyes again. The new voice spoke again. "It's all right, Steven. I'm here now."

Mahoney felt his left eyelid flicker open first. He started to move his head ever so slightly to the left. His peripheral saw the being first. It was a woman. He turned his head to face her. He looked upon a strange, shimmering woman, with green eyes that looked more like moving kaleidoscopes than the common iris. Her red hair seemed to be floating, the way that Mahoney had seen other women's hair float while splashing in pools or grabbing at their bikini straps underwater at Grand Beach in junior high. There was no water in the car. The hair moved as though there was.

Mahoney didn't know what to say to the being in the driver's seat. He knew he had to say something. He felt the words forming in his mouth. "So, uhm, you're the girl living in my radio?"

The woman smiled. "I haven't been a girl for a long time."

Women, thought Mahoney. *I'm always saying the wrong thing to them.* He regrouped. "Uhm, sorry about that. You're the *woman* living in my radio?"

"Not exactly."

"What do you mean, 'not exactly'?"

The woman smiled. "I'm not living anymore, that much I know. I was recently, then I wasn't. I know it sounds . . . strange. I don't know what this is. I just know that I can't leave this place. Not yet anyway."

Mahoney was starting to put two and two together. "So, you're a ghost?"

The woman's kaleidoscope eyes fluttered as she laughed. "I guess you can call me that, if you like. I don't know if you're supposed to call a ghost by her name or not. This is all so strange. I don't feel dead. And, yet, I don't feel alive either."

Mahoney remembered the name of the woman who had been found in the Camaro. "Heather Price. They said your name wa — I mean, is Heather Price."

"Yes," said the woman. "That sounds right. Heather."

"Do you remember how you got here?"

Price's expression went blank. Mahoney thought she might be remembering what had happened. If she was, she didn't share everything. "I remember the water. It was cold, so cold. It, it woke me up."

Woke you up? Mahoney remembered the morning of June ninth. He had told himself that he didn't want to see who was in the car. He knew that he had seen glimpses of her body in the car, heard the handcuffs being cut, heard the body fall out, heard her insertion into the body bag. He didn't want to remember. It was clear that he had.

Mahoney looked at Price. She was still off in a faraway place. He didn't know how to broach the subject, though he felt that there were probably certain things that you should or shouldn't say to a newly minted ghost. He tried to remember the prompts from the Ouija board instructions of his youth. He decided that simple yes-or-no questions might be the best course of action. "Heather, do you remember how you got into the car?"

"No."

"Do you remember driving the car?"

"No."

So far, so good. Mahoney decided to up the ante. "Heather, do you remember killing yourself?"

Mahoney knew he shouldn't have asked the question the second that he said it. The inside of the car grew darker, more sinister. The next thing he saw was a less-spectral Heather Price, inside the Camaro's former black interior, handcuffed to the steering wheel. The car was filling up with water, a water that he didn't feel, a water that wasn't making him wet. She was panting frantically in between screams, trying to free herself from the handcuffs that had secured her to the steering wheel. She kicked. She pushed on the top of the steering wheel rim, bending it forward, somehow catching the headlight switch in her furious efforts, an action that ensured that she would be found. The water rose to her neck, then covered her face. She hadn't taken enough of a last breath. Mahoney watched as she convulsed, her last screams muffled by the silty-brown water of the Red River. Then she was still. She had deep wounds on her wrists from trying to escape the handcuffs, her blood slowly mixing with the water. Her eyes were wide open. Her hair was moving just like it had when he had met her some 10 minutes before. Small bubbles were coming out of her nose and mouth. She turned her head to look at him. She blinked, revealing nothing but the whites of her eyes. Her lips spoke the answer to his question. "No."

Mahoney grabbed the door handle, falling out of the car onto the floor. He moved as fast as he could to the rear of the car, which seemed to be the safest place at the time. He couldn't see Price through the back window. He did see the radio dial flicker. The speakers were broadcasting the bits and pieces of the quickly scanning dial. It was stopping on various news stories. There was a familiar theme. Mahoney got the gist after the sixth mention.

"The Winnipeg Police said . . ."

CHAPTER
EIGHTEEN

Mahoney hadn't expected traffic to be light enough for him to make it downtown during the rush hour parking ban. He had been circling the Public Safety Building for 15 minutes. He was hoping to speak to Detective-Sergeant Patrick Milroy, though he wasn't exactly sure how to find him or know what he would say to Milroy if he *did* find him. He practised a few scenarios while crawling down King Street in his Plymouth.

"Uh, Detective Milroy?" *Dammit. Detective-Sergeant.* "I'm Steve Mahoney. I pulled that car with Heather Price in it out of the river."

Mahoney didn't like how it was sounding. He tried again, a little less formal. "Hey, Milroy. Mahoney. I don't think that girl in the car offed herself. What do you think about that?" *A little too ballsy*, Mahoney thought. He then said it the way that would get him into the wacko ward at the Health Sciences Centre right quick. "Detective-Sergeant Milroy. I believe the woman who died in my car is now haunting it, and she doesn't know if she killed herself." *Yeah, that totally works.*

"Who the fuck are you talking to?"

Mahoney looked to the right. The windows were down on his Plymouth, as were most cars in the rush hour scrum. The driver of a Red Patch Taxi was looking at Mahoney the way that most people look at someone who is completely nuts. Mahoney didn't know what to say. "Uh . . ."

The Red Patch driver asked again. "I said, who the fuck are you talking to?"

Mahoney figured out the best answer to be left alone. "The Lord. And God bless you."

The cabbie shook his head. Mahoney decided to roll his introductory speeches around in his head for the time being. Mahoney eventually found a spot near the Call Box Lounge, the cop bar across from the Public Safety Building parkade. He was about to jaywalk to the police department entrance when he heard a familiar voice. "You want a ticket for that, Tow-Job?"

Mahoney turned to face the voice. Detective-Sergeant Patrick Milroy had just come out of the Call Box Lounge. He was trying to light his cigarette, cupping the combustion away from the stiff breeze. The spark wouldn't take. "Hey, I was just going over to . . ."

"It's a good thing there are no uniforms around," said Milroy. "I think that was the last time I carried a ticket book. And you're a little late if you're paying a ticket. The office closes at 4:30."

"It's not a ticket," said Mahoney. "I'm actually looking for you."

Milroy looked up from his cupped hands, his unlit cigarette dangling from the corner of his mouth. "Me? Whatever the fuck for?"

Mahoney realized that all his practice speeches had left him. He decided to wing it. "Uh, you remember that car in the river, right?"

"Yes Tow-Job, I remember. What about it?"

"Well, I bought it."

"Why? Are your mom and dad cousins?"

Mahoney explained. "I have the same car, got its roof crushed."

"Roof crushed? Wow, you must be one shitty driver then, eh, Tow-Job?" Milroy chuckled to himself as he attempted a re-light. He stopped. "Wait a minute. Roof crushed. Was that the CAMAROWW at Kildonan Park?"

Mahoney was surprised Milroy would even know about that. "Yeah, that's my old car. Tree branch smashed it."

"Was that an actual SS, or did you just slap on the badges like most Camaro assholes?"

This cop is a car guy? Mahoney relaxed a little. "It's a real SS. Well, it *was* an SS. Now all its guts are in the car from the river."

"Well, I guess you saved it then, kinda." Milroy started walking south on Princess. "My car's on Elgin. I don't bring it out most days, usually take home one of those fucking K-Cars they bought for the plainclothes. But it's finally getting nice out."

Mahoney turned the corner and saw Milroy's car, a red 1970 Buick Wildcat coupe, topped with a black vinyl roof. Milroy started spouting the specs. "I rebuilt the 455, put a shift kit in the Turbo 400. It's got a 12-bolt Posi, front discs, and cop tires. Some banker in Fargo had it. The way it moves now, some bank robber would love it."

Mahoney gave the Buick a proper car-guy once-over. The Wildcat wasn't his thing, but he could certainly respect anyone who spent the time to build anything up, even if the car seemed a little old-man. "What's it putting out?"

"About four hundred horses," said Milroy. "The torque is nuts on these things. I can leave a strip for about half a block, if I feel like being a complete idiot."

Mahoney remembered why he was there. "Listen, I gotta ask about the Camaro."

"What about it?"

"How do you know for sure it's a suicide?"

Milroy finally got his cigarette to light. He drew in a long drag, exhaling before he answered. "You realize you're asking a cop this question, right?"

"I know. It's just . . ."

"It's just what?"

"It's just, what I mean is, uh, the girlfriend."

"What about your girlfriend?"

Mahoney realized he had discovered a way to ask without asking. He built on the story, thinking Diana would be stoked that he'd called her his girlfriend, if he ever told her about it. "Well, she's just a little weirded out by the whole thing, that someone died in it and all."

"What did you pay for it?"

"Twelve bills."

Milroy snickered. "Wow, you must really like Camaros!" He took another quick drag before he continued. "Look, as far as we're concerned, it's a straight-up suicide. There was water in her lungs. You don't get water in your lungs unless you try to breathe it. She cuffed herself in, rolled into the river, swallowed a couple of gallons, and it was done. Probably took less than a minute till it was all over."

Mahoney decided to keep using the girlfriend angle. "Well, the girlie watches a lot of those detective shows. All the new ones. Even old ones, like *The Rockford Files*."

"And?"

"Well, she wondered . . ."

"Wondered what?"

"If it wasn't actually a suicide. Just made to, you know, look like one." Milroy's expression went deadpan. Mahoney worried he'd gone too far. "So's I tell her she's watching too much TV."

"That's exactly what I'd tell her," said Milroy. "Look, Tow-Job, I've seen way too many dead bodies. I've seen suicides, death-by-misadventure, auto-erotic asphyxiation, even a full-on electrocution at a hydro substation. Real life isn't like TV or the movies." Milroy took another drag before he made his summation. "Every dead body tells a story. The chapters are the little bits and pieces of evidence that we find when we investigate. As for the girl in your car, there wasn't anything that pointed in the other direction. Besides, I don't have the luxury of going Hollywood cop on this stuff. If I thought every suicide was a murder, I'd never get a chance to investigate a murder that needs investigating. Let's say you've got 10 pieces of evidence. If seven of those pieces point to suicide, you call that puzzle solved."

Mahoney knew his fuzzy recollections of the late Heather Price wouldn't be part of any legitimate investigations. "Yeah, if only you could talk to their ghosts."

"I do," said Milroy. "Every goddamn night." He flicked his cigarette butt onto the pavement, then remembered that he'd scolded Mahoney. "Don't mention that, and I'll let the jaywalk slide."

"Thanks for the pass," said Mahoney. "See you around."

"See you around, Tow-Job."

Mahoney watched as Milroy started up his Buick. Whatever was under the hood, it sounded pretty great.

Traffic had thinned out considerably after Mahoney's cop chat. The weather was looking a little iffy. It always was when the Red River Exhibition was in town. Mahoney had mentioned it to Diana as a possible second date. The Ex was set up at the grounds for the Winnipeg Arena, the Winnipeg Stadium, and the Winnipeg Velodrome. He was pretty good at Skee-Ball — good enough to win an over-stuffed bear for Diana, which would probably send her into Full Spastic in appreciation. Apart from beating the carnies at their own game, there were only three things that Mahoney liked about the Ex: the oversized Ferris wheel, the little fried doughnuts, and the Kin Kar Raffle. The Kinsmen Club had been raffling off new Corvettes for the last few years. This year it was a blue ragtop. Mahoney always sprang for the three-tickets-for 10-dollars pack. The digital dashboard on the newer 'Vettes looked a little too much like the Trans Am on *Knight Rider*, but he knew that even he couldn't turn down a 10-dollar sports car. Most of the new Corvettes sold in Winnipeg never turned a wheel on a city street, ending up on transports headed for Toronto. Mahoney figured it must have been ex-Winnipeggers who had moved to Toronto and refused to pay marked-up GTA prices.

There were two messages on the answering machine at home. The first was from Diana, agreeing to Friday night at the Ex, if the weather wasn't "too shitty." The second was from Rick Scheer, reminding him about Thursday night. Mahoney couldn't believe that he had almost forgot about it. Thursdays were almost as important as Sundays to Winnipeg's gearheads.

Garage doors would rise throughout the city, in back lanes and suburban driveways, revealing cars both completed and in pieces. Friends would start to arrive around seven in the cars they cared about, with just enough beer to enjoy each other's company and still get to work on time and headache-free Friday morning. The crew would rotate locations each week. Tonight's open garage door was at Howard Petkau's place on Highway 44, the former Highland Glen School. The school had only been open for a few years when it closed in the early '70s. A previous owner had tried to make a go of it as a gas station, adding a shop with an in-floor hoist. Petkau had plenty of room for working on cash money jobs, as well as building up his hot rod, a primer-sprayed '64 Ford Falcon Futura, with a 351-cubic-inch Cleveland V8 block that was mocked up in the engine bay. The running joke was that Petkau had got the idea for the Falcon build when he was working on Jaguar V12s, that he somehow liked working in the tightest of spaces under the hood.

Mahoney debated which car to take that night. He knew that the crew would be curious about the Camaro and any concerns that may have presented themselves after the completion of the build. Mahoney doubted that "haunted" would be anywhere on that list. He thought about the recent broadcasts through the Supertuner before turning the key. He pulled its fuse just to make sure, or as sure as he could be, that the radio still observed the basic principles of electrical current. He stowed the Adidas bag in the trunk.

The Hot Rod enjoyed the Highway 59 run, about 25 minutes' worth, heading north from the city. Mahoney was glad he had opted for the Hot Rod. Scheer had brought his pale-blue 1960 GMC short box, a Pontiac Super Duty 455 under the hood. Fiddler had his Mopar, a dark green '69 Dodge Coronet

500 that had more Super Bee between the front fenders than most stoplight challengers would expect. They were looking under the hood of the Malibu sedan that Petkau had cut himself on and picked up for cheap at Bridgeway. What was good for Iraqi mechanics didn't translate into quick resale for local Winnipeg used car lots. Petkau had scooped it up for dead cost.

Mahoney steadied his six-pack of Black Label on the Malibu's fender, his Number Two beer when Club was warm or sold out at the vendor. Scheer immediately brought him into the conversation. "Whaddya think? Pull the six and put in a V8?"

Mahoney's beer cap flew off his Black Label, thanks to his Bic lighter. "Why bother on a fucking four-door?"

"That's what I say," said Fiddler. "No amount of money fixes that."

Petkau went to close the hood, making sure that Mahoney moved his beer before he did. "It's just for back-and-forth to work. I might put the F41 cop bits on the suspension, but that's just because I hate slowing down for off-ramps."

"Or on-ramps," said Fiddler. "Actually, when *do* you slow down?"

"For ten-dollar blow jobs on Higgins," said Scheer. "That's when he slows down."

"That reminds me," said Petkau. "Your sister says, 'Hi.'"

"HEYYYYYYYY!" said Scheer. He started to laugh, then paused. "Wait a minute. I don't even have a sister!"

"And could you get her to shave her moustache? That stubble stings, you know."

"That sounds like his brother," said Fiddler. He took a swig of beer, then acknowledged Mahoney's arrival. "How's she running?"

"Well, she made it here." Mahoney walked towards his Hot Rod. Scheer had already raised the hood, looking at the usual places that transplanted dormant engines might start to leak. The small block was bone dry. Scheer was impressed. "Wow. It hasn't barfed up anything yet."

Fiddler and Petkau strolled over to the Camaro for the inspection. Fiddler pulled a Mag-Lite out of his shirt pocket and crouched down to check the mating point for the engine and transmission. "No pee-pee out the main seal. Howie?"

Petkau was on his knees, looking underneath the Hot Rod. "Tranny pan is good; output shaft seal looks good." He scurried to the rear of the Camaro. "Rear end looks good."

"This is so . . . so . . ." Scheer couldn't finish the thought.

"Weird?" said Mahoney.

"Yeah," said Scheer. "Fucking weird. Mahoney's incredible No-Drip Camaro. Didn't it always leak when it was in the SS?"

"All the time," said Mahoney. "If it didn't, I used to get worried."

"Why's that?"

"I worried it was empty."

As the crew sipped, Mahoney opened the trunk. He looked at the Adidas bag, a bag that wasn't his, a bag he didn't feel like explaining to the crew. "Hey, Rickles."

"Hey what?"

"What size jacket you wear?"

"How the fuck should I know?"

Mahoney pulled the leather jacket out of the Adidas bag. He gave the pockets a quick check before tossing the coat to Scheer. He told him the lie that made the most sense. "Some guy left it in a Garage Keeper's Act car."

Scheer tried it on. It fit. He smiled at Mahoney. "That's what happens when you don't pay your fucking bills!"

CHAPTER
NINETEEN

JUNE 20, 1985
10:47 P.M.

Steve Mahoney had two bottles of Black Label left. He'd placed them with the empty bottles in the six-pack, stowing the box behind the passenger front seat. He listened to them clink with the surface breaks as he headed south on Highway 59.

The Supertuner was back in play. Mahoney had popped the fuse back in while at Petkau's. *Maybe it's all in your head.* He hoped that was true. The Black Label was doing its best to convince him. The Rolling Stones did the rest with "Can't You Hear Me Knocking." Mahoney drummed his fingers on the top of the steering wheel. He tapped his left hand on the outer sheet metal of the driver's door. He decided to join in on the backup portion. He figured Keith and Mick wouldn't mind.

Mahoney was getting ready to sing the line for a third time when he looked in the rearview mirror. Heather Price was looking back at him. It wasn't her sexy version. She was covered in Red River silt, her eyes missing their pupils. She finished the line for him, in her own special way.

"Could you help *me*, baby? If you're not too busy."

Mahoney mashed the brake pedal into the carpet. The Hot Rod was under full lockup, the back end swinging out to the left, then continuing to spin around on something greasy, possibly deer guts from the many night collisions with wildlife near Birds Hill Park. The Camaro came to a stop just shy of the centre ditch, its headlights pointing at oncoming traffic. A few frantic honks, some evasive manoeuvres, and at least two birds were thrown at the Hot Rod. Mahoney waited till the last car had passed until he pointed the car in the right direction and pulled over to the side to catch his breath. He didn't get a chance to do it for long. The late Ms. Price was now in the front passenger seat. Mahoney almost jumped out of his seat, hitting the horn for at least five seconds until he realized it wasn't going to scare her away. Mahoney was scared. He was also pissed.

"What . . . the FUCK . . . is your problem!?" He tried to calm his breathing. He didn't know how Price would take the question. He braced himself. She responded by slowly changing out of her freak-out persona. The transformation wasn't too otherworldly. She looked normal. She looked not dead. Her eyes looked like proper eyes. The only thing pushing her hair was the summer breeze. She wore a loose emerald green knitted sweater. Her jeans were extra baggy, acid-washed, something she must have bought recently, when she still bought things. Her red ankle boots didn't exactly mesh with the outfit. She wore no jewellery. Mahoney wasn't sure if she was wearing any makeup. He thought it best not to ask. She didn't look too impressed, which matched how Mahoney was feeling at that moment. He put on the hazard flashers before he spoke. "So was there . . . any particular reason you tried to get us . . . killed . . . back there?"

"*You* killed," said Price. "I've already had my ticket punched. Besides, you're fine."

Mahoney wasn't sure about that. He checked the steering wheel, making sure he hadn't cracked the horn button. Price rolled her eyes, the way most women do when a man is worried about his machinery. "And your precious car is fine. Nothing's busted, nothing's leaking."

"Don't be so sure," said Mahoney. "I think I just about pissed and shit myself back there."

"Well, I wouldn't know. I can't smell anything."

Mahoney was curious. "Why, is that like a ghost thing?"

"*Why, is that like a ghost thing?* Boy, you're a right-fucking genius, Steve-Oh. You must have seen *Ghostbusters* like, what, three times?"

Mahoney was doing his best to adjust to this snarkier version of the ghost in his Hot Rod. He was about to say that he had only seen *Ghostbusters* once, when the inside of the car was bathed in red and blue lights. "Shit. Look what you did."

Price would have none of it. "If you weren't such a chickenshit, you wouldn't have spun out and attracted all kinds of attention."

"If I wasn't . . . listen, just shut the fuck up for a few minutes." Mahoney checked his side-view mirror. The RCMP officer was getting out of his blue-and-white Malibu, the one with the cop suspension bits that Petkau wanted. "You think you can do —"

Mahoney looked at the passenger seat. Heather Price was gone.

Peter Scrapneck was still new to this. He warmed the spoon of heroin over the candle flame on his coffee table. The rest of his house was so dark a wandering deer had been resting in his backyard for over an hour. The house was a complete mess. At least the grass was cut, thanks to a neighbourhood kid who he had paid 20 dollars a month for a weekly trim, three months in advance.

Scrapneck had opted for an injection point between his toes, a tip from Heather Price. She had told him that it would keep him from doing the obvious jonesing scratches that would draw the wrong kind of attention at work. Price knew plenty about opiates. She'd started abusing painkillers after getting hit by a car in front of her Silver Heights apartment. The escalation led to her being fired from the accounting pool at Great-West Life, after she was found passed out in a bathroom stall with a needle in her arm. Her habit had reached the point of needing a better stream of revenue and accounting practices that were best termed as "creative." She got the idea of approaching car dealerships from a friend at a large Chrysler franchise that was bleeding about 50 grand a month, thanks to a planned expansion that wasn't going according to plan. Scrapneck became a client, a junkie, and eventually, a casual lover. He talked a different game in the showroom at Commonwealth. There were no ladies of the week, as he had told Loeb, which also meant he didn't have anyone to write a suicide note for Price. He had written it himself, using his left hand to disguise his handwriting, a tip he had seen on an episode of *Columbo*. The overdose was a bonus gone wrong, a balloon's worth of 90 percent pure heroin that Scrapneck's Minneapolis connection had thrown in during negotiations for the coke. Price, like most junkies, was used to 30 percent purity.

Scrapneck hadn't been at Price's apartment when she overdosed. When his knocks went unanswered, he tried the door-knob; it was unlocked. Price was on the floor, the needle in her arm, passed out cold. Scrapneck did what most men with a drug habit would do in such a situation: he panicked. He took the file boxes from her makeshift dining room office out to the car. He went back to the apartment to check on the scene, and that's when the paranoia kicked in. What if the cops found something Scrapneck had missed? Something connecting Scrapneck to the coke? He moved Price to the Dodge with the dealer plate, shielded by the dim of a rear parking lot that was in desperate need of replacement light bulbs. He covered her with an old sleeping bag from her closet. His paranoia, and his *Columbo* recollections, made him write the suicide note with yellow dish gloves from under Price's sink. He put the note on her nightstand and her plastic SIN card in her pocket for eventual identification.

The car. *That stupid, fucking car.* Scrapneck had seen the *Sentinel's* front-page shot of the late Guy Clairmont on Thursday morning, covered with a sheet. He hadn't got around to con-tracting with another "retrieval expert" yet. He wasn't sure if there was a need to do so. The cops had written off Heather Price's death as a suicide. Perhaps that was the end of it, per-haps not. All he knew for sure was that the car that he had put Heather Price into, the one that Jerry Waller had handcuffed her to, was still on the road. Something kept telling him that he had left something inside. He didn't know what.

The heroin was finally starting to mellow out Scrapneck's coke bumps. It was time to get to work. He walked to the dining room, which was now full of the boxes he had taken from Heather's apartment, and flicked on the light switch that sent the deer running from the yard. He had found the Commonwealth files, knowing which accounts he would need to reactivate for Loeb's phone venture on Monday, when the next shipment of American cars would show up, along with the second kilo of coke. He retrieved another folder from one of the boxes. It was stuffed with articles from various American magazines on the rising use of crack cocaine in major urban areas. Scrapneck flipped past the images of drug-related deaths and urban decay, feeling nothing. He focused in on the yellow glow from his highlighter. He smiled as he read about how addictive the drug was. He knew that he could have easily had the traditional coke cut down by his cook, still being able to double, perhaps triple, his initial investment. The problem was that the size of the market was limited. Winnipeg had its share of recreational cocaine users, mostly middle- to upper-class types who would dip in on the weekends. Few could be considered addicts, which meant the numbers had little chance of increasing. Crack had been proven to change that.

Scrapneck went over to a City of Winnipeg map taped to the wall. It was a festival of pins, highlighter touches, and coloured marker dots. The pins were used to denote Manitoba Housing projects. The highlighter swaths were used for the areas that had the worst levels of economic depression. The coloured marker dots were used to identify various schools in the target districts: red for high schools, blue for junior high, and green for primary. Community clubs were circled with a black Sharpie. Next to the map was a calendar from one of Commonwealth's auto parts suppliers, with pictures of different classic cars for each month. Scrapneck looked at the large red X on the 28th of June. He smiled as he looked at the date. Under it was a notation, written in the same red marker.

"LAST DAY OF SCHOOL."

CHAPTER
TWENTY

Steve Mahoney rolled down his garage door, securing his secondary locks. He turned around to look at the Hot Rod. He remembered what Freddie Rondeau had said at the Autopac auction. "Why don't you just go buy a decent Camaro for four grand?" *Why indeed*, Mahoney thought.

Heather Price wasn't anywhere to be seen. Mahoney knew she wasn't far off. He remembered a story that his Uncle Mike had told him, about an old house he had bought in a foreclosure sale. "The place made all sorts of weird noises for about a week after I moved in. Then one night, and I don't know why I did it, I just sat straight up in bed and said, 'Hi. My name is Mike, and I own this house now. I hope we can all get along.' After that, I never heard those noises again." Mahoney figured it was worth a try.

He walked around the car a couple of times, trying to figure out where the best place would be to address the late Heather Price. He decided on the last place that she drew breath. He walked over to the driver's door, and he opened it. *Better make sure she hears you loud and clear.* He cracked his knuckles. He felt the need to steady his legs, fearful that Price would leap from the car and cause him injury with his burgeoning request. He took a deep breath, hoping that his voice wouldn't shake. "Heather Price? This is Steve Mahoney. I own this Camaro now. My name is on the registration. I have a bill of sale from the Manitoba Public Insurance Salvage Department. I paid twelve hundred dollars plus tax for it."

The late Heather Price spoke into his right ear. "Wow. Even *I* know that was too much."

Mahoney spun to face her. Price was nowhere to be seen. He heard the driver's side door slam shut behind him. Price was sitting in the driver's seat, making car noises, pretending to steer the wheel down an unseen road of many curves. She almost lost it on a few of the corners, if her tire-screeching impressions could be believed.

Mahoney amped up his request, simple and to the point. "Get the fuck outta my car!"

Price screeched to a halt. She turned her imaginary engine off. She looked up at Mahoney. "Make me."

Mahoney didn't know how to answer that. He started by trying to open the door. It was locked. He went over to the passenger side. Price watched as he made the journey. The door handle gave him the same amount of grief as the driver's side. He was trying to figure out what to do next when the door button popped up. He looked inside at Price. She was smiling. It didn't look like an evil grin. He hoped that he had read it right. He opened the door. Price tried to allay his fears. "Just fucking with ya. Have a seat."

Mahoney hesitated at first, then entered the Camaro. The door closed for him once his feet were in the footwell. The two occupants looked at each other for what seemed an eternity. Price broke the silence. "So are you going to sit there like a big boy or are you going to run away like a pussy again?"

Mahoney bristled. "I ain't no fucking pussy."

"You sure run like a fucking pussy."

"When are you going to get out of *my* fucking car?"

Price started to speak, then stopped. Mahoney caught it. *She doesn't know the answer.* Mahoney thought for a moment about what little he knew about ghosts. Most of it was from bad horror movies that he had slept halfway through on KCND's Chiller Thriller in the early '70s. He remembered a DC Comic book series called *Ghosts*. He had read *The Shining* by Stephen King. Both the book and the movie had scared him in their own special way, as different as they were from each other. *Scooby-Doo* wasn't much help. The cartoon ghost would always end up being a fake. He had seen *Ghostbusters* the one time. He was starting to think that he'd have to reserve it at Video Stop for research purposes. *Should probably take the other movies back first, pay the late fees.*

Price snapped her fingers at Mahoney's head. "Steve-Oh, focus."

"How did you do that?"

"Do what?"

"You just snapped your fingers."

Price didn't know either. She looked at her hand. A thought

bounced into Mahoney's head that seemed reasonable at that moment. *Maybe she's a Scooby-Doo bullshit ghost!* He reached out and grabbed her wrist. It felt like a wrist. It didn't feel icy cold. It squished the way it should squish. He felt bone where there should be bone. He was just about ready to say so when he felt a shock. It felt electrical, like the zap you would get if you pulled a bad spark plug wire off a running engine. His hand flew into the windshield pillar, hard. He immediately started rubbing it, waiting for normal sensations to occur. He looked at Price. She didn't look happy. Neither was Mahoney. "Jesus, what the fuck?"

"Yeah, my thoughts exactly," said Price. She had moved the hand that had just zapped Mahoney to the top of the steering wheel. "I wouldn't suggest doing that again."

"How the fuck did you do that? How come you still feel . . ."

"Feel what?"

"You know, how come you still feel, like, *real*?"

Price looked at her hand. She flipped it around and touched the steering wheel a few times. Her hand didn't go through. She grabbed the wheel with both hands. She started to steer back and forth, the sensations of the tires moving on the garage floor felt by both occupants. She looked at Mahoney and started to laugh. "I think this qualifies as some pretty freaky shit."

Mahoney agreed. He turned himself in his seat to address her. She was still poking and touching parts of the car when he asked the question. "Heather, how did you get inside this car?"

Price stopped poking the car. The smile on her face started to fade. "I don't remember."

"Try."

Price tried her best. She started scratching at her left arm. The sleeve was pulled up enough for Mahoney to see the track marks. There had been the mention of drug use in the final telling of Heather Price's life by the media. They hadn't delved into the specifics for her drug of choice. Mahoney had run across his fair share of addicts at Hook Me Up. The vacant looks from the working girls. The weirdness of Waller, when he was jacked up on juice. If the hookers were successful in blocking out their day-to-day with Ts and Rs, then Mahoney knew that Price could have easily made her last day a blank tape. Mahoney rewound his memory tape to his last conversation with Price in the garage. If her recollections were correct, the only thing that Mahoney knew for sure was that Price had awoken when the car started filling with water.

The recollections of Mahoney's spectral comic books and B-movies were thin and jumbled in his mind. *Can a ghost be solid? Can you touch a ghost? Can a ghost touch you?* He didn't know what to ask or what not to ask of Heather Price. The tingle in his hand spoke to him. *Keep it simple, stupid.* "Heather: what do you want?"

"Home."

"Home?"

Price swivelled in the driver's seat. She looked at Mahoney. She reached out and touched him. He felt it. She looked at him with glowing green eyes of concern and sadness.

"I want to go home."

Mahoney checked his watch as he finished securing the locks on the garage. The witching hour had just ended as he knew it, 1:01 a.m. for everyone else. He remembered the reference from another ghost movie that he had added to the scary list, John Carpenter's telling of *The Fog*. The coincidence was a bit too much for Mahoney. He checked behind him to make sure that none of the red-eyed lepers of Antonio Bay were waiting to exact their revenge. There was a hint of a mist forming in the cool night air, the kind that hugs low on the grass. If there were murderous ghosts in it, they were only about three inches tall.

The answering machine had no new messages to illuminate the darkened living room. Mahoney flipped on the light to the kitchen. He thought about calming his nerves with a fifth Black Label, remembering the two remaining soldiers jangling about in the back of the Camaro. Instead, he grabbed a dusty bottle of Lamb's Navy Rum from the top of the fridge, pouring a healthy double into a stray Solo cup that still had some Pepsi residue on the bottom. He winced at the burn as he gulped it back. He poured a second, moving to the kitchen table. *Why didn't you just buy a decent one for four grand?* He sipped on the rest of the rum as he considered his options. Selling the Hot Rod was out of the question. Mahoney thought about the ultimate case of buyer's remorse for a *Buy & Sell* bargain hunter, a ghost that didn't seem to be in a hurry to find alternate transportation in the passenger seat of their purchase. He could drive the Hot Rod down to General Scrap, and insist that the car be crushed while he was in attendance, only to find Heather Price in a recycled can of Chunky Soup a year from now. Perhaps another Camaro, one that he could swap his parts into, like the current one. Mahoney knew it was a long shot, with most of the potential donors in the *Buy & Sell* needing about three grand in metal work just to look whole again. He also knew that the crew would not be pleased with doing another build for him, especially two weeks after the last one had left the garage. Besides, Mahoney thought, Petkau's Falcon was next on the list.

Mahoney pushed aside the empty pizza boxes on the table,

sifting through the collection of recent newsprint below. He found the last story the press had deemed worth writing about, along with the grad picture of Heather Price. It was from the '70s; the *Charlie's Angels* feathered hairdo was a dead giveaway. He dug deeper. The *Sentinel* had the nugget about Price's "last seen" whereabouts, the Silver Heights Apartments. Mahoney knew the area well enough; he stopped in at the Silver Heights Restaurant every few months to quell a craving for their signature ribs. *I want to go home.* Mahoney could hear Price's request bouncing around, in-between the sips of cheap rum. Was "going home" a literal request? Or could Price have meant that she wanted to go to the next home, the other side?

Mahoney thought of Heather's arm scratching. *What was she shooting?* He hadn't got around to asking Price about her preferred poison. For all he knew, she could have been getting it from the cab of a Hook Me Up tow truck. Mahoney made a mental note to ask the next time that Price tried to scare the shit out of him. He wondered if the drugs were the root cause of Price's behaviour. She had gone from shimmering fantasy to Silverfish bitch in six seconds flat. Mahoney figured that the Price he was talking to now was the authentic one. He saw a brief image of her alive in his mind, clattering away on some form of adding machine, working the numbers for the people who needed work on their numbers. He realized that there was something about her that was attractive. It was her eyes. It was hard to look away from her backlit greens, even when she was calling him a pussy.

Mahoney grabbed about five hours of sleep before the alarm buzzer intruded. The first call for Unit 36 was to a condominium on Wellington Crescent, a black Merkur XR-something that the building manager had been trying to get towed since Thursday morning. Mahoney had just left it in the Hook Me

Up compound when Dolores Favel hacked through the speaker of his two-way. "Base to thirty-six, base to thirty-six, are you ready for pickup? Over."

Mahoney picked up the microphone. "Just leaving now. Got an address? Over."

"In the rear, 2255 Portage Avenue, silver AMC Concord, plate number six-zero-four charlie-howard-delta. Estate sale car, we're storing it. Over."

"Got it. Is that a house or an apartment? Over."

"How the fig should I know? Just pick it up! Over."

Mahoney smirked. "Sounds like you ran out of milk for your Corn Flakes this morning. Unit thirty-six, over and out."

CHAPTER
TWENTY-
ONE

Dick Loeb watched as one of his lot boys transferred the license plates from a rusty Parisienne
Safari to the deeply discounted AMC Eagle sedan
in the Commonwealth Motors showroom. The
oversized doors that allowed for vehicle entry
into the showroom were wide open. Another lot
boy was using a razor blade to scrape the grease
pencil script from the windshield, stopping to
spray glass cleaner and wipe clean every word.
The remaining words spoke more to Loeb's current state of mind about everything in the car
business: LAST CHANCE!

A few minutes later, the new Eagle owners ambled out of the business office. The finance manager had sold the full deck of car dealer bullshit: fabric protection, security package, paint protection, rustproofing, and undercoating. He handed the couple a brochure on AMC's additional buyer protection plans, explaining they could opt in within the first 1,000 kilometres. The car would be back on Monday for all the applications, billed as a full-day service. It usually took about three hours in total, depending on how jacked up the detailers were. The extra time allowed the undercoating stink to air out from underneath and burn off the exhaust system.

Loeb exchanged pleasantries with the new customers, thanking them for their business. He looked around the showroom as the car was being backed out. Scrapneck had yet to make his presence known, which wasn't necessarily a bad thing. Fridays wouldn't pick up until the evenings at Commonwealth, and Saturday was the most important sales push of the week. The new car sales manager had announced an escalating cash spiff at the morning sales meeting. The spiff started at $20 for the first car, increasing in increments of $20 for the next sale, and paid off retroactively until the close of business on Saturday night. Top salesman for the weekend would also get one of those new Sony Walkmans that all the kids were wearing. Loeb had checked the specs on the box. Apparently, this Walkman had Dolby sound reduction and auto reverse, whatever the hell that was.

A healthy rumble from the lot got Loeb's attention. He looked outside to see Scrapneck pull up in his Bricklin. *Why the hell is he parking in the customer section?* Loeb walked outside and helped Scrapneck with the gull-wing door. Loeb's general sales manager looked rough. His five o'clock shadow was about 20 hours longer. He had forgotten his tie, probably counting on a pre-tied one that most salesmen kept stashed in their desk, in case of condiment stains from takeout accidents. He looked strung out. Loeb had seen it before. He knew Scrapneck could still sell cars, after a quick electric shave and a few Scotch mints. "Rough night, Scrap? Need a wash guy to hose you down?"

Scrapneck swung his legs out, doing the gull-wing limbo. Today's El Coredo hairpiece selection was a wavy sandy blond, the only part of him that looked right. His cheap sunglasses weren't dark enough for the approaching noonday sun. He held up his hand to block it as he greeted Loeb. "Late night, boss-man. Working on the books."

"Everything kosher?"

"Looks like, as far as I can tell. Everything looks paid up. She does good work."

"*Did* good work. At least that's all done with. So, we don't have to worry about the car?"

Scrapneck had finally made it out of the Bricklin. He steadied himself against the car as he lit a cigarette. "Cops have closed it. Whoever bought it can deal with her ghost, I guess, and the stray catfish in the trunk."

Loeb chuckled. "Well, it's a good thing I don't believe in ghosts." He moved in closer. "The only thing I *do* believe in are loose ends. What about this Clairmont guy?"

"No worries there," said Scrapneck, as he adjusted his belt. "Just a guy who didn't listen to Constable Finney in school about looking both ways before you cross the street."

"What about her apartment?"

Scrapneck looked confused. "What about it? It's a *suicide.* Done. Over. Nothing to worry about. I told you that's how the cops would see it. Seriously, we got nothing to worry about."

"And the Rice Krispies stuff?"

"Rice Krispies?"

"You know, snap, crackle, something-or-other."

It took Scrapneck a second to realize Loeb was asking about the crack cocaine. "It's almost ready. The rest of the coke comes in on Monday, gets cooked up, then the street. The first batch is done. My guy is going to do some, what do you call it, *market research* at the Ex this weekend."

Loeb moved in closer still. "You better be right about this crackle stuff."

Scrapneck rolled his eyes. "It's crack, boss-man. Crackles is pork fat. They serve it in Steinbach. Heart attack on a plate."

"You're going to give *me* a fucking heart attack if any of this shit goes sideways, understand?" Loeb stabbed his finger into Scrapneck's chest to make his point.

"Hey, owwww!" Scrapneck rubbed at his chest. The stab wasn't that painful, but it was enough to get his attention. "I get it. Don't worry about it. It's all going according to plan."

Loeb went to finger-stab Scrapneck again, then thought better of it. "Just . . . just make fucking sure, okay?" Loeb kept making the point, stabbing his finger in mid-air. "Just make sure."

Scrapneck took off his sunglasses, revealing bloodshot eyes that knew nothing of sleep. "Don't worry, Dick. I'm worrying enough for both of us."

11:21 A.M.

Steve Mahoney kept watch on the numbers as he rolled west on Portage Avenue in Unit 36. Once he had passed the Deer Lodge Hospital, he knew it would be an apartment building for the estate car pickup. The rest of North Portage was nothing but apartment blocks until almost Moray Street. He checked his hastily scrawled chicken scratch on his clipboard: 2255 Portage, rear, Concord. He remembered Dolores Favel coughing up something about the car being silver. Mahoney knew it would be an easy one to spot. An older AMC product was getting rare enough that it wouldn't be surrounded by other AMC products.

He slowed to a stop in front of the main entrance to the Silverfish. *It must have been something back in the day*, Mahoney thought. The Silver Heights Apartments name was spelled out in steel and attached to a mesh background, along with the building number. Most of the motorists driving past would miss the craftmanship, which included a long blade of stylized metal greenery. There were star-shaped metal flowers, culled from a division that wouldn't be found in any botany textbook. It was 1950s stock art at its finest, standing taller than one of the Silverfish storeys. Rust had erased most of the original paintwork. The windows were large by modern apartment standards, which made it easier to spot the fact that most of the paint that protected them had flaked off years earlier. The brick façade was about the only thing left of the Silverfish that commanded respect.

Mahoney cut through the shopping centre to get to the parking lot. It was only about a quarter full, with most of the tenant vehicles gone for the work day. Mahoney spotted the Concord easily, a late-'70s D/L model, topped off with a burgundy vinyl top. *Lipstick on a pig,* he thought, as he backed Unit 36 up to the car's rear bumper: the Concord was nothing more than an AMC Hornet that had been given more facelifts than Phyllis Diller.

A quick dip of the Slim Jim popped the driver's door. The

aroma inside was nothing new for Mahoney; the hot sun had been baking the car's contents of ash, sweat, and some petrified orange peels for at least a month, judging by the film on the windows. The litter bag on the passenger-side window crank was overflowing. The footwell was full of empty cigarette packs. The front seat had its fair share of burns from hot ash. The ashtray had just been emptied, though with anything but care, judging by the debris field around it.

Mahoney found the spare set of keys where most people stashed a set: under the car, in a little magnetic box that advertised boldly that it was the Magnetic Key Holder, and that you were Never Locked Out, in shiny gold letters. It was usually the first thing a thief, or a seasoned tow truck driver, would look for. The Concord started with minimal protest. Mahoney straightened the wheels, then secured the steering wheel with a length of rope, closing the driver door on the loose ends to keep the front wheels from wandering during the tow. He added a few extra knots to make sure.

It was just after noon when Mahoney pulled into the Hook Me Up compound. He didn't bother with a gingerly drop, not for a car that wasn't going anywhere but an estate auction. He grabbed the keys and headed into the office. The door buzzer tone was more of a flat than a sharp today as he entered. Dolores Favel was just hanging up the phone when he lobbed the Concord's keys at her. She was quick enough to catch them, but was not impressed that she had to exert herself. She looked at the keys, then at Mahoney. "Where is it?"

"Where's what?"

"The reggie, dipshit."

Mahoney realized he'd left the registration in the car. "Shit." He raised his open left hand for the key lob. Dolores threw the keys wide to the right, so far that it wasn't even worth the stretch to try to catch them. Mahoney exhaled as he bent down to pick them up. "Remind me not to tap you for softball pitcher."

"You almost hit me in the head with those fucking keys."

"And a scar *wouldn't* be an improvement?"

"Fuck you, Baloney."

"Fuck you, Delectable."

As Mahoney walked through the compound, one of the guard dogs followed him to the Concord. He opened the passenger side door, looking for the usual spots to stow a registration. The rubber bands on the visors didn't hold the paper, just a few parking lot slips and some coupons for Jet Car Wash, the full-service place off Portage. The glove compartment was full of service receipts, mostly from Commonwealth Motors. That was the dealer sticker on the trunk lid too. He found the registration at the bottom of the pile, a blue vinyl wallet that most insurance agents gave out. This one had gold lettering for Saper Agencies on the cover. Mahoney knew that the wallets didn't necessarily mean that the registration was inside; he flipped it open to check. The German-ish Shepherd standing next to the car cocked its head to the left at the sight of Mahoney's facial expression.

The Concord was registered to Heather Price.

CHAPTER
TWENTY-
TWO

Peter Scrapneck rummaged through his bottom desk drawer for the spare charger for his pager. Both units were stone dead. He then rummaged underneath his desk for an empty plug. Unaware that there was a considerable length of laminated particleboard directly above his hairpiece, he hit his head hard on the way out. After a quick curse, he planted himself in his chair. He winced at the pain as he pulled his hand mirror out of the top desk drawer. He assessed the damage. He smiled. He still looked like a million bucks.

Scrapneck had to run back out to the Bricklin to fetch his briefcase. He had brought in a few of the files that Heather Price had doctored. He was hoping for an amazing sales weekend, and it had nothing to do with cars. Scrapneck had cancelled 12 of the rooftop contracts in Winnipeg, contracts that had been made through Dick Loeb's shell companies to secure the space for future cellular antenna arrays. He had needed the cash to help with the start-up costs on the crack cocaine lab. Now he had to get them back, before Loeb noticed anything hinky in the accounting. Any new leases would be just like renting an apartment: first and last month up front, times 12.

Price had kept the cancellations as simple as possible for point of contact, with rooftop sites that were controlled by one property management agency. Scrapneck keyed in the number on his desk phone. The call was answered on the second ring. "Don't toss, ring Ross Realty, how may I help you?"

Scrapneck adjusted himself in his chair, leaning forward. His voice was half volume. "Hi, I was wondering who I would speak to . . ."

"Could you speak up please, sir?"

"Uh, yeah, sorry about that. I wanted to speak to the property management department, please."

"Please hold."

Scrapneck tapped his fingers to a Muzak version of Gordon Lightfoot's "Rainy Day People." Twenty seconds later, a man answered, quick and sharp. "Ross Realty Property Management, Curtis Craven speaking."

Scrapneck looked around from his half-walled office before he spoke. "Yeah, uh, yes. I'm calling on behalf of Skyview Ventures. We had some rooftop leases that were cancelled about four months ago that we need to secure again."

"Skyview?" Mr. Craven seemed confused at first. "Skyview, Skyview. Let me see here. Skyview." Scrapneck heard the tell-tale sound of a file cabinet door being opened and closed. "Skyview Ventures . . . here it is. Leases cancelled February 28th, possible renewal noted. Is that the reason for the call, uh, Mister . . .?"

"Scrapneck. I believe you had spoken to my associate, Heather Price?"

"Can't say for sure, Mr. Scrapneck. So, you want to lease the sites again, correct?"

"That is correct."

"Thank you, Mr. Scrapneck. Let me put you on hold for a moment."

Scrapneck listened as the Muzak played the next tune in the voiceless Gordon Lightfoot mix. It sounded like "Carefree Highway." He heard almost 30 seconds of it before Craven returned. "Mr. Scrapneck? Are you still there?"

"Yes, go ahead."

"Yes, Mr. Scrapneck, the leases are still available. We can do the five-year term you had specified. And the rate was . . ."

Scrapneck knew the rate: $575 a month. It still seemed pricey for a place to bolt an antenna. "I think it was about five-something,"

"Yes, it was five seventy-five per month. And it is now . . ."

"I beg your pardon?"

"Oh. Sorry, Mr. Scrapneck, but there has been an adjustment."

"What kind of fucking adjustment?"

Craven wasn't fazed by the F-sharp. "We've been tracking rooftop tower site leases since the initial interest in Winnipeg over the last year, after the Cantel plans broke."

"How much?"

"For the sites that Skyview has specified, the new rate on the five-year lease is eight seventy-five per month."

"That's fucking bullshit!"

"No sir, that's the current market value for Winnipeg. Other cities are already speculating between twelve hundred to fifteen hundred a month, perhaps twenty-five hundred a month in certain markets by 1987. It would be an opportune time to lock in now for the five years. Can I do up the paperwork for you?"

Scrapneck felt the sweat starting beneath his adhesive tape. *Eight-fucking-seventy-five per goddamn month!* He did the quick math on his desk calculator. First and last month up front, times 12 sites. He stretched the handset cord for a moment before he returned it to his mouth. "So, what you're saying is you'll need twenty-one grand to secure the sites, is that correct?"

"Plus the government's share," said Craven. "Can I get the paperwork ready?"

"Fuck me."

"Sir?"

Scrapneck found the half-cup of composure he needed. "Yeah, do up the paperwork. I'll have the cheque to you on Monday."

"Certified cheque, please."

"Yeah, certi-fucking-fied cheque."

"Have a good weekend, sir."

"Yeah, don't get hit by a bus or anything." Scrapneck threw the handset on the desk. With what he had in the bank, his wallet, and the outlay for the second key of coke arriving on Monday, he knew one thing for sure: he was 17 grand light. He picked up the handset and punched the button for the outside line. His call was picked up on the third ring. "National Pagette call centre, can I have the pager code number please?"

"One, zero, four, two."

"And the message?"

"See you at the Ex."

1:23 P.M.

Jerry Waller felt the buzz on his hip as he ate lunch in the front seat of his Corvette Stingray at the Dairy-Wip Drive-In. He pulled his new Motorola Optrx that Peter Scrapneck had recommended out of its holster to read the message. He smiled. He put the rest of his cheeseburger on the dashboard as he exited the car, heading over to the wall-mounted pay phone. It was a new phone, not as greasy as the last one that had been marinated with years of salt and oil. He flipped open a little black book for the needed number. He dialled, hung up, then dialled again. The voice was unsure at first. "Wallbanger?"

"Yeah, Ray," said Waller. "It's me. Can you talk?"

"Yeah, boss-man's out getting new bells. Are we good to go?"

"Yeah, we're good to go. How many guys working the Ex tonight?"

"The Group of Seven. They're all cool, Ray Fontaine– approved. Two hundred a head?"

"Only if they sell out, a hundred if they don't. And I know exactly what I'm handing out, so no fucking around. I get everything back that don't sell, okay?"

"It's cool. Still four hundred for me?"

"Like we talked about."

"So, do I get a taste of this new shit or what?" Fontaine pushed.

Waller hesitated. He knew it wasn't a good idea to start handing out samples, especially to subordinates like Fontaine, who were either full-blown junkies or apprentices-in-training. Anyone with Videon or Cablevision could tune into the coverage of the ravages of crack from the American television-feed every night. "Ray, I don't think you wanna go down this road. This is fucking hardcore, no-coming-back kinda shit. It's at least Smack Light. I'll get you some better weed instead, okay? How about some coke?"

"Yeah, sure I guess. Okay."

"And Ray?"

"What?"

"I'm keeping track. For real. Don't fuck me around on this shit, understand?"

"Okay, Wallbanger. It's all good."

The call ended. Jerry Waller returned to his cheeseburger.

CHAPTER
TWENTY-
THREE

JUNE 21, 1985
2:47 P.M.

Steve Mahoney had yet to dig into Heather's car at the Hook Me Up compound. First, he needed a reason to go into the compound, which meant dropping off another car. The two-way in Unit 36 had been pretty quiet for a Friday afternoon. The spare change in his pocket was enough to call Diana about the Ex. The forecast was 50-50 for thundershowers, the expected forecast for any evening the Red River Exhibition was in town. Diana gave the okay for a 7 p.m. pickup at her apartment. The Ex took over the parking asphalt at the Winnipeg Stadium, a sizable chunk of Empress Street, and much of the property for the Winnipeg Velodrome. The Winnipeg Arena was stuffed with vendors, hawking everything from miracle knives to the world's smallest juicer. Some of them even had PA systems to heighten the excitement. Mahoney would only venture inside if the sky opened up. The hawkers were worse than the carnies on the midway.

Was there anything in the car? Mahoney knew it was anyone's guess. The late Heather Price remembered little of the events that had led to her current place of residence in the Hot Rod's cabin. Mahoney remembered the most recent of interactions, how Price felt more human than spectral. *Could she leave the car if she wanted to?* Mahoney was deep in thought and halfway through his Pepsi Slurpee lunch when the radio crackled to life. "Base to thirty-six, base to thirty-six, what's your twenty? Over?"

"Just gassed up. Watt and Talbot, over."

Dolores cleared her throat. "Got a lockout, Richardson Building parkade on Lombard, second level, brown Pontiac J2000, plate number five-eight-three delta-bravo-tango, over."

Shit, fucking lockout. "Got it. Is owner with car? Over."

"Yeah, owner with car, locked her kid in it. Freaking out. Over."

"Got it, freak-out lockout, brown Pontiac Richardson, on my way. Over and out."

The lockout took about five minutes to pop, the mother in a state of complete meltdown, while the toddler within amused himself by gnawing on a Little Golden Book. At least the car wasn't in the hot sun. The Pontiac had plenty of previous lockout entries, judging by the battered driver's door window-rubber on a three-year-old car. He gave the mother the empty key locker-box that he had retrieved from Heather Price's Concord.

Mahoney knew that Larry Ballendine wouldn't approve of the generosity. He swore the mother to secrecy.

Summertime construction was in full swing in the downtown, which made for slow going. Mahoney had hoped to be out of the downtown by 3:30 when the calls for the no-parking removals would start. Dolores the dispatcher had crackled his two-way speaker at 3:25: at least four imminent illegal parkers on Kennedy Street, next to the law courts complex. It was the city contract, a must-go. Two of those vehicles were probably police units. Mahoney made it just in time to see that three of them were unmarked cruisers, most likely detectives who were testifying for court cases. One of the other Hook Me Up trucks had already hoisted an offending Ford Pinto by the time Mahoney arrived. *Shit,* Mahoney thought. *Nothing for the compound.*

Mahoney was home by 5:30, and freshened up by just after 6. He decided on the Plymouth for transportation. Most of the parking lots around the Ex were of the five-dollar variety. That annual surprise would always amp up people's anger flinging their doors in frustration into the cars parked next to them, not to mention the whining kids in the back seats who were in desperate need of cotton candy and rides that maximized their upside-down time. He fiddled with the AM radio as he backed out of the Video Stop. The late fees had cut into his carny budget by 90 bucks. He hoped his aim was true.

The Plymouth's sound system was usually parked on one of the two AM rock/pop stations in Winnipeg: 13 CFRW or KY-58. Mahoney's preset switch punches weren't finding them, unless you counted unintelligible static. Manual tuning didn't seem to help. Perhaps the thunderhead clouds massing overhead had something to do with it. Mahoney stopped dialling when he hit the only station of strength. The announcer came in strong and purposeful. "From coast to coast on CBC Radio and around the world on shortwave, this is *As It Happens*."

He listened to the theme music, a catchy jazz tune that he'd heard before, on the odd occasions that the radio dial would land on the CBC. Alan Maitland and Peter Downie chimed in their greetings. It was white noise at best. At least, it was until Mr. Maitland began the segue into the first story. "We begin tonight with the things that go bump in the night, and a Winnipeg medium who claims that she has not only been able to speak to the dead, but can help counsel these spirits in limbo, assisting them in their journey to the other side. We spoke to Madame Marie Marshall at her favourite haunt, The Chocolate Shop restaurant in downtown Winnipeg."

Another voice chimed in. Mahoney figured it had to be the Downie guy. He listened as he drove towards the city centre. "Madame Marie, thank you for joining us tonight."

"Good evening, Peter, thank you for the invitation."

"Madame Marie, we understand that you have worked as a medium for some time."

"Yes, Peter," the woman replied. "In addition to my regular work with tarot and tea leaves, I have been involved in the field for almost thirty years."

"When did you first discover that you had the ability to communicate with those who have passed on?" Mahoney listened a bit more intently.

"It was actually at a very young age. When I was about four or five, I remember going to my parents' bedroom almost every night, telling my mother that I couldn't sleep because it was too loud."

"What was too loud?"

"All of the voices."

"What kind of voices?"

Yeah, Mahoney wondered. *What kind of voices?*

The Madame continued. "It was as though I was listening to a myriad of conversations, as if a hundred people were all talking at once, desperate to be heard. And not only heard. They wanted to send a message, to let someone know that they were all right, or to warn them."

"Warn them of what, exactly?"

Warn them? Mahoney was doing his best to listen carefully while piloting the Plymouth.

Miss Marshall continued. "Sometimes, a spirit may wish to communicate a caution of a sort, a subtle advice to someone they care for. A . . ."

Mahoney was so focused that he didn't see the red light. He swerved just in time to miss the Beatrice Dairy delivery truck, its angry horn accompanied by equally angry obscenities from the driver, easily seen through the open sliding doors on each side of the van. Madame Marie continued, "with the right skills, I try to relay this information in a way that the living person can understand and act upon."

Mahoney scrawled "Marie" and "Choklit" on an old envelope as he waited outside Diana's apartment. She didn't seem too impressed by Mahoney's choice of transportation. "Where's your Hot Wheel?"

"Tucked away," said Mahoney. "Too many door-ding clowns at the Ex."

"Not to mention real clowns. They're just as scary." She gave him a playful kiss before settling into her seat, struggling with the sticky seatbelt. "I guess there's more room in this shitbox for all the stuff you're going to win for me, right?"

"Don't forget the trunk," said Mahoney, thumbing towards the rear. "We still might need two trips."

CHAPTER
TWENTY-FOUR

Ray Fontaine sat in the cab of the Ice-Cycle Frozen Treats company truck, a well-worn 1-Ton Dodge with dual rear wheels. The heavy-duty Dodge was used to move multiple ice cream pedal carts to special events. Seven carts were strapped down to a flatdeck trailer, waiting for their riders to arrive at the usual muster point on Westway, next to the Mercury dealership. At the Ex, the shift was nine at night until one in the morning. Fudgesicles, Creamsicles, and ice cream sandwiches took up most of the cart's cooler cavities. The rest of the space was home to a new flavour that would have its Winnipeg debut at the Ex: Scrapneck and Wallbanger's Old-Fashioned Crack Cocaine.

Anyone with eyes could see that Fontaine used. He had a Harry Dean Stanton after a Hunter S. Thompson Las Vegas weekend look about him. He looked 60, with a driver's license that said he wasn't quite 40. Crack was one of the few drugs that Fontaine had yet to try. Waller had warned against it. The way Fontaine saw it, his money was his to do as he pleased. He had been able to handle everything else that he had snorted, shot, and swallowed. *Why would this shit be any different?*

The ice cream riders were starting to arrive. They shared the general sketchy look of their supervisor, with gaunt faces, lanky frames, and twitchy eyes. Fontaine knew that most of them would be customers as well as vendors. The Group of Seven ranged in age from early twenties to mid-fifties. They all looked as though they were related.

Fontaine exited the truck cab, heading to the back of the trailer to off-load the carts. Each cart had received a stock of a hundred rocks, about a 10th of a gram for each. Scrapneck and Waller had decided on $20 a rock. It was a premium, though with zero competition and a get-in-get-out business plan the pricing made sense. Fontaine knew most of the carnies would balk at the price. They would be used to $10 rocks, if they had spent any time in the carnival route Stateside. Fontaine's riders still had their regular loads from Waller, the drugs that the HRs knew about. The two hundred bucks Waller was offering per rider was over and above the usual take that a rider would make for peddling weed, hash, and pills. The Group of Seven usually threw in the ice cream for free as a bonus. There was little doubt about the crack being a hit, though there still needed to be a solid night of regular sales to keep the HRs eyelids from lifting. Friday nights at the Ex were always good nights for weed and acid, for those wearing all-you-can-ride wristbands. The location was inspired for selling illicit substances. There were the suburban kids with money to burn and the inner-city youth who were only a five-minute bus ride away from the grounds. How they got their money didn't require a lot of guesswork. The West End was rife with thefts from parked cars and back-lane garage break-ins.

9:02 P.M.

Peter Scrapneck was winding down for the day at Commonwealth Motors. The last customer exited the business office at five minutes shy of nine o'clock. The business manager flashed five fingers to Scrapneck, indicating another full house of protection add-ons. Old-man Loeb had gone home around six, after his wife had informed him earlier in the day that she was heading to the cabin at Big Whiteshell Lake with her girlfriends. He wouldn't be back till Monday. The front door was firmly locked at nine sharp.

Scrapneck went out one of the auto-locking side doors to check on his Bricklin. The SV-1 was locked up tight and sitting up high on one of the ramps in front of the dealership. *If only the gull-wings would stay open*, Scrapneck had thought, as he inched the car onto the ramp. It would have looked more airplane than earth-bound. The price was a bit of a reach: $7,995 RARE SPORTS CAR had been drawn with care on three-quarters of the windshield. Scrapneck needed every penny he could get to ensure his cheque didn't bounce for the realty company on Monday. He didn't have any issues plating a used car for wheels for the rest of the summer; any of them would be easier to get into than his Bricklin. He knew Friday night at the Ex would be lucrative, but he was still skeptical. There was still the return on investment that Loeb was expecting, plus Waller's end, and the crack cook. Scrapneck felt that things were getting closer and closer to a successful conclusion for everyone involved. He used his key to re-enter the dealership. The rest of the staff had already left through the rear. He walked around the showroom a few times, doing a wide-and-sloppy figure-eight around the wheeled inventory. *I could have this,* he thought, as he let his fingers drag along the fenders. He stepped into Dick Loeb's office, flicking on the light switch. He sat himself down in the well-used chair. He looked up at the buzzing Nash clock.

"That's the first thing to fucking go."

CHAPTER
TWENTY-
FIVE

Steve Mahoney's touch was bang on, much to
the chagrin of the carny at the Skee-Ball Row
on the Red River Ex midway. A combination
of wrist angle, speed, and follow-through were
paying off handsomely. Diana was hanging on
to an overstuffed panda bear, with a little red
velvet tongue sticking out from its synthetic fur.
Mahoney was two throws away from a Lloyds
stereo system. The carny was doing everything
he could to jinx it with his play-by-play, while
using the potential for a big win as a lure for additional marks. "That's right, folks, big winnah,

big winnah comin' up here, only two throws away, just two throws away, and . . . AND JUST ONE THROW AWAY! Big winnah, folks. WHO'S MY NEXT BIG WINNAH?"

Mahoney rolled his last ball to secure the win. The carny reacted to the ball drop by looking furious and festive at the same time. His exuberance distorted the dried-out speakers of his Skee-Ball PA system. "BIIIIIIIG WINNNNNNAH! A brand new supah-dupah ray-dee-oh stereo cassette record playah for the BIG WINNNNNNAH!!!" The carny motioned Mahoney over to the microphone, but switched it off before he spoke. "No more winnin' for you tonight, mistah. Time for root beah and Bavarian pizzah, doncha think there-ah, mistah?"

Mahoney played along, trying to guess whether the carny's voice was an accent or an occupational affliction born of the midway. "No worries there, *mistah*." He motioned to the microphone switch. "Let's find some suckers to make up for the ray-dee-oh."

The carny gave him a crooked wink as he flipped on the microphone. "All right, mistah! Tell us how easy it is to win this here Skee-Ball. What's your special secret there-ah, mistah?"

"It's all in the wrist." Mahoney mimicked his style at the gathering crowd, a show of skill that maybe one of them would be able to half-master. The wannabes would spend at least 30 dollars trying, usually ending up with the carny's pity doll for their dates, in hopes that the mark would reinvest. The pity doll made for an excellent study in offshore textile pathos. The sandpaper texture of the fabric, the cheap creepy eyes, even the stuffing felt wrong. It was also a potential case-study for identifying true love, if any professor of the mind chose to make it part of their annual funding requests. The girl who looked at the pity doll sideways was a short term.

The one who gripped it as tightly as her arm around her beau would be with him until the end of time.

Mahoney had picked the perfect time to win the stereo. The thunderheads grumbled, released a spat of drizzle, then cleared just enough to showcase the dying sunset. He decided to take the carny's advice, stopping with Diana at one of the oversized root beer keg stands for a frosty beverage and then to the pizza stand with the Oktoberfest decor. Diana kicked in dessert, springing for a bag of the miniature doughnuts with at least a pound of cinnamon sugar holding in their deep-fried heat. The least-moist of picnic tables presented itself for their midway feast. Diana hung on to her new panda friend with one hand, steadying the slice of pizza in the other. "What did that carny say to you when you won?"

Mahoney smiled. "It wasn't exactly congratulations."

"He sure made a big deal out of it, though."

"They always do. That's how they let the other carnies know you're a bad risk."

"So it's all rigged?"

"Just like wrestling," Mahoney confirmed. He kept a firm elbow on the top of the stereo box, something resembling security, as he devoured the pizza slice. Then he remembered. "Aw, fuck!"

Diana stopped digging into the little doughnut bag. "What is it?"

"We can't go on the Ferris wheel with all this shit."

Diana looked at her new panda partner with fabricated sorrow. "Awww, sorry Mister Panda. I guess I'll just have to go on another ride." She kicked off her left flip-flop and placed her foot firmly into Mahoney's crotch, the bold flirtation shielded by the picnic table. She held her hands apart to an approximate size. "And you must be 'this tall' to ride."

Mahoney smiled. He checked his front pocket, pushing aside his new Kin Kar Corvette tickets. The Ferris wheel wouldn't have happened anyway; there was only one ride coupon left. "Will this do?"

Diana was about to answer when she was interrupted by a commotion on the midway. Even with the clangs and whoops, something else punched through. It was a panicked voice.

"Somebody call an ambulance!

Mahoney turned to see. A pair of St. John Ambulance volunteers were running up to someone lying on a picnic table, obviously in distress. The victim was partially blocked from view by curious onlookers, security guards, and a group of teens who looked like his friends. Judging by what could be seen, it seemed like a young man was having a seizure. "Maybe it's a bad trip."

Diana reached for another little doughnut, but she kept her eyes on the developing scene. "I've never seen a bad trip like that before." The convulsions reached a fever pitch. The friends of the patient were looking one of three ways: panicked, tearful, and ready to run like hell. The victim went limp, and one of the St. John attendants jumped on the table to begin administering CPR. Three of the teen's friends started to back away, slowly, then bursting from the scene at full speed. The other St. John attendant was on his two-way, calling for paramedics, stat. It took a minute for the paramedics to arrive. One of the paramedics readied something in a syringe as the CPR continued. The injection did nothing. Mahoney saw the look on one of the paramedic's faces as they readied the stretcher, and the nod, the left-to-right nod that never meant anything good. It was the nod of death.

On the drive back to Mahoney's house, there was little talk of the frantic events that Diana and Mahoney had just witnessed. There would probably be a mention of it in the papers on Saturday if the death nod was correct, maybe a follow-up story if there was any heart-tug to the tale.

Diana wanted to cash in Mahoney's remaining ride ticket when they arrived at his house. Mahoney obliged, opting for a doggy-style romp that wouldn't reveal the mood-killing thoughts that were showing up on his face. *What the fuck was that kid on?* As far as he knew, there weren't any new concoctions being distributed from the cab of Jerry Waller's Unit 32. This overdose was downright scary. He wondered if there would be more in short order.

Mahoney's eyelids fluttered open around 9:30 on Saturday morning. Diana had found just enough meat, potatoes, and recently expired eggs in the fridge to pull off a breakfast hash. A friend paged her as the last morsels left their forks. The phone number that accompanied the page was a reminder for a baby shower that afternoon in Portage la Prairie, a reminder that sent her into the full spastic mode that Mahoney was becoming accustomed to. He dropped her and the panda at her apartment just before 11. She planned to stay overnight in Portage. Mahoney's Sunday had been earmarked for Petkau's Falcon. They agreed to meet up at his place Sunday night, eight-ish.

Mahoney stopped for gas on the way back from Diana's apartment. He grabbed the Saturday edition of the *Sentinel*, a one-dollar indulgence that included the comics insert and the new TV listings guidebook for the coming week. He saw the small story about the overdose at the bottom of the front page. He pulled his Plymouth off to the side of the pumps to read it.

TEEN CLINGS TO LIFE AFTER SEIZURE
AT RED RIVER EX
By Jil McIntosh

A 15-year-old St. James teen is in critical condition at the Health Sciences Centre, after suffering a seizure at the Red River Exhibition late Friday night. Braeden Westmacott, a Grade 10 student at St. James Collegiate, collapsed on the midway of the Ex shortly after 10 p.m. First-aid volunteers from St. John Ambulance gave assistance to Westmacott until paramedics arrived. Westmacott was transferred to the Health Sciences Centre in unstable condition, which has since been upgraded to critical condition as of press time. Anyone with information is asked to contact the Winnipeg Police Department at 986-6222.

Mahoney put the paper down on the seat. Making this a police matter right out of the gate meant this wasn't a nut allergy gone wrong. The Westmacott kid had OD'd, plain and simple. It could have been any number of products, though it was most likely something that fell under the distribution arm of the Heaven's Rejects. Mahoney wondered if Jerry Waller had sold the kid the dose. He wasn't sure if he cared one way or another. The only thing on his mind today was assuming full ownership of his Hot Rod. He opened up the Saturday Classified section of the *Sentinel*. The Personals section had the ad Mahoney was looking for:

MADAME MARIE
PSYCHIC READINGS
MASTER OF THE MYSTICAL TAROT
BY APPOINTMENT ONLY
CALL THE CHOCOLATE SHOP
947-9109
268 PORTAGE AVENUE

Mahoney circled the ad with a well-chewed pencil from the grubby dashboard and headed for the pay phone next to the gas station's icebox.

CHAPTER
TWENTY-SIX

JUNE 22, 1985
1:04 P.M.

Peter Scrapneck couldn't believe his good for-
tune. The new owner of his former Bricklin
SV-1 was waiting to exit onto Portage Avenue,
blissfully unaware that one of his brake lights
was out. The recent graduate from Kelvin
High School had been promised a car for his
successful completion of the 12th grade. His
dad didn't seem too impressed with the choice,
considering that a new Renault Encore with
a warranty was also priced at the same $7,995
ask that was on the 11-year-old Bricklin's windshield. The base Encore was a non-starter: the

kid couldn't drive stick. However, he did have the upper body strength needed to fling up the Bricklin's gull-wing door like it was made of cardboard.

The showroom was thick with traffic. Three Cherokees had just received the "SOLD TO A NICE CUSTOMER" placards on their rearview mirrors. The used car department had just sold the Impala coupe that was part of the recent American shipment, with an extended warranty, plus a $200 service fee to change the miles-per-hour speedometer to kilometres. The owner of the Fast Pink Lady courier company had just inked a deal with the fleet department for six Encores. There was even a deal pending on the '84 Renault Fuego Turbo that had been on the lot since last February, a car so loathed by management that it had earned a $200 spiff to get it off the lot at any price. Scrapneck cringed slightly at the prospects of the lot-rot that would gum up the semi–sports car's mechanicals in short order. Maybe he could get the new owner to trade it in on a new Cherokee in the fall.

Scrapneck's high was natural. There were still the remnants of heroin and cocaine in his bloodstream, though this sensation wasn't as illicit as the current urine analysis would have shown, if Commonwealth Motors had cared about such things. Waller had dropped off the previous night's take from the Ex, as well as his own crack sales from the cab of Unit 32. The cancelled leases for Loeb's rooftops would be easily secured. The kilo of coke due for Monday would also be covered, thanks to the ongoing sales push for the crack derivative. He even had enough left over for lunch for the staff. The scent of Gondola Pizza wafted through the showroom.

Waller had explained how the rest of the month should go for the remaining crack stock, as well as the new shipment.

"We don't want to poke the bear," he'd warned, as he handed Scrapneck the manila envelope of cash from his Corvette's front seat office. "We'll stay away from the Ex till Monday. There's plenty of weekend junkie-business that we'll do well off of, plus the bored kids in the housing projects. We're gonna sell a lot of ice cream."

"Was there any trouble?" said Scrapneck. "Any ODs or freaky shit?"

"Just one," said Waller. "That's a regular night at the Ex. And that's why we'll stay away this weekend. Don't want the narcs to get wise."

Scrapneck agreed. "So, by the end of the summer, we'll be kinda rich. What are you going to do with your share?"

Waller stretched out in the driver's seat. "I've got my eye on a fishing lodge north of Kenora. American plan, on Separation Lake. It's amazing what those rich assholes will pay for eating fresh pickerel full of mercury over a campfire. And it's only May to September. Maybe get a condo in Florida for the winter."

"Make sure I get a couple of weeks at the condo," said Scrapneck. "As for the black flies and fish guts, you're on your own."

Waller smiled as he fired up the Corvette. He chirped the tires as he headed towards the rear exit of the Commonwealth lot. Scrapneck watched him as he left. He wondered how long before he had enough money to buy Dick Loeb out. Waller had said by the end of the summer.

Scrapneck looked over at the shit-brown Dodge Aspen, tagged with his dealer plate. He decided he didn't want to wait that long.

Steve Mahoney waited patiently at the Chocolate Shop Restaurant on Portage Avenue, wedged into a booth where the hostess had left him. He had cleaned himself up somewhat, with a shave detail around his moustache and sideburns, a fresh blue shirt untucked over the cleanest dirty jeans he owned. The Chocolate Shop was a favourite destination for those who enjoyed a vague foretelling of their future. One patron was hunched forward in awe, as her tarot card reader explained the meaning behind the King of Pentacles, The Lovers, and the card of Death, which apparently wasn't as bad as it sounded.

Mahoney's eavesdropping stole his focus long enough to believe that Madame Marie Marshall had simply materialized in front of him. She certainly looked the part of her profession: a deep red velvet dress with a shawl of black lace and poker-straight black hair that hung past her shoulders. Her nails were long, with multiple coats of blood-red polish. Mahoney couldn't put a guess on her age. Maybe 40, maybe 50, maybe even 60. Something told him that he shouldn't even put the number into his mind, for fear that she would immediately see it with her hazel eyes and tear out his heart for his insolence. She stared at him with an intensity that was anything but comfortable, her face expressionless as she spoke. "It is an invitation to darkness to listen to the fortunes of another without express invitation."

Mahoney felt the words hit his mind like hot oil. "I'm, I, I mean, I . . ." Mahoney felt as though his throat was closing off, the way that Darth Vader could close off throats. He struggled to find the words. He decided on formality, with a touch of Chiller Thriller Theatre for effect. "Madame Marie, I seek the help that only you can provide."

The medium seemed pleased by his answer. Her smile broadened. She closed her eyes and instinctively reached for Mahoney's hands. She massaged his fingers, cocking her head slowly from one side to another, stopping every so often with a twitch or a tick that must have been terribly important. Mahoney did his best to keep a straight face. He didn't know if it was all an act. Even if it was, it was well worth the $40 he'd paid for the performance.

Madame Marie's eyes fluttered open. She looked intensely into his eyes. "You have a secret that you are afraid to share; a secret that few mortals would ever be able to comprehend. Is that correct?"

Don't we all have secrets? Mahoney didn't think that this statement was more than a 50-50 chance in the realm of clairvoyance. At the same time, she wasn't wrong in saying it. "That is correct, Madame Marie. I heard on the radio how you can, uhm, how you can, uhm, talk to the, talk to the . . ."

"The dead?"

"Yes, exactly. Talk to the dead. Yes."

Madame Marie closed her eyes again. After a minute of head bobs, she opened her eyes. "The spirit is not here."

No shit, Sherlock. "That is correct. She's not here. She's . . ."

"In your house?"

"No, not in my house, she's . . ."

"A she. A former love?"

"What? No, we've never . . ."

"An unrequited love, perhaps?"

"No, I don't, I mean I don't think . . . anyway, she's in my car."

"In your what?"

"My car. It's a Camaro. A Chevrolet. A nineteen—"

"The spirit is in your car?"

"Yes! Exactly. She's in my car. She died in the car. And she won't leave."

Madame Marie closed her eyes again. After a minute more of twitches and bobs, she opened her eyes. "I will speak to the spirit in the car."

Mahoney was relieved. "Thank you, Madame Marie, I appreciate . . ."

"One hundred and fifty dollars."

"Say again?"

"This is my standard fee to cleanse a domicile. I have not yet had such a request for a motor vehicle, though I do feel that this qualifies as the same realm."

Mahoney did the math in his head. He had spent almost three times that amount for his car stereo when it was new. Not hearing voices and not seeing dead people would certainly make for a more enjoyable ownership experience. "When can you . . ."

"Tonight," said Madame Marie. "It must be tonight, the witching hour."

"I can do that. Should I bring the car here?"

"No. I shall come to you."

"Alright. I'm at —"

"Plus twenty dollars for gas."

Oh, for fuck's sake. "And twenty dollars for gas."

Madame Marie removed a card from an ornate holder on the table. She slid the card towards Mahoney. "Write the address down and give the card to the hostess. I will be there . . . at midnight." The medium closed her eyes and bowed her head. Mahoney didn't know what to do.

She broke the silence after a solid minute with a mediocre whisper. "You can go now. My 3:30 is here."

CHAPTER
TWENTY-
SEVEN

Mahoney was worried. An I-should-have-told-you-about-my-plans kind of worried, since he hadn't informed the late Heather Price about the visitor that would be arriving to meet her in the next few minutes. *She said that she wanted to go home.* Mahoney had opened the garage door, inviting in the warmth of an evening usually suited for late July. He thought about what Madame Marie had asked him at The Chocolate Shop. *Unrequited love.* How could he be in love with someone who was already dead?

Mahoney busied himself with under-hood checks of the Camaro's condition while he waited. There were no new leaks. Oil consumption was practically nil. The drive belts were right tight. Other than the four-wheel lock-up event near Bird's Hill Park, the Hot Rod had seen little stress since it returned to the road. He saw headlamps in the driveway as he closed the Camaro's hood. He turned to see a car that most people wouldn't expect a medium to drive: a rusty white '73 Chevy Vega Kammback, with woodgrain panelling holding most of it together. *Well, the Vegas were kinda scary*, Mahoney thought. He had dealt with enough of their evil tendencies while working at Terry Balkan.

Madame Marie exited her suburb-friendly compact, wearing the same outfit that she had worn at The Chocolate Shop that afternoon, with the addition of oversized amber-tinted glasses that she must have needed to drive. She carried a small black bag, the kind that was normally seen in the hands of doctors making house calls in black-and-white movies. She offered no greeting, walking past Mahoney to his workbench. She removed something that looked like a band of twigs from the bag. She rummaged further. "I require sacred fire."

"Fire?"

"Yes, to light the sage."

Mahoney had nothing in his garage that qualified as sacred, as far as he knew. He grabbed a propane torch from the workbench, lighting it with a flint striker. "Will this do?"

Madame Marie nodded. She turned the bundle of sage slowly in the outer reaches of the blue flame. Once it was lit, Madame Marie let the bundle burn for a moment, then smudged out the flame in one of the ashtrays on the bench. She walked the smoky stalk around the Camaro three times, waving the sage in a slow weaving motion. "This will help to diminish the negative energy of the spirit." Judging by the smell, Mahoney figured it would make Heather Price as mad as Dolores Favel was whenever he lit up a Colt in the Hook Me Up office.

Madame Marie asked Mahoney for a place to lay the smouldering sage. He looked around the garage, finding a battered wheel cover that was hanging on a nearby nail. She produced a hand fan that must have been tucked up the sleeve of her red velvet dress and used it to spread the smoke throughout the garage. Mahoney knew it was only a matter of time until Madame Marie started to recite some-thing, something that ghosts were supposed to respond to. She closed her eyes for effect. "Greetings to you, oh lost and gracious spirit. I am the Great Madame Marie. I have come to you at this, the witching hour, to ask your favour, to assist you in the journey that will release you from this earthly realm and bring you to the afterlife you desire. I command you to reveal yourself . . . NOW!"

Mahoney was squinting slightly as the medium spoke, tightening his eyelids as the command to the late Heather Price was spoken. He was sure that some form of intense light would fill the garage and the Camaro, the garage doors would slam behind them. Then, if all the Video Stop horror movies that Mahoney had rented could be believed, the floor of the garage would open, sending Mahoney, Madame Marie, and the Hot Rod to the bowels of Hell.

Mahoney waited for the lightning strike and the thunder crack. They didn't come. The radio didn't start playing by itself. There were no bubbles of soft, shimmering light inside the Camaro, or anywhere else in the garage. The only sound was the buzzing from the fluorescent light fixtures overhead. Even the stench of Loveday's mushroom manure was the same pungent aroma it always was. *Maybe she's gone,* Mahoney thought. *Maybe the car is finally mine.*

Madame Marie thought so. "The spirit that had inhabited your vehicle has left us. She has gone over to the other side, and is at peace."

Mahoney was skeptical. "That quick? How do you know for sure?"

"A professional knows. This car is clean."

Mahoney remembered where he had heard that before, from another so-called professional, right after the cleansing of the house in *Poltergeist*. That flick had cost Mahoney a six-dollar late charge at Video Stop. He asked about Madame Marie's customer service policy. "So what if the ghost comes back?"

The medium was not impressed. "Are you doubting my ability?"

"It's not so much a doubting," said Mahoney. "I'm asking for, like, just in case."

Madame Marie closed her eyes again. After a minute, she opened them. She smiled at Mahoney. "There are no wandering spirits here. The realm is empty. I have brought you peace." She gathered her tools into her physician's satchel. She bowed slightly to Mahoney as she held out her hand for payment. "That will be one hundred and seventy dollars."

Mahoney handed her eight twenties and two fives.

JUNE 23, 1985
12:37 A.M.

Peter Scrapneck had just untied the rubber tubing from his left arm. He hoped that the hit, mixed with his daily coke regimen, would assist him in finding the nerve — the same nerve that Waller had exerted without hesitation when faced with Heather Price in full overdose. *How am I going to get rid of that tow-truck fuck?* He leaned back in his recliner. Waller was the lowest character he knew, not counting the cook who was awaiting the next kilo of coke. He didn't know the crack cook well enough to bring him on board. The guy could just as easily inform Waller there was a hit coming, and then it would be Peter Scrapneck's mug on the front page of the *Sentinel* and his body being removed from a soggy shit-brown Dodge Aspen with a dealer plate attached. No, if Waller was to go, Scrapneck would have to do it himself. That was the only way to speed up his payout.

Scrapneck noticed movement outside. There was a good chunk of moon overhead, with enough light and a clear sky to illuminate the young buck that was sampling his sod. Scrapneck knew he had to be the buck: He knew that Waller didn't see any of those qualities in him, especially after the night Heather Price went into the river. Waller was the alpha male. Waller was the hero that night. He'd been the fixer. Scrapneck let that idea swim with the chemicals in his brain. Then it hit him with acute clarity: *Waller can't say no to a call for help. ANY call.* Scrapneck figured that it was part alpha exertion, part self-preservation, in the case of Heather Price, and part old-fashioned job description, as the dealership and Hook Me Up had a long-standing contract. When he had made the panicky call from the dealership, Waller was there faster than one of the shit-kicked yellow Chevettes from Gondola Pizza. When a call went out for a run-of-the-mill tow from Commonwealth, Waller jumped to the legitimate duty just as quickly. Scrapneck knew that he could lure Waller to the scene of his ultimate demise.

And he wouldn't need a body to do it.

CHAPTER
TWENTY-
EIGHT

Mahoney steadied the Salisbury House coffee in his right hand as he headed north on Highway 59, towards Howard Petkau's former schoolhouse. The Hot Rod had started that morning like a freshly minted 1985 model. The Supertuner fed the 92 CITI FM Sunday morning classics through the speaker cones. The DJ must have needed to drop a deuce. That usually meant one of three songs on CITI FM: the full version of "Time Has Come Today" by the Chambers Brothers, the fattest run of "In-A-Gadda-Da-Vida" by Iron Butterfly, or the current weirdness, a 13-minute telling of the demise of the *Titanic* by Jaime Brockett. Mahoney figured the DJ must have had a touch of the 26-ounce flu to choose that track.

The RCMP had pulled over an older Winnebago near the exit to Bird's Hill Park. That meant they'd be busy for a while. Mahoney waited till he was just past the park entrance to toss the coffee cup and drop the shifter into second. He held the throttle to the floor, ignorant of the speedometer reading, slapping the shifter forward just enough to avoid neutral once the tachometer crested the 4,800-rpm mark. The soundtrack was now a Humble Pie standard, "30 Days in the Hole," mixed with small-block Chevy. Mahoney chimed in for the chorus.

The crew was already under Petkau's Falcon, fine-tuning the alignment of the dual exhaust piping, when Mahoney pulled up. "Not too low," said Petkau, as he eyeballed the driver's side section from the rear of the hoist as Fiddler and Scheer adjusted the hangers. "Not with all these new speed bumps they're putting in the parking lots."

"I scraped my crossmember on one at the IGA," said Scheer, holding the pipe at the right height as Fiddler tightened the clamp. "I think they owe me some paint."

Mahoney looked at the pipe. "I think you can tuck it in another half-inch."

Scheer went for the low-flying fruit. "Didn't your new girlie say that the other night?"

"Ouch," said Fiddler. "Or, I guess she won't be saying ouch if there's still room."

"Hey, stop talking pussy and hold the pipe," said Petkau. "Now it's too low!"

Mahoney stepped in with an extra hand as Fiddler tightened the clamp. Petkau eyeballed the two pipes against the bottom of the rear bumper. "Eh, we're out by a quarter of an inch."

"That's not the pipe," said Scheer. "That's your bent-up bumper."

Petkau protested. "Bent? It's straight as an arrow!"

"It's bent," said Scheer. He went for the automotive jugular. "Just like everything else on a Ford."

Petkau bristled. "Fuck you, Rickle-Dick. Hey, Fiddy, help me out here."

Fiddler was busy checking the connections at the exhaust headers. "If you think this car's bent now, wait till Howie hits the gas pedal. It's gonna twist in half with that Cleveland under the hood."

The good-natured bashing of Petkau's Ford continued. Mahoney felt his stomach growl. "Hey, Fiddy, what did your mom make for lunch today?"

"She's doing up a stew," said Fiddler. "Brought Gramma too."

Mahoney's eyes lit up. "We get fresh bannock too?" Fiddler would head out to Peguis on most weekends, bringing his mother and grandmother into the city for Saturday shopping. Stores were closed tight on Sunday, and after a few too many visits to the zoo, Fiddler would bring his mother and grandmother along during his visits to Petkau's garage. They were mechanics of all things food, quickly overtaking Petkau's schoolhouse kitchen. Mahoney cast his nose into the air of the shop. The stew was a given, the fresh-baked bread hard to detect.

"Fresh yesterday," said Fiddler. "That's like a workout for her now. She's like eighty-four, man."

"Evan! I'm only eighty-three." The crew turned to see Maria Fiddler in the doorway. She steadied herself with the door frame on her left and used a hospital-issue cane to manage her right. No one in the family called her by her first name, which included the extended family that was the crew. It was Gramma for Fiddy, Biddy for everyone else. She grabbed the door frame tight, aiming her cane at her grandson to punctuate her disapproval. "Evan, if you want to get a wife and keep a wife, never give her more age than she's got." Biddy's speech was a little jumbled, which meant her teeth were probably back home on the reserve. She brought the cane back down to hobble into the shop, an official frame of five feet that was hunched over to four-foot-six, and had been for the last five years. The march of time had tried to shrink her into submission with various health issues, with little success. Mahoney knew she was back in her garden a week after her last stroke in May. Her cheek had dropped slightly on her right side as a result, the accompanying eye in a permanent state of squint. She looked up at the Falcon on the hoist. "What kind of car is that?"

Petkau stepped forward. "It's a '64 Ford, Biddy. A Falcon."

"A Ford." Biddy ambled closer to Petkau. "My husband had a Ford once." She craned her neck at the undercarriage as the crew listened. "Then he got a job."

The crew roared with approval. Petkau took it the way a good surrogate grandson always should. Biddy ambled away from the crew into the midday sign, using the fenders of the crew's cars to steady her stroll. Fiddler's mother, Ada, appeared at the doorway, drying her hands on a well-worn tea towel. She was the spitting image of Biddy, but in her early 50s, without a squint, a cane, and the effects of a stroke to slow her down. "Lunch is ready, come get it while it's hot!" Ada's stew was the stuff of legend, with Biddy's best potatoes, turnips, and a mix of Interlake rabbit, moose, and venison, a ratio that varied throughout the year with what was in the freezer and what was in season. Biddy's bannock would ensure that the plates were wiped squeaky clean.

The interior of the former Highland Glen School had little remaining that spoke of school days, except for the kitchen, and two former boys and girls bathroom doors that had become an oversized dining room table. The signs for Dick and Jane were still screwed tight to the doors, which were mounted on sawhorses culled from scrap lumber. The rest of the space was at least two years away from being renovated, with gutted walls, naked framing, loose drywall sheets, and a few buckets placed strategically around the house for the leaks from the flat roof. Petkau had hung a protective tarp over his most prized indoor possession, a massive Sony VideoScope projection TV. The curved screen was about three times as big as a regular console unit. Petkau had picked it up at a sheriff's auction last summer. It was fed by a satellite dish on the front lawn that looked big enough to talk to ham radio operators on Jupiter.

The crew dug into the lunch, worrying little about the ladle slop that was splashing the makeshift table. Ada shook her head. "I don't know why we use a table. You boys could get by with a trough."

"As long as you don't send us piggies to market," said Mahoney. He threw in a trio of hog snorts, quickly imitated by the crew.

Ada rolled her eyes. She brought out the tray of Biddy's warmed bannock from the oven. As the plates were wiped clean with the bread, Mahoney noticed that Biddy hadn't come back in. He got up from his chair to look outside. She was standing in the driveway, leaning against the driver's door of the Hot Rod. He looked closer. She was talking.

Talking to someone who wasn't — or maybe was — in the car. "Shit."

"Shit what?" said Fiddler. "Is Gramma okay?" He started to get up from the table.

"Yeah, left my lights on. I'll go turn 'em off." There were plenty of signs along Manitoba's highways advising drivers to turn on their headlamps for added safety, a tip that Mahoney figured was believable enough to exit the house and check on Biddy without someone tagging along. He grabbed his half-eaten piece of bannock from the table.

Mahoney exited through the shop's side door. Biddy was chatting up a storm. No one had to tell him who she was talking to. Mahoney thought about how to play it. For all he knew, Biddy talked to dearly departed relatives on a weekly basis, so it was worth a shot. "Hey, Biddy, who you talking to out here?"

"Oh, just talking to Heather. I was going to bring her some stew, but I don't think she's too hungry."

Mahoney looked inside. Heather Price must have been hiding, most likely in the Supertuner. "Uh, that's nice. So, what did you two, uh, *talk* about?"

"Mostly about your wallet."

"My wallet?"

Biddy gave him a crooked smile with her squint. "Sounds like some lady gave you quite the show last night for a lotta money."

His jaw dropped. Mahoney had just learned two things about the spectral resident inside his Hot Rod: she wasn't gone, and she wasn't exclusive. She had played a game of spectral hide-and-seek with the medium, probably laughing her ghost head off about the whole thing after Mahoney locked up the garage for the night. No amount of burnt twigs, carny spells, and stacks of fives and twenties were going to get her to leave the Hot Rod. Sweat was starting to run down his back. *Who the fuck is she going to make friends with next? What's she going to tell them?* He grabbed on to the coolest composure he could muster. "So, uh, Biddy. Did, uh, did Heather . . ."

"What about her?"

"So, like, she's still in there, right?"

"Yup," said Biddy. "She's still in there. Said something about going home."

Home. He wasn't any closer to getting the answer. "Biddy, what does Heather mean by *home.*"

Biddy started to hobble back towards the house. *Maybe she didn't hear me.* Mahoney stared at the empty Hot Rod. He kept staring inside as he called to the eldest Fiddler on the property. "Hey, Biddy?"

"Yawp?"

"Did Heather say what she left in her apartment?"

"Nothing."

Mahoney turned to look at her. "Nothing?"

Biddy squinted at Mahoney, shielding her eyes from the noon-day sun with her left hand as she steadied herself with her cane. "Nothing in the house. She said it's in the car."

CHAPTER
TWENTY-
NINE

The Falcon was finally running. Petkau had to search the inner crevasses of his tool cabinets for the four pins needed to hold his Thunderbolt-style fiberglass hood in place. The car was still a long way from an oversized trophy at the annual World of Wheels car show at the convention centre. It needed paint, interior, a matching set of wheels, and a rear bumper that wasn't bent. For now, it was a driver. The crew took turns putting it through its paces down Highway 44. They worried that the Cleveland block was over-heating, even though the gauges said otherwise.

The culprit was the engine's tight fit. Petkau wouldn't have any interior heat issues on cool summer cruise nights.

The late hour and another meal from Biddy and Ada had sapped the energy of the crew. Fiddler still had to drive his mother and grandmother back to Peguis. Scheer was beat. Petkau would probably be up till late, continuing his tweaks and checks on the Falcon. Mahoney waved heartily at the crew and the two extra Fiddlers as he backed out of the driveway.

He took the slow-and-easy cruise home, choosing to tune into the Hot Rod's small-block song instead of the Supertuner. He checked his rearview mirror often, wondering if Heather Price would make an appearance. She must have taken the night off.

When Mahoney backed into his driveway a little after nine, Diana was relaxing in a better lawn chair from her open hatchback, sipping on a wine cooler that must have come from the Playmate cooler next to her. He had told her he'd be home by eight-ish. Mahoney waved as he reversed to the garage door. Mahoney could see that Diana was in the mood as she approached, judging from the lack of bra and the half-buttoned Daisy Dukes in danger of slipping off her hips. She closed the overhead door, then did the same to the side door. Mahoney watched her stroll towards him as he leaned on the Hot Rod's nose. She pounced. They squeezed, pulled, and bit till it hurt just enough to still please. Mahoney traded positions, yanking down her Dukes as he lifted her up onto the Camaro's hood. He plunged into her with pleasurable ease. "How you doin'?"

Diana wrapped her legs around Mahoney's torso as he thrust. "Pretty . . . good . . . now!" The position wasn't as comfortable as originally thought. Less than a minute later, she pushed Mahoney off and invited him back into the rear as she steadied herself against the front of the Camaro. Mahoney figured that it could have been because of the heat from the hood, the engine still going through its cooling ticks. Judging by the noises that weren't the engine cooling down, the new position was anything but a mood killer. That is until the noises changed. The first change was the lack of noises coming from Diana. She then started to make new noises that could have been mistaken as pleasurable if they were heard through the paper-thin walls of a cheap hotel room. But from where Mahoney stood, the new noises sounded wrong. Mahoney stopped. Diana's noises did not. She pushed herself off the Camaro, backing up quickly into the closed garage door, her Daisy Dukes still around her ankles. Mahoney looked back to the Hot Rod. Heather Price was looking out of the windshield, in her full-scare best, with extra silt, full whiteout eyes, and flowing hair that looked like a cut-and-perm from the House of Medusa. Mahoney calmly hoisted up his pants as Diana exhibited both cower and confusion. He decided that introductions were in order. "Diana, Miss Heather Price. Heather, Miss Diana McRae."

Diana continued to cower at the garage door. The words didn't come easy, but she managed to push out a few. "What . . . the fuck . . . is THAT?"

Mahoney continued his matter-of-facts as he knew them. "*That* is Heather Price."

Diana inched closer, hitching up her shorts. "Who . . . the fuck . . . is Heather Price?"

"She's the one they found in the car."

"Which car?"

"This car." As soon as Mahoney said it, he realized that he'd never got around to explaining to Diana the events surrounding the arrival of the donor shell for the Hot Rod.

"She, uhm . . . they found her, uh . . . handcuffed to the steering wheel."

Diana's look was now 60 percent fear and 40 percent disgust. "Wait a minute. Are . . . are you saying I've been riding around in a car that someone . . . that she *killed* herself in?"

Mahoney thought about it before he answered. "Well, I'm not a hundred percent —"

"A hundred percent what?"

"That she killed herself."

"And that's why this . . . this *thing* . . . is sitting in your car?"

Mahoney was starting to get frustrated. He looked at Diana, then back at Heather, still wearing her Halloween. He spoke to Heather first. "Hey, could you turn off the *Nightmare on Elm Street* for a minute?"

Diana watched wide-eyed as the image that Mahoney knew would forever haunt her dreams melted away into an attractive redhead. As Diana tried to process the transformation, something happened that Mahoney had yet to experience, so much so that it put him on immediate edge; Heather opened the driver's door of the Hot Rod. He watched as the first red boot contacted the floor, then the other. Heather raised herself up out of the Camaro, with her right hand on the top of the door. Mahoney couldn't see what the left hand was holding until Heather moved out from behind the driver's door; her fingers were holding up her acid-washed jeans. She walked to the front of the Hot Rod.

Diana broke the silence, using Mahoney as a shield. "What . . . the *FUCK* . . . is going on?"

Heather looked at Mahoney, slightly perturbed. "So, you haven't told her anything?"

Mahoney rolled his eyes. He motioned to Diana. "Does she *look* like I told her anything?"

Heather tried to peek around Mahoney to get a better look. Diana was still visibly upset, her face a mess of tears and running makeup. Heather tried to lighten the mood. "You should probably spring for the waterproof stuff, instead of that cheap Zeller's shit you got on."

Mahoney saw Diana's eyes go wide. For a moment, Diana looked like she might retaliate, but the fight within her calmed down quickly. Mahoney figured that it might have been the realization that going toe-to-toe with someone from the afterworld could have consequences that a Band-Aid couldn't fix. Mahoney looked at Heather's left hand. "So, what's up with your jeans?"

Heather looked down at the wad of acid-wash denim that was bunched up in her hand. She looked back at Mahoney. "These jeans . . ."

Heather unfolded the wad of denim, holding the jeans up with both hands. She held the waistband of the jeans in front of her. The image looked like those on the weekly women's magazines that were displayed near the cashier lanes at the neighbourhood Safeway. There was at least eight inches of space between Heather's torso and the waistband of the jeans. "These aren't my fat pants. They're —"

Mahoney finished her realization. "Somebody else's."

Heather looked at Mahoney. "Yeah. Somebody else's." She looked down at her red boots. "I can't remember the last time I wore these." She secured the pants again as she examined the sweater. She peeked down the front of it. She held her pants open to peek down them. "Uhm, where's my gitch?"

"What gitch?"

Heather checked again. "My gitch. Bra, panties." She looked inside the Camaro as Mahoney and Diana watched. She walked to the back of the car. "Are they in the trunk?"

"There was nothing like that in the trunk," said Mahoney. "This is all you've had since you . . . since you, uhm, *arrived*."

Heather kept looking at her ensemble. Then it hit her. "I didn't dress myself!" She looked at Mahoney and Diana, their looks still puzzled as Heather became more elated. "I didn't dress myself! Someone else did! *I DIDN'T KILL MYSELF!*" Heather raised her arms in victory, jumping up and down as her jeans hit the floor around her ankles. The bottom of her sweater covered most of her, when she wasn't jumping up and down. "I DIDN'T KILL MYSELF! I KNEW IT! I FUCKING KNEW IT!"

Mahoney and Diana watched as Heather continued her celebration. About a minute later, Heather stopped jumping. She pulled up her pants, bunching the extra denim into her left hand. She steadied herself against the Camaro with her right hand. She looked at the pair, then asked the question that neither of them could know the answer to. "So who killed me?"

"That's what we're trying to figure out," said Mahoney. He remembered what Biddy had said at Petkau's. "Heather, Biddy said you told her that there was something in the car, something you need to get, uhm, *home*. What is it?"

Heather thought about it. "The car . . ."

Mahoney asked again. "Heather, what's in the car?"

"I don't, I mean I know it's . . . something is in the car. I need it to get home. I just don't—"

Diana finished for her, "You don't know what it is."

Heather nodded in agreement. "I don't know what it is. All I know is that it's in the car. I need something in the car to get home. I don't know how I know that. It's just . . . just, *there*."

Mahoney asked the question that had been nagging him ever since he had heard Heather mention the destination. "Heather, where is home?"

Heather looked at him. "It's not here."

CHAPTER
THIRTY

JUNE 23, 1985
10:12 P.M.

Mahoney slid the barrel bolts into place on the side door of the garage. Once the door was padlocked, he walked over to the open hatch of Diana's EXP. She was leaning against the driver's side of the car, rocking back and forth, her arms folded in front of her in some form of self-hug. Mahoney wasn't sure if she needed or wanted his reassurance. The late Heather Price had calmed down considerably after the realization that she hadn't put herself behind the wheel of the Camaro on the night of her passing. Someone else had, someone who had felt that the action was necessary, someone who had dressed her in whatever was handy, including a pair of jeans that might not have even been for a woman. Someone who had no idea that Heather Price never went commando, even in her comfy clothes. Someone who didn't know that she hated the green sweater, that the red boots always gave her blisters. Someone who was in a hurry. Someone who wanted her dead. Someone who didn't know, or care, that she was still alive.

Heather had returned to the confines of the Hot Rod cabin, slowly fading from view as Diana and Mahoney watched.

"That must be how a ghost goes to sleep," Diana had whispered. Mahoney could tell Diana had plenty of thoughts cascading through her grey matter. Maybe everything she had ever been taught, believed, or perceived about the after-life had been tossed firmly on its head. Mahoney decided to give her a nudge. "Hey . . ."

Mahoney reached for her, slowly, cautiously, but surely. She hesitated, eventually moving to the safety of his arms. He dispensed with something resembling an apology. "I didn't mean to freak you out like that."

Diana's voice was muffled against his chest. "You didn't freak me out, but she sure as hell did."

"I should have told you about her."

"I would have said you were nuts and lost your number."

"That would have been fair." Mahoney rubbed her back as they rocked. About a minute later, something stopped Diana. She pulled back enough to look Mahoney straight on. "So, uhm, you two haven't . . ."

"Haven't what?"

"You know."

"No, I don't think I do."

She went for blunt. "You haven't *fucked her* have you?"

Mahoney looked at her — *you're nuts* written all over his face. "She's a *ghost*! I don't even think that's *possible*!"

"But what if it was possible? Would you fuck her?"

Mahoney had to think about it for a moment. Heather Price would have been more age appropriate. The flowing red hair trick was pretty cool. Diana snapped her fingers at him. "You want to, don't you?"

"I can't believe we're having this conversation."

"It's not like you'd be cheating. I mean, she is dead and all."

"This is getting weird." Mahoney turned away from Diana, walking slowly down the side of her car. She followed, cutting off his escape. "It's not like it's that hemophilia stuff or anything."

Mahoney blinked. "I think you mean necrophilia."

"Oh, so you *have* thought about it!"

Mahoney let out a hard exhale. "Look. This is all really weird shit, and I'm still trying to figure it all out. Biddy . . ."

"Who's Biddy again?"

"Fiddler's grandma. She figured out that Heather was still in the car after Madame Marie—"

"Madame who?"

"Marie, reads tarot cards and stuff. She did her witch doctor shit on the Camaro, said that Heather was gone, then she came right back again this morning. Biddy starts talking to her at Howard's place, says Heather wants to go home, just like she told me the other day. Maybe it's Heaven, maybe it's Hell, maybe it's the fucking loony bin for all I know. Wherever she's going, she needs something, says it's in the car. That's the problem."

"Why is that a problem?"

"Heather's car is at work, the storage compound. I towed

it there the other day. I didn't even know it was hers until I dropped it on the ground and brought in the paperwork."

"Isn't that place twenty-four hours?"

"Well, yeah, but that doesn't mean I can start poking around. At the least, they'd can my ass."

Diana pondered the dilemma a little more. She looked over at her EXP. "What if we had a *better* way in?"

JUNE 23, 1985
11:37 P.M.

Jerry Waller was checking his accounting for the night, parked in front of the Patricia Hotel on Main Street. The crack was a hit, especially with the hardcore clientele that used the Main Street hotels as their shooting and smoking gallery. He had taken a run through the Manitoba Housing projects in North Kildonan and planned to visit the St. Vital properties when the next call to the south end came in. He had rolled up to the Patricia after outfitting most of the roomies at the New Occidental Hotel with fresh rocks. The only initial complaint from his customers was their lack of pipes, though Waller knew that there was nothing more ingenious than a junkie in need of a fix. He hoped to hit the Leland by one, the McLaren by two. He still had to keep tabs on a couple of his regular girls at the Savoy. He wanted to take a run at the one that Larry Ballendine had been favouring, the one he kept saying was crazy tight.

"Base to thirty-two, base to thirty-two, go for dispatch. Over." *Shit,* thought Waller. There was hardly enough time to handle the current docket of illegal activities for Hook Me Up

Towing, let alone his new freelance business venture of crack cocaine. A tow, a lockout, a battery boost. *What the fuck did they think this is? A tow truck?* Waller picked up the mic. "Go for thirty-two. Over."

The night dispatcher detailed the call. "Got an illegal park on Kimberly, at the fire hall near Golspie. Over."

"You mean it's on Kimberly or Golspie? Over."

"I mean its parked *in front* of the fire hall. Probably some drunk who got out and walked home. Over."

Shit. City contract. Waller knew anything for the City of Winnipeg was a drop-everything-and-roll situation, especially with a new tender expected in September. He hit the mic button for the details. "What am I getting? Over."

"A little red Ford hatch, no plates. It'll be hard to miss. Over."

Waller acknowledged and signed off. He headed towards the fire hall.

Diana McRae watched the fire hall on Kimberly Avenue through the smudged windshield of Mahoney's Plymouth. She'd followed him to the rear parking lot of a church on Golspie Street that offered a good view of the front of the fire hall. She had even offered to tuck herself underneath the musty sleeping bag in the back of the EXP. Mahoney explained that as much as he appreciated the gesture, and that she was a far better fit, the dogs in the Hook Me Up yard had no idea who she was and might bite first and ask questions later. He removed her car's license plates and took the registration from the glove compartment. Then he tucked himself into the hatch and had her drive the car to the fire hall driveway with the lights off. She parked the car in front of the centre door that separated the two overhead doors, then ran across the street, cutting through an unfenced backyard to the back lane that led back to the church. The car's placement wouldn't block the fire trucks if a call came in, but its presence would be quickly discovered, probably when one of the night owls went outside for a smoke. Diana watched as a fireman opened the man door. He looked at the Ford. He called to someone inside. Another man appeared at the door. They inspected the vehicle, which they found to be locked. A third man checked on the situation. Judging by his hand gestures, the call for the tow would be imminent.

It took about 12 minutes for the Hook Me Up tow truck to arrive and another three minutes for the driver to open the car and roll it into position for a front-end tow. There was plenty of room on the fire truck–sized driveway to manoeuvre. The driver switched on the tow truck's amber beacon. Diana started the Plymouth.

Steve Mahoney may not have seen the driver that picked up Diana's EXP, but he knew where he would be going. It took about five minutes until Mahoney felt the washboard surface of the Bowman parking lot, a surface that became even rougher as the truck entered the Hook Me Up compound. The car came down quick and hard into the rutted gravel. Mahoney made a mental note to promise Diana that he could buff out most of the scratches. He listened as he heard the driver unhook. The driver's side door swung open, hitting whatever was parked next to it. *Drakkar Noir.*

Mahoney figured it had to be Jerry Waller. Mahoney kept quiet as Waller quickly rummaged through the places where spare change might be, better known to the Hook Me Up drivers as "the tip." Waller pocketed the loot from Diana's ashtray. *What a cheap asshole.* Waller locked up the car and headed back to Unit 32. Mahoney heard the truck leave the compound, and the Bowman yard, assured by the sound of the tow truck's gears being changed as it picked up speed towards Watt Street.

Mahoney waited another five minutes to be sure before unfolding himself out of the cargo hold. He wriggled through the passage between the bucket seats, opening the passenger door to exit. He was immediately greeted by the guard dogs, licking his face and demanding ear scratches. Mahoney obliged, and the time spent bonding with the canines helped the feeling return to his hatchback-cramped legs. The extra Slim Jim tool that Mahoney had found in the bag of the would-be Camaro thief was at the ready. Mahoney worked it into the weatherstrip of the Concord's passenger door. He kept an eye on the Hook Me Up office and the rest of the Bowman compound, in case anyone popping outside for a smoke developed a case of curiosity.

Heather Price's Concord was still the mess he remembered. He pulled a cheap flashlight out of his pocket to check the interior. He fished through the fast food bags, looking for anything that could have had some importance. The glove compartment presented no additional clues. He was trying to figure out how to get into the trunk when he realized that the Concord was a hatchback model, something he hadn't remembered from the tow at the Silverfish. He folded down the rear seatback, revealing a well-stuffed cargo hold of empty washer fluid bottles, jumper cables, an old snowmobile suit, a compact snow shovel, and a few shopping bags with the Eaton's logo on them. The bags were in varying degrees of half-empty and full, stuffed with paper. He checked under the front seats, finding a few plastic bags that had been tied shut. *They might be important.* He threw the additional items into the half-empty Eaton's bags. He was just about ready to leave when he noticed another bag at the rear of the cargo area, a dark blue vinyl travel bag, with *Wardair Canada* written in white script. It had some heft to it. He added it to the pile. He also had plans for the snowsuit.

Mahoney carried the bags to the rear of the compound. The chain-link fencing had seen better days, thanks to a few impacts from cars that had been dropped a little too quickly. This was where the junk lived, like the old milk truck that the guard dogs were squatting in. As bent as the fence was, the barbed wire on the top was still intact. A rusted-out Dodge Tradesman boogie van with teardrop rear windows would supply the ladder, a small aluminum unit bolted to one of the rear doors for roof access. Mahoney took two trips to get the bags to the top of the van. He could see Diana parked on Raleigh Street in his Plymouth. The bags were easy enough to toss to the other side. Mahoney laid the snowsuit on top of the barbed wire. He could still feel the sharp bits as he slid over, but he wasn't slicing himself open in the process. The guard dogs watched as he retrieved the bags. Diana had seen him coming. She pushed open the passenger side door to help with the getaway. "Looks like you found some stuff."

"Yeah, there's stuff all right." Mahoney threw the bags into the back seat and got in the front. "Let's hope that whatever she's looking for is in here."

Diana put the Plymouth into drive. "Are we going to show her now?"

Mahoney looked out at the night sky. A full moon was shining back. "Tonight's probably as good a night as any."

"I hope she's not cranky."

Mahoney nodded. "I hope so, too."

CHAPTER
**THIRTY-
TWO**

JUNE 24, 1985
12:21 A.M.

Steve Mahoney flicked on the overhead fluores-
cents. He grabbed a well-used Black & Decker
Workmate to use as the presentation table
for what was in the bags from Heather's car.
Diana grabbed a couple of short shop stools
with wheels from a dusty corner. Mahoney
opened the driver's side door of the Camaro.
He kept the Workmate platform at its lowest
level to go through the bags. The position was
anything but comfortable. Mahoney hoped
that they wouldn't be sitting in the position
for too long.

Mahoney and Diana sat and watched the cabin of the Hot Rod for a solid minute. He was about to ask Heather if she was in when the lights overhead started to flicker. A nodule of light began to emanate from a space on the driver's seat, a space that must have been where Heather's heart would have resided in life. The light grew enough that Diana had to turn away slightly as it reached its peak. Then she was there, Heather Price, in the same green sweater, red boots, and acid-wash jeans that were never going to fit. She looked at the presentation setup. She smiled. "You guys look like you're sitting in the kindergarten chairs on parent-teacher night."

Mahoney was busy fishing through the first Eaton's bag. "Yeah, well, if this was elementary school, your homework is pretty sloppy." He pulled a stack of papers from the first bag, bringing them closer for Heather to see. "What is all this shit anyway?"

Heather looked at the papers. She reached slowly, then clamped her fingertips on the sheets and pulled the pile closer. She flipped through the stack. She shook her head as she handed them back to Mahoney. "Just my taxes from '83," said Heather.

Mahoney rolled back to his earlier position. Diana rolled forward, her arm outstretched with a new stack. "These look like taxes too," she said, as Heather gripped the papers and brought them closer. She agreed. "I kept most of my tax stuff in those Eaton's bags. They're worth the four-bits they charge for them." The rest of the Eaton's bags drew similar responses, as the remaining stacks of papers were passed into the Hot Rod for examination.

Diana uncoiled the knotted plastic bags that Mahoney had found bunched up beneath the front seats. It was wise on her part to unfurl the bags instead of digging in; the bags held a collection of Heather's spent syringes. Diana showed the contents to Heather. "I guess that's one of the pluses of being dead," Heather sighed.

Diana pulled back the bag. "How so?"

Heather smiled. "I haven't been jonesing for a fix for more than two weeks."

Mahoney was working the zipper on the Wardair Canada bag. It finally came loose, though the bounty inside was just another selection of personal papers for Heather Price. There were no scribbles, no paper-clipped addendums, not even one of those yellow sticky notes that Dolores Favel liked to plaster around her desk at Hook Me Up. The something that was supposedly in the car simply wasn't there.

Heather Price faded once again into nothingness. Mahoney figured that he had to stow the bags somewhere. He put them in the trunk of the Hot Rod.

That night, sleep didn't come. Mahoney and Diana shifted into multiple positions, trying to capture it in the lumpy mattress. The shifting was almost a conversation that didn't require any vocalization. Diana heard it, so did Mahoney. *Will I ever sleep again?* They watched as the digital clock readout mocked them with every minute. Mahoney wondered if Heather Price was thinking the same thoughts, sitting in the Hot Rod, watching the sweep hand of the clock in the console gauge cluster that had been transferred in from the smashed donor car. That's when Mahoney remembered.

The clock in there had never worked.

The clock radio had been blasting the CITI FM morning show for at least a couple of minutes. Mahoney hadn't slept a wink. Neither had Diana. *Something is in the car.* Mahoney wasn't sure if that was simply in his head, or if he was listening to Diana's thoughts next to him. The only thing he knew for sure was that both of them needed to get out of bed. This Monday would be crueller than most. The soul-sucking day jobs would be the icing on the proverbial shit cake.

There was little conversation. Coffee was instant, the cream was no-name powder, the toast stale. Diana went to say something as she left to catch the bus, then seemed to think better of it. Mahoney sipped on his black instant, with dried creamer blobs refusing to dissolve. His head was pounding. *Something is in the car.*

He headed to work early. No one had touched Unit 36 all weekend, thanks to its quirks. He pulled the wrecker up to the front door of the office to let it idle up to operating temperature. Dolores Favel had already arrived, currently indisposed in the washroom. Mahoney checked the desk for any immediate pickups. None of the sticky notes spoke of such a task. He hollered through the washroom door. "Hey Dolores! Can I roll or what?"

Dolores was busy, and said as much. "Christ! I can't even pinch off my morning loaf without somebody fucking bugging me!" Mahoney heard the telltale fumble of toilet paper being unrolled, a toilet being flushed, and a toilet handle being jiggled. Dolores burst out of the door faster than Mahoney had expected, or wanted. Her evacuations were the stuff of stinky nightmares. She knew it too. She fanned the door back and forth as Mahoney gagged. "What's the matter, Baloney? Can't handle a proper dump?"

Mahoney's voice went nasal, as he pinched off his nostrils. "You should really get that looked at, Delectable. Even Luscious Larry's don't smell that bad."

"You probably sit down to pee, Missus Mahoney." Dolores made a beeline for her chair, the *Winnipeg Sun*, and a cigarette half-reduced to embers. She flipped through her sticky notes. "Nothing, nothing, nuth-, wait a sec. That silver Concord."

"Yeah." *Heather's car.* "What about it?"

Dolores squinted at her chicken scratch. "It's gotta go to Commonwealth on Portage. Outstanding lien or something, in-house finance deal."

"I thought that was going to an estate sale."

Dolores looked at Mahoney as sharply as she could. She tossed the keys at him. "Who cares what you thought? Just take it where I fucking tell you to take it!"

The dogs in the Hook Me Up compound seemed slightly curious as to why their ear-scratcher was back so soon. After five minutes of puppy love, Mahoney, Unit 36, and the Concord were rolling west on Watt Street. He knew he couldn't just swing by Diana's work and ask her to help search the Concord for whatever it was that they had missed. He had maybe 10, possibly 15 minutes of extra time to give Heather's car one last look before he dropped it off at the dealership. He hoped it was enough.

He headed towards Fort Gibraltar. With schools shutting down around the city for the summer break soon, he figured that there would be few field trips to the historical site. It would be quiet. He pulled into the parking lot and gave the Concord a final once-over. Nothing. He headed towards the dealership.

CHAPTER
THIRTY-
THREE

Something is in the car . . .

Mahoney couldn't shake the phrase, first from Biddy Fiddler, then from the late Heather Price. He remembered the teardown of the Lincoln Continental in *The French Connection*, one of the movie car chase–contestants that the crew had recently enjoyed from Video Stop. The movie car was practically in pieces before the rocker panels were popped open to reveal the heroin shipment from Marseilles. Mahoney doubted that the Concord was playing such an important supporting role. It simply wasn't big enough for smuggling.

The front of Commonwealth Motors was impassable; a new Jeep was being wheeled out of the oversized showroom doors. Mahoney drove around to the rear of the dealership, which wasn't doing much better than the front. A car transporter was a third of the way through its deliveries, blocking off the easy entrance points for a tow truck to make a quick drop-off. Mahoney drummed his fingers on the steering wheel and the shaking shifter knob as he waited. He noticed that the cars were without plates, with some type of grease pencil scrawl on the windshields that wasn't retail car-dealer language. *Probably auction stuff.* The bulk of the shipment looked like former economy rental cars with minimal flash, the kind that most people would immediately upgrade at Tilden Rent-A-Car. The last car was almost ready to be off-loaded, a car that definitely wasn't like the others. Mahoney watched as the transporter driver slowly backed a light-green Oldsmobile Toronado off the rickety ramps. It was the last of the big 1970s' Toros, with a wraparound rear window that must have been part of a special option package. *That is one ugly boat,* thought Mahoney, as the monstrous coupe touched down on the Commonwealth Motors asphalt. It must have been a bargain. Something had fallen on the trunk lid, almost caving it in. Something heavy.

Mahoney watched as the lot jockeys assisted with the off-loading. A man with a light-khaki sports coat and neon green pants was checking a clipboard with the driver of the transport. *Looks like Crockett has really let himself go,* Mahoney thought, as the tedium of crossing t's and dotting i's played out in the parking lot. The Don Johnson–wannabe's dirty blond hair didn't look right, maybe a rug. He did something that looked like a signature on the clipboard page, judging by the flourish of his wrist. The transport driver hopped into the cab of his truck and moved the empty transporter out of the lot. Mahoney pulled in with the Concord. He found a spot next to the wholesale units at the back of the lot.

As Mahoney lowered the car, a familiar beige Corvette convertible flew into the rear lot at a speed that would have immediately fired one of the lot jockeys on duty if they were the pilot. *Fucking Wallbanger.* Mahoney figured that the Hook Me Up drug dealer was there to top off the salesmen and possibly a few of the mechanics on flat rate that needed to keep their speed up to maximize their take-home. Jerry Waller didn't head for the shop or the showroom. Instead, he ambled up to Mr. Miami Vice with a fat manila envelope. The man who signed things with great flourish nodded at Waller, took the envelope, then walked over to a shit-brown Dodge Aspen with a dealer plate. He stowed the envelope in the trunk. Mahoney thought it odd that Miami Vice didn't produce his own envelope to pay for whatever Waller had dropped off. *What kind of drug deal was that?* Waller hopped back into his Corvette, leaving just as quickly as he had arrived.

Mahoney grabbed the keys and the paperwork for the Concord and headed through the shop to the reception desk. A chesty brunette was busy filing her nails at the desk, keeping time with the popping of her bubble gum. Her name plate stand was something that Mahoney had never seen at Terry Balkan. The woodgrain slab said *Lisa Bentley: Director of First Impressions*. Mahoney silently agreed; her cleavage was the first thing that impressed him. He plopped the Concord's remnants on the counter. "Got a drop-off for you guys."

Ms. Bentley kept at her filing and gum-popping without looking up. "Second office on the left." Mahoney scooped up the keys and the papers. The first office was empty, one of the business offices, judging from the posters on the walls extolling the virtues of rustproofing and fabric treatments. The second office was less sales, more executive. The occupant wasn't around. The top of the desk was thick with paperwork, file folders, and extra keys. It looked like a great place to lose the keys that Mahoney had in his hand. *I'd better wait.* He let his eyes wander around the office. It was hard not to notice the old Nash clock. Mahoney figured the light and the buzzing clock movement were responsible for at least a quarter of Commonwealth's monthly hydro bill. He noticed the black-and-white picture of two men, one holding a large trophy and a Plymouth banner. Mahoney had heard about the old-school diagnostic competitions when he was an apprentice, but they'd fallen by the wayside in the early '70s. He was staring at a black-and-white picture of a 1940 Ford when he heard a voice behind him. "Something I can help you with?"

Mahoney turned. The man in the doorway reminded him of the rumpled salesmen and sales managers from his days at Terry Balkan, the ones who complained incessantly about the repairs that were required on the dealership's fresh trade-ins. *This must be the boss-man.* He then noticed that the boss-man wasn't looking at him; he was smiling at what must have been his Hot Rod. "That's my old Deluxe coupe," the man said, as he shimmied around his desk to his chair. "Built it up like one of those moonshine cars that the old NASCAR drivers cut their teeth on."

Mahoney remembered an episode of *The Dukes of Hazzard* that showed some of the old cars from the '40s in action on the dirt roads of moonshine country. "What was in it?"

"Cadillac V8. Pulled it out of a hearse from Bardal that got T-boned leaving the Elmwood Cemetery." The boss-man pulled the picture down for a closer look. Mahoney saw the twinkle in his eye. "Had an Isky cam, dual Offenhauser intake with a couple of Strombergs on top."

"Sounds pretty fast."

"It was, for the time." The man put the picture back on the wall.

"Ever race it?"

"Every weekend."

Mahoney looked around the office, hoping to see a trophy or a dragstrip picture from back in the day. "Where did you race?"

The man smiled. "Wherever some smartass was dumb enough to open his mouth. Paid for my first house on Polson with that car."

The man kept smiling. Mahoney didn't know if he was expecting a racing story in return, but he did his best. "Yeah, hoping to take my car out to Gimli one of these days."

"That's sensible," said the man. "Fewer tickets that way. Watcha got?"

"Older Camaro. Three-fifty, thirty over, four-hundred crank."

"A stroker?"

"Yep."

"So more like a three eighty-three now."

"More like it."

The man pointed at the keys in Mahoney's hand. "I'm guessing those are for me?"

Mahoney had almost forgotten about the Concord. "Oh, yeah, right. We picked it up the other day. From an estate." He handed the keys and registration over. The boss-man had found his chair by then and reached for his glasses to read the documents. He smiled to himself before he looked at Mahoney.

"Do you know what you've got here?"

Mahoney had no idea. "Uh, what?"

"A very rare bird. Probably an American car. Most of the Canadian ones didn't get loaded up like that, especially a hatchback."

Mahoney remembered the car transporter. "I saw a bunch out back that just got delivered. Are they from the States too?"

"Probably. My sales manager brings them in. Gotta be five years old to get across the line easy. A lot of ex-rentals, a few repos."

Mahoney nodded. "I'm guessing that Toro that came off the truck isn't a repo."

"Toro?"

"Yeah, one of the big ones. The *really* big ones. Mashed-in trunk lid."

"Then I hope we stole it from the auction. Nothing worse than paying for an empty space on a truck coming back from Minneapolis. Sometimes you fill it with the car that nobody wants." The boss-man pointed towards the director of first impressions. "Let Lisa up front know who we're paying for the tow. It's Hook Me Up, right?"

"Right."

Mahoney turned to leave. He heard the creak of the chair before he heard the voice. "And don't forget the most important thing on race day."

"What's that?"

The boss-man smiled. "Keep the shiny side up and the rubber side down."

Peter Scrapneck was enjoying his Monday. Jerry Waller had just dropped off the weekend crack take. The second batch of coke had arrived from Minneapolis, stashed in the damaged trunk lid of a light green 1978 Oldsmobile Toronado XS. *That is one ugly boat,* Scrapneck thought, as one of his lot jockeys drove the car over to the open overhead door of the body shop. The replacement trunk lid was waiting to be installed, resting on a padded panel stand in the morning sun. The Toronado went for just eight hundred bucks at the American auction.

With the replacement trunk lid, quickie paint, and the bill for the space on the transporter, the car would still net about $1,500 once it sold at a No Dicker–Sticker price of $2,995. Scrapneck checked his watch. The camera crew from CKND would be arriving shortly to record the latest commercial for Commonwealth's used car department.

Scrapneck loved TV ads. The cooperative advertising dollars he spent among the local TV stations for his new inventory was sizable enough that he got late-night commercials for the used cars thrown in at no charge. The time slots were anything but plum, though there were definitely enough insomniacs who needed wheels. The sales numbers had confirmed it for the last few months. The only caveat from the stations for the bonus spots was minimal production. That meant price signs painted by the most artistic of the lot boys, a portable camera unit that filmed the cars as they rolled past, and Peter Scrapneck on two fat lines of high-test cocaine.

Scrapneck headed through the shop towards the men's room for the coke bump. Dick Loeb was coming through the shop door as Scrapneck reached for the door handle. Loeb put a set of keys in his hand instead.

"They just dropped off that in-house finance Concord. I left the paperwork on your desk."

Heather's car. "Yeah, I'll get one of the guys to check it over."

Loeb nodded and returned to the showroom. Scrapneck tossed the keys up and caught them in his other hand. Loeb must not have bothered to look at the paperwork closely. That could have started a new group of questions, questions that Scrapneck didn't want to answer. He knew the Concord was a tight ride; he had personally picked it out for Heather six months ago and had the shop foreman go through it front to back. Her credit rating had been blown to smithereens when she was still using at Great-West Life. He called in a favour with the business office for the in-house financing, a favour that required a few grams of Waller's utility-grade cocaine to swing. He couldn't remember if he'd ever told Heather that he loved her. He had said it with the car. He tossed the keys to one of the lot boys. "Give it a quick clean," said Scrapneck, as he headed for the men's. "It's part of the No Dicker this week."

JUNE 24, 1985
10:59 A.M.

Dick Loeb looked at the sales numbers from the weekend that he had booked off from the dealership. Scrapneck had done an admirable job: 12 new cars delivered, three pending, and seven used cars off the lot. The six trade-ins hadn't taken hard stretching to get, and three were new and low-mileage enough that they might be candidates for full reconditioning. He decided to stretch his legs, shimmying around the desk to the showroom floor. He smirked as he looked out the window at the front lot. The overhead streamers were dancing madly in the wind, just like Peter Scrapneck. Loeb's sales manager was moving frantically around the No Dicker–Sticker deals of the week. Loeb had seen Scrapneck stuff at least five cars into a 60 second commercial, although he thought the commercials were as bad as the local-yokel American advertisement assault from WDAZ in Grand Forks. The Weivoda Carpet Girl's voice was usually cause enough for Loeb to launch a slipper at the TV, if he happened to be home that night. As low-rent as they looked and sounded, Scrapneck's commercials brought in the customers.

The overhead speakers started to squawk. "Dick Loeb, call holding on line three. Dick Loeb, call holding on line three." The canned music returned. Dick Loeb walked back to his office, closing the door behind him. He shimmied around the desk and parked himself comfortably in his chair before he answered. He had a feeling he knew who the call would be from. He picked up the handset, pressing the flashing button that connected the third line. "Commonwealth Motors, Dick Loeb speaking."

"What in tarnation are you up to out there, Dick Loeb?"

Dick smiled, pausing a moment before he spoke again. "Can I ask who's calling?"

"You know darn well who's calling."

Loeb couldn't resist poking the bear, and it was a very big bear at that. "I'm sorry, sir, are you a customer at Commonwealth Motors? Was there a problem with your vehicle?"

"Problem with my vehicle . . . *problem with my vehicle?* Yes, I'd say there's a problem with my *vehicle*, except my vehicle doesn't have whitewalls or power steering."

Loeb's smile widened "Well, sir, if you don't have a Jeep, AMC, or Renault product, I don't know how I can help you. Oh wait, is this about a used car? I can direct you to our—"

"THIS IS TED ROGERS FROM CANTEL!"

Loeb was starting to look like a stand-in for the Grinch, running out of face to curl upwards. "Oh, hello, Ted, I've been reading about you a lot in the business section of *The Winnipeg Sentinel*. So, I guess you're getting pretty excited about Canada Day, eh?"

"I know what you're up to, Loeb. And now we're going to take care of it." Loeb could hear the shuffling of chairs and people over the line. The next voice that spoke was cooler, calmer, and collected. "Mr. Loeb? Are you still there?"

"Yes, and to whom am I speaking?"

"Mr. Loeb, this is Lance Harzan speaking, legal counsel for Mr. Rogers and the Cantel wireless venture. We are calling today to discuss the acquisition of the rooftop leases through your various companies throughout Western Canada."

Loeb stated the obvious. "Acquisition? I don't remember offering them for sale."

Ted Rogers had heard the exchange, saying something that Loeb couldn't quite hear. It was obvious that he was anything but pleased. Harzan continued. "Mr. Loeb, as I'm sure you're aware, this isn't the first time we've encountered speculators such as yourself."

"Speculators? Maybe I just like the view."

Harzan paused for a moment, calming another meltdown in the background by the head of the new Canadian cellular phone network. "Mr. Loeb, as much as we applaud you for your business acumen, we both know that securing these sites and not building out a cellular network is something that your coffers cannot sustain."

"I wouldn't bank on that," Loeb said. He pulled out a file with notes from his earlier feasibility studies. "You'd be surprised at how much people pay for these Jeeps and what it costs to fix them when they break. And, boy, do they love to break."

"And what does that have to do with the cellular phone business, Mr. Loeb?"

Loeb lost his smile and brought forth his sizable balls. "It *means* I've got a fucking boatload of cash coming in on a monthly basis to maintain those leases into the next millennium if I want to. Sure, you can probably find alternate sites, sites that will be seeing hefty increases to their lease rates, plus the purchase of all kinds of technical equipment to boost the signal to standards. And that signal has to be beyond acceptable, Mr. Harzan. If it isn't, then Mr. Rogers might have to go back to fixing radios like his old man."

"Mr. Loeb, can I put you on hold for a moment?"

"Certainly. Talk to Teddy Bear and see what he wants to do." Loeb tried to push out his chair enough to put his legs up on his desk, the way he imagined a business tycoon would when he finally arrived at the point of his career known as The Upper Hand. After four attempts, he realized the space and his frame simply wouldn't allow it.

Harzan came back on the line. "Mr. Loeb?"

"Yes?"

"We would like to buy out the rooftop leases of your holding companies, effective immediately. I will forward the paperwork to you by overnight courier. You will have our offer in its entirety by 12 noon Winnipeg-time tomorrow."

"I'm looking forward to it."

"Have a pleasant day, Mr. Loeb."

"You too, Mr. Harzan."

Loeb listened as the call disconnected. He leaned back in his chair as far as the confines of his office and frame would allow.

JUNE 24, 1985
9:19 P.M.

Steve Mahoney made a call to the Madame at
The Chocolate Shop. The hostess promised
to relay the message. That was at 5:30 p.m.,
shortly after Mahoney had got home. He'd been
checking his answering machine for new messages every hour or so while organizing his tool
bench in the garage. There was nothing from
the Madame or from Diana. The garage door
was open, the night air warm. Heather Price
must have been asleep in the Hot Rod.

The Monday night DJs on Winnipeg radio
must have been afflicted with various degrees of

heartbreak, with little in the way of garage-savvy music. *Ugh, Corey Hart.* Mahoney killed the radio on the bench, opting for whatever background noise he could find on an old Viking black-and-white TV that he had hung from the ceiling. He'd got the idea of hanging it from the rafters from a billiards hall, a handy thing to have during the Stanley Cup play-offs. Hockey had ended in May, and Blue Bombers football wouldn't hit the regular season until July fourth. There was a lot of news on CBC's *24 Hours* about an Air India flight that had blown up over the Atlantic. Mahoney glanced up at the video of the space shuttle *Discovery* coasting in for a landing in California. He tuned in and out to an episode of *The Nature of Things.* It was something about whales mating in BC. He didn't know what kind.

A set of headlights shone into the driveway. They belonged to Rick Scheer's Chevette. Mahoney noticed that he was still wearing his work shirt with the name 'Rick' embroidered on it, which probably meant one of two things: a raft of pre-delivery inspections on new inventory at Garden Gate or a very large job that needed finishing. Judging by his appearance, it was something very greasy and very broken. He had a six-pack of Extra Old Stock with him. *Ouch! High-test!* Mahoney figured that the job must have hurt, the reason for the dark-brown painkillers.

Scheer plopped the six-pack on the bench without any pleasantries, cracked open the box, and used the edge of the tool bench to slap off the bottle cap. He pulled a third of the high-test back before he spoke. "Do me a favour, Steve-Oh."

"What's that?"

"Don't ever buy a front-wheel drive anything. *Ever.*"

Mahoney fished into the box of beer. "Tough day at the office?"

Scheer was just finishing his second pull of medicine. "Fucking Cadillac! Those new ones are fucking bullshit! A Caddy should never be a front-wheel drive. A Citation maybe, but a Caddy?"

Mahoney nodded in agreement. He gave a second nod, in the direction of the Hot Rod. "They'll never build shit this simple again."

"That's for sure. So, are you going to introduce me to your girlfriend?"

Mahoney looked at Scheer. "Well, sure I guess. She's not here right now."

"Then who's that in your car?"

Mahoney stopped organizing his tools. *Great. She wants to socialize.* He didn't have a bullshit speech ready for such instances. He decided to state something truthful before he turned around to face Heather. As he turned to say it, he realized that Scheer was already moving in her direction for an introduction. "Oh, *Heather*? She's not my girlfriend. She's my, uh—"

"Neighbour," said Heather. She extended her hand, but not so far past the seat that she thought Scheer's hand would pass through hers. Scheer shook her hand without issue, exchanging stock pleasantries. He gave her the kind of smile that most guys give when they think they might have a shot. He nodded towards Mahoney. "I guess there's nothing on TV tonight if you're hanging out with this loser."

"Well, it is mating season for these whales they're talking about." She pointed up at Mahoney's fuzzy black-and-white TV. "It could get interesting."

Mahoney was watching the conversation, trying to communicate with Heather in a way that he wasn't sure if he could: his mind. *Don't do any of your freaky ghost shit, okay?*

You hear me? Don't freak out Rickles. Just be nice. For Christ's sake, just be nice.

Heather leaned back in the seat. "So, it's Rickles, right?"

Mahoney leaned in. *Don't freak him out!*

Scheer moved in closer. "Yeah, that's what they call me."

"So what kind of Cadillac made you look like that?"

Mahoney exhaled a silent sigh of relief in his mind. Scheer went through the inner workings of the new Cadillac Fleetwood as Heather listened intently. She seemed to be enjoying the conversation, probably because it wasn't a conversation about her demise, who did it, and what to do about it. The banter continued right up to 10:30 p.m., when Mahoney flipped the TV over to channel nine for the CKND news. There wasn't much to raise an eyebrow on the local news broadcast: a few stabbings, a rooming-house fire on Broadway, and something about an overdose at a one-star Main Street hotel. The commercial break got Scheer's attention.

"Steve! Turn it up!"

Mahoney reached up to the TV without looking. He realized why Scheer was so excited when the volume reached 70 percent. The ad was for Commonwealth Motors, and it was so frantic that it easily deserved a minute of your time. Mahoney took a sip of Hi-Test as Scheer smiled like a little kid as the announcer ramped up his pitch. Mahoney figured that the guy must have been on at least a gram to talk that fast, maybe a Wallbanger gram, considering that he had seen him there that morning while dropping off Heather's old car. The three watched the pitch for the used car deals. They didn't catch his actual name.

The announcer was talking wildly as the selection of used cars drove up, stopped for a moment, then drove off camera, the cameraman trying to keep the announcer in focus as he went. The "No Dicker–Sticker" tag line was flashing on and off at the bottom of the screen. The prices were drawn on white cardboard, secured under the passenger side wiper. Some of the No Dicker script had been misspelled, probably on purpose.

"Check out this No Dicker deal, a '79 Concord hatchback with whitewalls, tinted glass, and automatic for just *twenty-seven ninety*-five!"

Holy shit! Mahoney was a little surprised at how quickly Heather's car had made its way from the hook of Unit 36 to the front line of the dealership. *Did the lot guy find what was in the car? Was there anything in the car?* He wanted to say something to Heather, though he didn't want to explain to Scheer that he was currently chatting up a ghost for her phone number. He glanced at Scheer and Heather. She offered no obvious tell.

The announcer continued. "Need something bigger for the family? How 'bout this '78 Mercury Colony Park wagon, big V8 power, leather and air conditioning for just *thirty-four-ninety*-five! Or cruise in style to Grand Beach in this 1978 Oldsmobile Toronado coupe, with sure-footed front-wheel drive for just *twenty*-nine *ninety*-five! Only at Commonwealth Motors, home of Winnipeg's No Dicker–Sticker used car deals, open till 9 p.m. Your best deal on used cars on the Portage Avenue strip!"

Mahoney reached up to the TV to turn down the volume. "That guy's the fastest talker I've ever heard."

"Those Commonwealth ads are almost as good as Kern-Hill," said Scheer. "Or that Flam guy at Transcona Dodge."

"Flam?"

"Yeah, Flam. Monty Flam!"

Mahoney rolled his eyes. "It's Flom, you idiot. Monty Flom. The would-you-care-of-course-you-would guy."

"Whatever." Scheer took another sip. "Where does this guy find all this shit anyway?"

"It's auction stuff," said Mahoney. "I was there this morning. That Toro had a mashed-in trunk lid when I saw it. Must have had a fresh one ready to go. Even looked like they matched the colour pretty good."

Scheer shook his head. "It's still ugly as fuck."

Mahoney clinked Scheer's bottle. "No argument there."

"Yeah, whaddya think, Heather? Would you be seen in that? Heather?"

Scheer and Mahoney turned to look at the Camaro. Heather Price was gone. Scheer looked around the garage. "Hey, where'd she go?"

"Probably taking a leak. Or she's, uh, letting out the cat, or something," Mahoney fumbled.

"Gotcha." Scheer gave him an elbow. "So, she like, got a boyfriend?"

Mahoney thought about it for a moment before he answered. "Yeah, she kinda does."

JUNE 24, 1985
10:37 P.M.

Peter Scrapneck was sorting the information
into his mind as he watched the news on CKND.
The ambulance in front of the Savoy Hotel was
anything but out of place for most nights, and
the overdose was news enough for a Monday.
Scrapneck breathed a sigh of relief when there
was no follow-up as to the drug type that took
the life of the 34-year-old male victim. He was
pronounced dead on arrival at the Health
Sciences Centre.

Waller had told him to expect a few overdoses,
until the users settled into an understanding of

how the crack would affect them, especially when mixed with their current drug diet. "We can probably rule the summer until somebody gets wise," Waller said, when he had dropped off the weekend take at the dealership that morning. "Let's just call it collateral damage."

Scrapneck looked at the stack of bills on his dining room table. The money to cover the rooftop leases had already been converted into the certified cheque that the leasing company had requested, done and delivered. The pile of money was hefty, not buy-out-the-old-man-hefty, but very respectable. By week's end, he figured that he might hit six figures. He'd have even more if Waller was out of the picture.

Loeb had brought him in earlier in the day to tell him the good news. "I made Ted Rogers blink," said Loeb, as he bragged about the conversation. There hadn't been a hard-and-fast number on the buyout for Commonwealth yet. Scrapneck knew that there had been talk about an "image program" in the works for the AMC/Jeep/Renault dealers. That would mean a considerable infusion of cash for renovations, maybe even the construction of a new dealership. Loeb would have to spend that money if he stuck around. Scrapneck was betting that Loeb wanted out. He wasn't going to give the dealership away, but he would be reasonable.

Waller wouldn't be reasonable, especially since he had dreams of his own. Scrapneck kept contemplating as he tied off his arm for a hit. *He's in a dangerous business.* Bad things had been known to happen to people in dangerous businesses. These were the risks of the trade. Scrapneck thought about how Waller's business could be his undoing as he heated the spoon and reached for the syringe.

Dick Loeb looked at the number in the legal documents from the Cantel lawyer who had kept Ted Rogers from jumping through the phone and strangling Loeb. It had the right number of zeros on the end. He had already signed off on the copy to be sent back to the lawyer to transfer ownership of the rooftop leases, witnessed by his director of first impressions. His luck was continuing to come up sevens. His wife had informed him at breakfast that she was leaving him, for the recently widowed neighbour at their summer cabin. The affair was two summers old. The neighbour's wife had passed away peacefully in palliative care from breast cancer at the beginning of June. The neighbour was wealthy enough that Loeb's wife was asking only for the deed to the cabin and half of their investment portfolio. Loeb could have won an Academy Award for his performance as the dejected/easily agreeable pushover of a soon-to-be ex-husband. With the money that would be coming from Cantel and the money owed by Scrapneck, he could easily pay out the amount of the second mortgage, sell the house, and head for the West Coast with a trunkful of retirement funds. He was thinking about Tofino on Vancouver Island, the end of the Trans-Canada Highway for those heading west. The end of the road.

Loeb wasn't completely without worry. The accountant that had brought the venture to fruition was as dead as disco. He couldn't be 100 percent sure that there wasn't a paper trail that could come back to bite him. But he was as sure as he could be, somewhere around 85 percent. It would have to do. He was about to have his sales manager paged when Scrapneck entered the front door of the dealership. He was carrying a large manila envelope. Loeb waved him into his tight office. "Close the door, Scrap. Looks like I'm just about to wrap this up."

Scrapneck clicked the door behind him. He handed Loeb the envelope. Loeb checked the contents, the money owed for financing the crack venture. Loeb smiled, placing it on top of his desk. "So, I understand you're in the market for an American Motors dealership."

Scrapneck grinned, still wearing his sunglasses. "Yeah, I've heard this one might be available soon. Any truth to that?"

"That there is." Loeb pushed a piece of paper towards Scrapneck. "I'm thinking this is more than fair."

Scrapneck looked at the figure. He looked confused. He pushed the paper back to Loeb. "Are you sure that's all you want for it? I'll bet Jack MacIver at Midway would pay that just for the land."

"He probably would, but then it gets into all the nitty-gritty of paper, lawyers, land surveys, and all the other shit. I tell the Zone Manager, sign a few papers, and cash your cheque. Then it's yours."

Scrapneck pulled the paper back and looked again. "When do you need it by?"

"I'm thinking half by the end of July. I've had enough hot Augusts in Winnipeg for one lifetime."

"Fair enough." Scrapneck got up from his chair and extended his hand. Loeb shimmied up out of his chair to seal the deal. Scrapneck headed back to his desk. Loeb picked up the phone and dialed three ones. Lisa Bentley answered on the first ring. "Reception."

"Hi, Lisa. Can you order lunch for the guys? Maybe Gondola? Thin crust."

"Yes, Mr. Loeb, I'll take care of it."

"Thanks, Lisa."

The call disconnected. Loeb looked up at the buzzing Nash clock. He thought he might take it with him. He'd grown accustomed to the buzz.

11:45 A.M.

Peter Scrapneck was doing the quick math at his desk. His timeline had been effectively cut in half. He had originally budgeted for a one-million-dollar price tag to be scribbled on the piece of paper that Dick Loeb had just passed him. The amount in its place was half that. If he went through the summer with Waller and the current crack venture, he would easily have the amount required, with enough cash to cover the acquisition of additional kilos to be converted into crack.

The problem was exposure. It was no secret: the longer he stayed in, the harder it was going to be to get out. He knew it would start attracting the wrong attention, the wrong partners. If Waller wasn't in the picture, the current batch of product would be enough. *He's in a dangerous business.* Scrapneck's eyes popped wide open. He scribbled madly on a notepad next to his desk. He had his answer.

12:05 P.M.

Steve Mahoney's morning had been spent at the Manitoba Public Insurance satellite claims offices, transferring fresh accident write-offs to the Autopac compound. He had driven past Commonwealth Motors a couple of times already that morning. The light-green Toronado from the TV commercial the night before occupied a lofty perch on one of the raised ramps in the used car section. *It really is ugly as fuck,* Mahoney thought, as he headed towards something resembling a lunch date at VJ's Drive-In on Main Street. Diana had left a message while he was in the shower that morning. It said she wanted to "talk." It didn't sound spastic.

Mahoney pulled up in front of the eatery. It was strictly takeout, though there were plenty of picnic-style tables for good-weather seating. Diana had already arrived, wearing work togs that did anything but line up with Mahoney's tow truck rags. She waved as she chowed down on a cheeseburger and fries. Mahoney ordered the same, with extra chili. No one in Winnipeg knew what was in the chili topping that all the Greek burger stands used. All they knew for sure was you couldn't order one without it. Even the "no-chili" orders still got a little bit thrown on top, to keep the onions from sliding off the burger. Safety first.

So far, Mahoney felt good about the vibe. The two talked about the simple stuff first: how was your day, get any sleep, how's your burger. When it was time to get into the "talk," Diana got things started. "So, I've been doing a lot of thinking about this, uhm, you know . . ."

Mahoney tried to help. "Situation?"

"Yeah, situation. What do we, like, *do* about it?"

Mahoney finished his chew before he answered. "She keeps saying that whatever 'it' is, it's in the car. I just don't think it's in her car."

"Why do you think that?"

"If there was something in *her* car, she'd probably just come out and say it. 'It's in the glovebox, under the Air Supply cassette, next to the extra tampons,' you know? Anything that was worth grabbing, I grabbed, even her druggie garbage. I still can't feel parts of my left side from being crammed in the back of your car."

Diana smiled. "Now you know what one of those clown-car clowns from the Shrine Circus feels like!"

Mahoney nodded as he dug into his fries. "Yeah, not a job I'm looking to fill." The mention of a job jogged his memory. "Speaking of jobs, what was her day job, anyway?"

"Accountant?"

"Yeah, that sounds right. For who?"

"Dunno. Maybe we should ask her."

Mahoney smiled. "You're starting to be quite the detective there, McRae."

Diana answered through a mouthful of fries. "Yeah, a regular Laura Holt."

CHAPTER THIRTY-SEVEN

Mahoney hadn't entered the garage yet. He was waiting for Diana to show up, his lovely assistant for the interview. *You're starting to be quite the detective, McRae.* Mahoney wasn't sure if it was a job description he wanted for himself. All he knew for sure was that he wasn't getting a clear title to his Hot Rod until the whole Heather Price mess was figured out. He needed all the help he could get. He was in his kitchen attempting to scrape petrified Kraft Dinner from one of his pots when the phone rang. It was Evan Fiddler.

"Hey, Fiddy, how's it hanging?"

"It doesn't hang. It *drags*."

There was a moment of laughter between the two motor-heads, then an awkward silence. Fiddler shattered it into a million pieces.

"So Gramma says you got a ghost in your car or something?"

Mahoney blinked. *It was a good haul back to Peguis,* Mahoney thought. *They had to talk about something.* "Uhm, yeah. It looks like it."

"So that's like the girl who was in it, in the river?"

"Yup. That's the one."

"And she's still in it?"

"Oh yeah, she's alive . . . no, I mean, she's in there."

"Cool."

"Yeah, I guess so."

"So, you gonna keep her?"

Mahoney thought about that for a second. "I don't think she wants to be *kept*. She wants to . . . I mean, she keeps *saying* she wants to go home, then something about something in the car, but I didn't find anything in her car." He could almost hear the gears turning in Fiddler's head as he processed the information.

"Something in the car."

"Yeah. Got any ideas?"

"Fresh out." Another awkward pause ensued until Fiddler made it *very* awkward. "So, can I like meet her?"

"Uh, I guess so. Rickles did on Monday. He actually tried to pick her up."

Fiddler laughed. "I thought the minimum requirement for Rickles was a pulse. I guess I stand corrected."

"Yeah, but Rickles doesn't know she's like, you know . . ."

"Dead?"

"Yeah, dead."

"I guess you'll have to tell him sooner or later. Or maybe we can scare the shit out of him for fun first."

Mahoney knew that Fiddler didn't mean anything by it, but it still set him off. "Listen, Fiddy. She's not some kind of fucking seance Ouija-board bullshit. She's somebody who might've got fucking *murdered*."

"Hey, I know, it's freaky shit. My grandma talks to ghosts all the time. The only thing I know for sure is that they don't leave until they get the help that they want."

Help me, baby. "Yeah, she's already mentioned that. Any other Biddy tips?"

"Yeah, don't get 'em mad."

"Way ahead of you, brother." Mahoney explained that Diana was coming over to help interview Heather.

"Maybe me and Howie can help too. And we better break it to Rickles, before he buys her a ring at Consumers Distributing."

Mahoney hadn't thought about enlisting more help. He knew it was needed, and it was a big ask of the crew. He thought of the builds they had participated in, how everyone seemed to anticipate the next one's move. He couldn't remember the last time any of them even dropped a wrench when they were together. Teamwork like that was a rare thing. "Yeah, sure. More the merrier. Might as well get a pizza while you're at it."

"Ham and pineapple?"

"Bring that, and we'll be dealing with *two* ghosts."

"See you in a bit."

Mahoney hung up the phone. As he did, he heard Diana's car roll into the driveway, recently retrieved from the Hook

Me Up compound. She was already rummaging around in the hatchback when he reached her. "Watcha looking for?"

"This!" She pulled out her red cassette blaster. "It's got a condenser microphone. We can tape the interview."

Mahoney frowned. "Don't you think we should ask her first?"

"It's just in case we miss something, so we can go back to it."

"I still think we should run it past her first."

Diana smiled. "You *do* have a thing for her, don't you?"

Mahoney rolled his eyes. "No, but Rickles does. Oh, and Fiddler's coming by tonight too. Biddy told him about Heather. He's bringing Howie along."

Diana had yet to meet the crew. "Jesus. Anybody else you want to invite?"

"Naw, that should do it."

Diana shook her head, chuckling as she headed towards the garage.

Fiddler had picked up Petkau and pizza on the way to Mahoney's. Judging by the look on his face when he exited Fiddler's Dodge, he'd been told about the late Heather Price. Mahoney had already hustled the pair into the garage when Scheer pulled into the driveway. Fiddler had called him over, said it was "important, non-car-related stuff." Judging by the getup, Scheer definitely had Heather on the brain. He was wearing a fancy purple paisley shirt, new acid-washed jeans, and a hand-tooled belt with cowboy boots straight out of *Urban Cowboy*. The ensemble was topped off with the leather jacket Mahoney had given him, the one that must have belonged to whoever was trying to steal the Camaro. Scheer had even switched up his usual garage beer selection for wine coolers. Mahoney felt bad that he was about to kick Scheer in the nuts of his twitterpated heart. It's not like he had any choice. "You clean up nice, Rickles."

Scheer gave himself a quick once-over to confirm that he agreed. "Yeah, not too shabby. Soooo, what exactly is going on here? All's I know is Fiddy said it's kinda important."

"Kinda," Mahoney said. He grabbed the box of wine coolers, worried that Scheer might lose his grip when Mahoney dropped the bomb on who Heather was. He put his hand on Scheer's shoulder, guiding him as they went. Scheer looked at the hand, then at Mahoney. "So, what's going on?"

They were almost at the threshold. Mahoney stopped and looked at Scheer. "You remember Heather?"

Scheer smiled. "Yeah, sure I do. What about her?"

"She's a ghost."

"Say again?"

"She's a ghost." With that, Mahoney gave Scheer a quick shove through the open door, almost tripping him onto the floor of the garage as he closed the side door firmly behind them.

The garage was getting crowded. Fiddler had placed the pizzas on the workbench, with no ham and pineapple in sight. Petkau was nervously munching on a slice of pepperoni, standing as far away from the Camaro as the space would allow. Diana introduced herself to Scheer, then returned to setting up her ghetto blaster to record the interview. Scheer was looking around the garage, still processing what Mahoney had told him. He was smiling as he did.

"So, let me get this straight. You're saying that Heather is a ghost, right?"

"Right," said Mahoney. "The one you were talking to in the car the other day."

"The girl in the green sweater?"

"Yeah. I mean, no."

"No, she isn't a ghost?"

Mahoney was having a hard time breaking through. "She doesn't like being called a girl."

Scheer started to laugh, shaking his head. He lifted his arms to show off his jacket. "So I guess I should've dressed up for Halloween instead, right? Un-fucking-believeable!"

Mahoney pressed on. "I'm serious, Rickles. I'm not making this up, I swear."

Scheer grinned at Mahoney. "Bull-fucking-shit!" He looked at the rest of the attendees. "Okay, you guys, you got me. Very funny. Fiddy, did you put him up to this? Fiddy?"

Mahoney decided that he had to get the ball rolling, regardless of Scheer. "Well, thanks for coming everybody, I guess. So, the, we're gonna try to . . . the thing we want to figure out is . . . uhm . . ."

Diana cleared the confusion. "Okay, here's what we know. The woman in the car is Heather Price, the one they found in the car in the river. She says she didn't kill herself, and she's told us that she doesn't remember how she got there or who put her there."

"*Oh*. So now she's been *murdered*," Scheer had found himself a Club in the beer fridge. He grabbed a slice and looked at Diana. "Please, *continue!*"

"She keeps telling us that something is in the car, and that she needs to get home, wherever that is." She motioned to Mahoney. "Steve checked her car at the compound, and we brought back the stuff that was in it." She pointed to the Eaton's bags, which had been laid out on the workbench, next to the pizzas. "We went through it all with her, and there's nothing there."

"This is fucking hilarious," said Scheer. He looked around the garage, still smiling. He poked Petkau as he nervously chewed. "Okay, Howie, where's the camcorder? Beta or VHS?"

Mahoney continued. "The *Sentinel* said she was some kind of accountant."

"Who'd she work for?" Fiddler asked, his mouth half-full of pizza. The revelation of something spectral in Mahoney's Hot Rod hadn't fazed him in the least. He'd seen enough of Biddy's conversations with the afterlife to know.

"I plan to ask her tonight," said Mahoney. "She might've been killed by someone she knew." He was about to continue when he heard a pizza slice fall onto the floor, then another, then the shatter of a half-full bottle of Club. Mahoney looked over at Petkau and Scheer. Petkau's mouth was wide open, half-chewed pizza in view. Scheer's mouth was also open, equally stunned. Mahoney turned back to his Hot Rod and saw the reason why: Heather Price's grand entrance had just begun. Diana pressed Play and Record at the same time on the cassette deck. Fiddler chewed his pizza and sipped his beer with a collected casualness. The light show started to dissipate and Heather appeared, sitting in the driver's seat, her head resting on her crossed arms on the top of the driver's door. Her red hair was flowing slowly back and forth, the underwater effect. She decided to start with Scheer.

"Hey, Rickles. You clean up pretty nice."

Scheer blinked. He rubbed his eyes a few times to make sure he wasn't dreaming the visual in front of him. "Uh, uhm, uh, *thanks*?"

"Who's your friend?"

Petkau realized she meant him. "Uhm, I'm how, how, how . . ."

Heather pointed at Petkau's face. "You've got some . . ."

Petkau just stared. Scheer looked over at him slowly. He carefully flicked the piece of pepperoni that was stuck to Petkau's chin onto the ground.

Heather smiled. "Yeah, that's much better."

Mahoney got things back on track. "Heather, we're going to, uh . . . record this, if that's okay."

Heather looked at Mahoney, her hair still flowing. "Audio or video?"

"Uhm . . . just audio."

"Good. This sweater looks like shit." Mahoney never thought a ghost would be vain.

Diana leaned in. "Heather, who were the guys you worked for?"

"They were . . . uhm . . . how do I put this?" She tapped her fingers on the top of the door. "They were all looking to cook their books, someway, somehow. There were a couple of construction companies. Inflated invoices and stuff, sticking it to the City. There was a sand and gravel outfit. Some quarry out of town . . . can't remember where. There was an RV store. I think they sold motorcycles too. A few car dealers, a couple of swimming pool contractors . . ."

Now they had something. "Car dealers?" Diana said. "What kind of car dealers?"

Heather rubbed her forehead. "Let's see. There was a used car place in Transcona, Jeep guy on Portage, a Mazda place in Steinbach, a Chevy dealer in . . ."

Jeep guy on Portage. Mahoney knew that it had to be Commonwealth Motors. The Concord that he had dropped there. Wallbanger in the parking lot. The manila envelope changing hands. The Miami Vice guy with the fancy signature, even the shit-brown Aspen. It was all starting to come together. "Heather, what was the name of the dealer?"

Heather wagged her finger. "Yeah, the one by Midway Chrysler. Commonweath Motors."

Mahoney pressed. "Yeah, Commonwealth. What was going on there?"

"Commonwealth . . ."

Diana chimed in. "Something in the car."

"What car?" Everyone turned to look at Scheer. It was finally dawning on him: this wasn't a joke. This was happening. A fucking ghost in Mahoney's car. For real. Scheer repeated the question. *"What car?"*

Heather Price's expression had suddenly changed. She looked at Mahoney.

"The car . . ."

She had remembered.

CHAPTER
THIRTY-EIGHT

Heather Price paid no attention to the banging noise from the floor below her Silverfish apartment as she rode her casual partner. She had named the tenant "Broom-Hilda," from the comic strip. She had assumed it was a witch, or at least a woman with a high-pitched shrieking voice who had initially tried to shout for quiet in the wee small hours. When that didn't work, the banging commenced, most likely the whack of a broom handle on the stipple ceiling below. *So much for your damage deposit, bitch.*

There was plenty of banging, creaking, and squeaking coming from Heather's bed, as she searched for her elusive orgasm. Before she was hit by the car in front of the Silverfish, the accident that had pushed her into an escalating dependency on painkillers, and eventually heroin, she had enjoyed sex with the cliché fervor that most men had associated with redheads. Now she didn't feel much of anything anymore.

Judging by the noises from her partner, Heather realized that she would have to fake it. She looked down at the contorted face of Peter Scrapneck as he came. She dismounted. "I gotta go pee," she said, as she finished off with a sloppy, slightly detached kiss. She could still hear his panting as she headed down the hall.

Heather flicked on the fluorescent fixture, illuminating the bubble-gum pink tile. She turned on the sink tap before she sat on the toilet, a trick for number one that had worked since grade school. She silently wondered why she bothered with such a mediocre lay. Peter Scrapneck was *convenient*. He was her contact at Commonwealth Motors, for the cellular antennae sites that were the brainchild of the owner and the hinkey drug shenanigans that were Scrapneck's bailiwick. He'd helped her when she needed wheels, financing her new-to-her Concord when nobody else would lend her a nickel. She thanked him by introducing him to the needle.

Scrapneck was lying in the same position that she had left him in, his soldier more at ease. She curled up next to him, running her fingers through the shag carpet on his chest. His breathing was sounding less and less like a medical emergency.

"That . . . that . . . really . . . hit the spot," Scrapneck gasped.

"It sure did," said Heather.

"Did you come?"

Heather lied into her pillow. "Absolutely!"

"Awesome." Scrapneck stood and began to rummage through the inner pockets of his Miami Vice linen sports coat. "I got you a little present."

Heather looked up from her pillow. "It better not be an engagement ring from Consumers Distributing."

"Better." Scrapneck dangled the tied-off balloon in front of her. The carrier and its contents were obvious to anyone who used heroin regularly. The amount within the balloon appeared to be meagre. Heather said as much to Scrapneck.

"Looks more like a grade nine promise ring to me."

Scrapneck explained. "I got it from my Minneapolis guy. He says this is sirloin, the best shit out there."

Heather took the balloon from Scrapneck, checking the heft. "I hope so." She put the balloon on the opposite night-stand. "I'll save it for a rainy day."

"Be careful with it, babe. My guy says it's high-grade."

Heather rolled her eyes. "That's what they all say." She grabbed a pack of Matinées from the same nightstand, a blue Bic lighter in the empty half pack. After a healthy drag, she put the cigarette in Scrapneck's mouth. "Minneapolis," she said, as he inhaled. "You sure like to live dangerously, don't you?"

"It came in with that coke I told you about, the test run."

Heather couldn't remember. "Test run?"

Scrapneck handed the lit cigarette back to Heather as he exhaled. "The coke I need for the crack. It was in one of the auction cars."

"Don't they check those cars when they come across the border?"

Scrapneck chuckled. "Well, if they did, you wouldn't have your promise ring right now. Besides, the border guys like us. They're all driving Commonwealth Jeeps."

Heather took another drag and handed the cigarette back. "So how much can you make off this crack shit?"

"Enough to buy out the old man," said Scrapneck. "Oh, and I don't think he has any idea about those rooftops that got cancelled."

Heather chuckled. "Portable phones. You couldn't pay me enough to carry one of those things around. I hate answering the one that's bolted to the wall."

"Just as well," said Scrapneck. "You probably couldn't afford it anyway."

Heather took the dig but threw in an elbow to his side that was enough to get his attention. "Fuck you, Scrapheap."

"Fuck you, Price is Right."

At that moment, they decided to act on their suggestions.

Heather Price had remembered quite a bit.

She explained what she knew about select used cars that came into Commonwealth Motors. She was a little fuzzy on the details, but she remembered the "it" in the car was cocaine, probably as much as a kilo per damaged trunk lid. Mahoney knew little about the coke trade, other than what he'd seen for sale by Jerry Waller. He knew nothing about crack, aside from the odd news report from the States. He remembered the kid at the Ex, the one who was flipping like a fish in one moment and still and unresponsive in the next. He hadn't heard if the kid had lived.

The crew shouted questions.

"How much is this crack shit worth?" said Scheer.

"Is it on the streets now?" said Fiddler.

"Do we go tell the cops?" said Diana.

"So, she's like a ghost, right?" asked Petkau, taking his time to catch up.

Mahoney shouted over the din. "HEY!" Everybody clammed up. Mahoney grabbed one of the rolling stools to park himself. He held his hands over his eyes for a moment, massaging his temples with his fingers. Then he stopped. He looked up at the rest of the crew, Diana, and Heather. He got up from the stool, walking briskly to the back of the Hot Rod. He opened the trunk and removed a blue Adidas bag. He grabbed a pair of fender covers, slapping them on the hood of the Camaro, then emptied the contents of the bag. He stood back from the items.

Fiddler broke in. "What is all this shit?"

"Wait," said Mahoney. He went over to the workbench, retrieving the notebook that someone was using to log his movements in his Hot Rod. He tossed it onto the pile. "Okay, so Heather's *it's-in-the-car stuff* is drugs. This is *my* it's-in-the-car shit."

"Where did it come from?" Scheer asked.

"It was in the back seat," said Mahoney. He looked at Diana. "I found it after we went for dinner on Corydon. I thought it was your purse or something." He addressed the group. "Then I found this shit inside, and the book, and Rickles's jacket. Somebody was casing the car, and I don't mean a bunch of junior-high dropouts."

Scheer looked down at his new-to-him leather jacket. "This was in there?"

Mahoney flipped through the book page by page. "Whoever's shit this is, it wasn't anything they thought they'd ever lose." Mahoney thought a little more about why the bag would have been left in the back seat of the Hot Rod. Then it hit him: *they left in one hell of a hurry.* Mahoney remembered back to his own hurried escapes from the front seat of the Camaro, the freak-out spin out on Highway 59. He looked over at Heather.

"Heather, did you scare the fucker out of the car?"

Heather looked down at the floor. "Uh . . . maybe."

"It would have been helpful to know that."

That set her off. "I thought you'd be happy to not have to take the bus home after your hot date. So, fuck you, fuck you very much."

Diana hoped to calm the situation. "Heather, what did the guy look like?"

"I don't know, just some guy. Had a blue hoodie, I think. And . . ."

Mahoney leaned in. "And what?"

"Sunglasses. I, I think he had sunglasses."

Mahoney remembered the pair of Ray-Bans he'd found on date night, well-worn but in one piece. He pulled them out of his front pocket. "These sunglasses?"

Heather's eyes went wide. "Yeah! That's them! I . . . I think they were pushed up on his head. They must have fallen, when he, when . . ."

Diana was right there. "When?"

"I scared the shit out of him, and he ran."

Mahoney thought back to the events of the date night. The sunglasses, the flashing lights on Wellington Crescent. The body covered with a sheet in front of the bus. "Heather, which way did he run?"

The group waited patiently as Heather remembered.

"To the rear."

Mahoney moved in closer. "The rear? The rear of what?"

"The car. The rear of the car."

"So, away from Corydon?"

"Yes, away from Corydon."

Mahoney looked at the items on the hood. He looked over at Scheer and his new-to-him leather jacket. "Well, Rickles, I think you're wearing a dead man's jacket."

Scheer looked down at the coat of the dead John Doe. He stepped back and gripped the lapels. "As long as it ain't haunted like your car."

JUNE 25, 1985
9:06 P.M.

Jerry Waller was sitting in the cab of Unit 32, letting the truck warm up before he started his shift. He had received plenty of messages on the new pager Peter Scrapneck had recommended. The crack had been very good for business, contributing to increased sales for the regular menu of drugs from Unit 32. The Monday night at the Ex had been responsible for a much fatter envelope for Scrapneck. Waller let his mind wander to baiting hooks and cleaning walleye, somewhere in Northwest Ontario.

The two-way crackled to life. "Base to thirty-two, base to thirty-two, what's your twenty? Over?"

Waller gave the air horn a quick blast before picking up the mic. "Look out the window, Dolores. Over."

She continued the call-out without a snide comment. "Got an abandoned over on Douglas, west of Rothesay. Mustang coupe, red. No plate, over."

Waller confirmed he would take the call, then signed off. Douglas Avenue was a rough stretch of asphalt that ran east to west. There were houses set back from the street on the north side, with a large green space to the south and the street's dim lighting made it a good dump spot for stolen joy-ride cars.

He stopped at the 7-Eleven on Edison first, pulling the trigger on a hot dog with the best cooking marks off the stainless-steel rollers. He bought a six-pack of Pepsi to help fuel the evening. He alternated between bites, sips, and gear-shifts as he headed towards the call.

It took five minutes for Waller to get to the offending pony car. He didn't see any damage, other than the usual Winnipeg rust on the rear fenders. It was one of those Mustang II hatch-backs, or as one of his Ford-hating friends had said, "The nicest Pinto ever built." Whoever had stolen the car must have had the keys to do it with; the steering column hadn't been cracked open. Nothing on the visor, nothing under the floor mats. They had probably been tossed in the tall grass.

Waller got out of the Mustang. He walked back to the open window of Unit 32, reaching inside the cab to flip on the overhead beacon. He turned towards the rear of the tow truck just in time to hear the throttle open on a dark shape that was almost on top of him. The mass hit Waller, slam-ming his body against the driver's door of Unit 32 as the mass flew past him. Waller couldn't feel much of anything after the impact. He thought he would have fallen to the ground by now. He slowly looked down to see why.

The side mirror of the tow truck was lying on the ground. The support arm that secured the mirror to the door was sticking through Waller's chest. His shirt was soaked with blood, a sensation he couldn't feel. He was starting to slip off the supports. His arms couldn't help him; he hit the roadway with a sickening thud. He figured it wouldn't be long until he bled out.

The last thing he heard was the sound of the same dark mass, coming back to make sure.

CHAPTER

FORTY

Steve Mahoney's Plymouth was almost at capacity. Diana had squeezed next to him as close as she could. Scheer rode shotgun. Fiddler and Petkau were in the back seat, quietly processing the evening's events. They were heading to the intersection of Wellington Crescent and Hugo Street. Mahoney hoped that the intersection could provide some answers. Whoever the thief was, he wasn't out for a joyride. The bag, the book, Scheer's new jacket. The guy was a pro. *Was*. Mahoney knew that the thief's attempt to steal his Camaro may have cost him his life. There had to be a way to confirm it.

Mahoney parked in front of the Pasadena Apartments, a sandy brick-and-stucco building that probably rented for three times a McTavish Street mortgage payment. The Plymouth dieseled for about five seconds after Mahoney had shut it off. Fiddler tried to use the automotive concern to break the tension.

"You know, my Coronet was doing that for a while, and I figured out that . . ."

"Fuck the car," Mahoney growled. He exited the Plymouth as its coughing fit ended. Diana followed. The rest of the group got the hint, meeting at the rear of the car. Mahoney looked towards the intersection. He had stared at it for an entire traffic-light cycle before anyone spoke.

"So, what's the plan?" asked Scheer.

Mahoney turned back towards the rest of the group.

"I have no fucking idea."

Diana pointed to where the Camaro had been parked on that Wednesday. "I think the car was on the next block."

Mahoney nodded in agreement. "That's right. All the spots in front of the apartment building were taken."

"So, the guy got creamed by the bus?" Petkau had finally returned to the land of the living.

"I think I saw something about it in the *Sun*," said Fiddler.

Diana stepped out from the group, looking at the intersection. "So, we're actually going to do this. We're going to try to talk to two ghosts. In one night."

"That's the plan. Unless anybody else has any suggestions," said Mahoney, looking back at the intersection. The westbound Route 68 bus had just passed. "Shit! The bus will be here soon! Let's go!"

The group trotted the short distance to the bus stop shelter, an aluminum frame with half of its windows broken. The smell of urine was enough to keep a five-foot buffer from its entrance. The eastbound bus approached. Mahoney checked his pockets. He wasn't sure what the rate was for regular fare, not since he had aced his driver's test on his 16th birthday. He pulled a couple of two-dollar bills out of his pocket. One of them was pretty old; the Queen looking back at him was kind of hot.

"I got four bucks. Is that enough for all of us?"

"Should be," said Fiddler. "I think it's like eighty cents or something."

The Winnipeg Transit bus rolled to a stop in front of them. The rear door hissed and popped as a rider exited. The driver looked at the group, waiting for one of them to make a move. No one did.

"I'm guessing one of you guys needs a ride?"

All at the same time, the group went for the open door. The driver watched as the mash of humans made their way to the fare box.

"How much for five adults?" asked Mahoney.

"Four bucks," said the driver. "Unless one of you guys has a student card."

Mahoney looked at the group. He smiled at the thought of any of them furthering their education. "Naw." He went to stuff the pair of twos in the fare box. The driver slammed his hand over the opening.

"No bills, jams everything up."

Mahoney panicked. "Uh, okay. Guys?" The group started digging in their respective pockets, depositing what they had found in Mahoney's palm.

"C'mon, c'mon, c'mon. I got a schedule to keep here."

Mahoney looked at the driver's name tag. "Sorry, Mr. Blatz, uh, we're just, I mean we should —"

"I can tell from here you don't have enough." The driver's hand was still covering the fare box.

"How about just one of us?" Mahoney asked.

The driver looked at the pile of change. "Yeah, just one of you guys. C'mon, c'mon, c'mon . . ."

Diana looked at Mahoney. "Who's it going to be?"

Mahoney looked at the group. He grabbed Scheer, pushing him in front of the rest. "Here's your guy."

"Here's your *what*?"

Mahoney patted Scheer's shoulders. "You're the only one the jacket fits." He backed down the steps with the rest of the group, tossing him the notebook of the jacket's former owner. He gave Scheer the thumbs up as he left. The door hissed and popped as it closed. Scheer looked out the window as he saw his "friends" waving goodbye.

Driver Blatz jolted him back to reality. "Behind the yellow line, sir."

Rick Scheer hadn't been on a bus in a long time. It almost felt like he was on a boat, a sensation that he had always felt uneasy with. The bus was practically deserted. He headed towards the rear, using the grab handles at the top of the seats to steady himself. He chose one of the empty elongated benches that straddled the rear inner fenders, the one with the least amount of graffiti on its heavy blue vinyl hide. He looked towards the front. Someone was reading what looked like a textbook and was wearing cheap Sony Walkman–knock-off headphones. A little old lady was sitting on one of the elongated benches near the front of the bus. She appeared to be sleeping, though the pitch and movement of her body led Scheer to believe she was awake, just not up for company. Even her snore sounded rehearsed. Scheer breathed as calmly as he could, and closed his eyes to try to steady his resolve. They didn't stay closed for long.

"Nice jacket," said a voice. "I used to have one just like it."

Scheer opened his eyes and looked to the right. A man wearing a navy-blue hoodie was seated on the bench that bordered Scheer's. His left hand was stuffed in the front pocket, and he was steadying himself from the to-and-fro motions of bus 751, his left foot pressed against the bottom of Scheer's bench. Scheer knew he should say something. The man beat him to it.

"You won't find anything in that book."

Scheer looked down. He was gripping the notebook like a waterski tow-rope in choppy waters.

"Hey, don't come down on me, man. I don't know anything about this shit. They pushed me on the bus because of the jacket."

The man smiled. "Wow, with friends like that . . ." He chuckled as he looked out the window. Scheer followed his gaze. He immediately wished he hadn't. While the man before him exhibited none of the trauma that would have occurred from an impact with a city bus at roughly 35 miles-per-hour, the face in the reflection was a bloody pulp of tissue and bone. His right eye had completely dislodged from its socket. He wasn't sure if the man could see his own "after" picture.

"I got that jacket at Maxy's Leather. They sell this stuff, "leather honey" I think. Make sure you hit it twice a year — keeps it from cracking."

Scheer looked at the jacket. The man was right: no cracks.

"Uh, thanks. I, I'll take good care of it Mr., uhm, Mr. . . ."

"Clairmont," said the man. "My friends call me . . . *called* me Guy."

"Got it. Guy."

"So, what can I help you with? I'm assuming that's why you're here."

Scheer drew a blank. His recruitment as ghost whisperer happened so quickly, there hadn't been any time to discuss a game plan. Mahoney had mentioned trying to talk to the man that the bus had creamed, though he wasn't sure if getting slammed by the front of a city bus would automatically transfer the spirit of the mashee into one of the blue vinyl seats. "That's gotta be one hell of a whack," Mahoney had said. "It might've, I dunno, *absorbed* him."

Scheer heard the finger snap. He turned to look at the late Guy Clairmont and saw the reflection in the window. The view was the back of Clairmont's post-impact head, a cracked mess of hair, blood, skull, and brain. Scheer looked away from the reflection. He knew he still had to answer before he threw up.

"Uhm, uh, I think I, uhm we —"

Clairmont helped fill in the blanks. "The guy whose car I tried to boost."

"Uhm, yeah. the Camaro."

"And the girl with the big tits, right?"

Scheer thought about it for a moment. *Yeah, they are pretty big.* "Why were, I mean, why were you —"

"Good fucking question. All's I know is Scrap wanted this car bad."

Scheer honed in on the scrap mention. "Scrap? You mean General Scrap?"

Clairmont chuckled. "There are plenty of rust buckets out there for General Scrap. They don't need, and they can't afford, my help, not for thirty bucks a ton. The guy's name is Scrapneck, over at Commonwealth on Portage. That American Motors place."

"He hired you to boost it?"

"Not at first. He wanted me to buy it at the Autopac auction, then get it crushed and melted down in Selkirk. 'Leave no trace' is what he told me. Then your buddy comes along and outbids the shit out of the thing. And then he *fixes* the submarine! I'll bet it still smells like hot-buttered assholes!"

Scheer thought about it for a moment. *The Camaro did have a slight funk.* Anything old did. Even after reupholstering the bench seat in his truck, a tinge of sweaty farmhand lingered, the kind who rolled their own and didn't care where the ashes landed.

Clairmont continued. "Anyway, the next step was just to steal it, then get it crushed. I was inside that thing faster than the guy who actually had the keys. Everything was going fine until *she* showed up."

Heather. "What happened?"

Clairmont looked at Scheer, puzzled. "What happened? Look in the fucking window!"

Scheer didn't want to see it again. Whatever Heather had done to spook Clairmont, it had worked like gangbusters.

"So, it's Scrapneck, right?"

"Right. Tell him I said, 'Hi.' Hell, send him over. I'd love to say hi in person."

"I'll bet you would."

Clairmont chuckled at the thought and turned back to the window. Scheer kept his eyes forward at a downward angle.

"Oh, there's one more thing," said Clairmont.

"What's that?"

"I think I saw your buddy tow my car from that condo

on Wellington, black Merkur. Not much else to do all day on the bus, you know? Anyway, there's a spare key in the tire well, assuming he can open the door without fucking up the weatherstripping."

Scheer flipped open the notebook. He made a note about the key, worried that he might forget in all the excitement. "Okay, I'll let him know. Thanks Guy. Guy?"

Scheer turned slowly to the blue vinyl seat next to him. The late Guy Clairmont was gone.

CHAPTER
FORTY-ONE

Peter Scrapneck was wondering when the vomiting would stop. He had parked the rusted-out '71 Buick Centurion behind a motor home, at the Shell service station on the corner of Douglas and Henderson Highway. He wouldn't report the car as stolen until the morning. Around 5 p.m., a couple had traded the Buick in on a Renault Alliance and had decided to treat themselves to a new set of license plates. That meant the Buick's tags would still be active for the evening.

Scrapneck was trying to be as self-congratulatory as he could, in-between the queasiness of his first kill. He had thought about playing damsel in distress, luring Waller the way that he had when he had stuffed Heather Price's over-dosed body into the back seat of his shit-brown Dodge. There was only one problem with that scenario: Waller could have just as easily told him to go fuck himself. Waller was getting ready for outboard motors and pickerel jigs in Northwest Ontario; he wouldn't be rescuing anyone from their own stu-pidity, especially not for a second time. Instead, Scrapneck had bought a portable scanner at RadioShack and followed Waller at a distance, providing the all-important element of surprise.

Scrapneck's stomach was finally empty. He checked the damage on the front of the dark green Buick. The initial hit had done little to the front of the car, with the exception of a broken low beam headlamp on the passenger side. The passenger-side mirror had been instrumental in pushing Waller into the framework of the tow truck's exterior mirror. It had broken free of its moorings, though still technically attached, thanks to the cable that controlled its adjustments from the instrument panel. Scrapneck knew that the heavy chrome mirror wouldn't break off easily upon impact, not like the plastic ones that were on much of the new inventory at Commonwealth. He'd seen enough of them broken off by fired lot boys to know.

The light was dim on the driver's side, though the spray of blood and brains could still be seen on the lower part of the front fender. Most of it was caked on the inside of the fender well. Waller's head felt more like an annoying bump than a living breathing thing when Scrapneck hit it. *I'd better make sure.* He was hoping for joyride-gone-horribly-wrong, in the eyes of the traffic division, but Scrapneck knew that his insurance policy had taken this from an unfortunate roadside accident to murder-by-Buick.

Scrapneck removed a couple of grease rags from his pocket. He wiped down the obvious bits that he would have touched: steering wheel, seatbelt buckle, and the door-mounted controls. He had thought about setting the car on fire, though a fire would attract immediate attention, which could involve the questioning of his pedestrian shoes by a curious black-and-white. He was only about three blocks from the Nor-Villa Hotel. There would be a cab or two in the parking lot. He gave the keys a good wipe before throwing them and the scanner in the bush.

JUNE 25, 1985
10:12 P.M.

Steve Mahoney had been following bus 751 since he had shoved Rick Scheer into the capable hands of Driver Blatz. The bus was easy enough to catch up to, especially when the driver stopped to pick up a takeout coffee at a mom-and-pop convenience store on Stradbrook. It was hard to see exactly where Scheer was on the bus, or how things were going inside.

When Scheer had made his way off of the bus, he looked anything but right. Mahoney gave the horn a quick tap to get his attention. Scheer didn't get the cue.

Diana touched Mahoney's shoulder. "I'll go get him." She exited the door, slowly walking up to Scheer. He was exhibiting much of the catatonic tendencies that Petkau was first displaying at the garage. She knew she had to be careful not to spook him.

"Hey, Rickles. How's it going?"

Scheer looked at Diana. It took a moment to remember he actually knew her.

"Uh, I think I'm okay. I guess."

"Wanna get out of here?"

"Yeah, that, that'd be nice."

Diana led Scheer back to the open door of the Plymouth. She motioned him into the middle seat position, next to Mahoney. There was at least 15 seconds of awkward silence after she closed the door. Mahoney took second 16 as his opening.

"Who's hungry?"

"I am," said Fiddler.

"Me too," said Petkau.

"Maybe a little something," Diana said.

Mahoney put the shifter into drive. "Junior's?" He looked around the car to get the needed nods. Scheer stared straight ahead.

"Four outta five," said Mahoney. He hit the gas to make the yellow light.

Junior's could be relied on for two things: easy parking and burgers that truly needed both hands.

Mahoney leaned up against the window, picking away at his French fries. Diana had a cheeseburger with extra chili, sloppy enough that a plate and utensils were mandatory. Petkau and Fiddler were halfway through their Double Fat Boy's. Scheer had yet to say much of anything since the curbside pickup and looked the same as he had in the Plymouth. The rest of the group gnawed in silence until he spoke.

"Cheeeburger…"

Diana perked up. "Cheeseburger?"

"You want a cheeseburger?" Mahoney asked.

Scheer finally started smiling. He looked at Mahoney, then Diana, then Fiddler and Petkau.

"C'mon, you know. Cheeeburger, cheeeburger, cheee-burger . . ."

The rest of the table wasn't getting it. Scheer continued.

"Pepsi, Pepsi, cheeeburger, cheeeburger . . ."

Fiddler caught it. He pointed at Scheer with a French fry. "*Saturday Night Live*, right?"

"Yeah, *Saturday Night*. Cheeeburger, cheeeburger . . ."

Diana chimed in. "Pepsi, Pepsi!"

After a minute, the whole table was doing their best impressions of the Not Ready For Prime-Time Players homage to the Billy Goat Tavern. The staff at the counter shook their heads.

Scheer interjected during the laughter. "So that guy was a ghost, right?" He went for volume over discretion.

Mahoney immediately shushed. "Hey, keep it the fuck down."

Fiddler asked about the ghost's condition. "So was he like all fucked up?"

Scheer kept talking. "You know, he looked not bad, until I saw his — his *head*."

The group had little warning. Scheer threw up over most of the table and their burgers. He then turned around to the other table, which was thankfully empty. Round two brought one of the staff over to the table with speed. He wasn't happy.

"Get your drunk asses outta here, NOW!"

Diana had already pushed herself from the table when Scheer first vomited. Mahoney had received minimal splash-back. Fiddler and Petkau had raised their Fat Boy's out of harm's way. They were still chewing on them as the group ran out the door. They had to pull Scheer towards the parking lot as he apologized like an eight-year-old with the flu.

Mahoney threw the driver's door open. He pushed Scheer into the seat, then Diana towards the middle position. "Better roll down his window." Fiddler and Petkau hopped in the back, still holding their burgers, as Mahoney spun gravel as they tore out of the lot.

It took about 15 minutes to get back to Mahoney's house. Diana had been doing her best to keep Scheer as calm as possible. He was hanging his head out of the window like a dog, the exception being that he wasn't enjoying it to any degree. He kept apologizing.

"I'm sorry, guys."

"Don't worry about it," said Mahoney, as he turned into the driveway. "At least you didn't yack in the car."

"Yeah," said Fiddler. "That shit never comes out."

The group proceeded to the garage. The lights had been left on inside. Heather, sitting in the driver's seat of the Hot Rod, noticed Scheer's condition straight away.

"Wow. He looks like he's seen a ghost."

Scheer felt the bile rise again. He pushed his way out to the driveway. Petkau watched from the door, wincing.

"Yikes," said Petkau. "It's like when they cut into that shark's stomach in *Jaws*."

Fiddler reached into the old fridge, retrieving a leftover OV from the Camaro build. "If he yacks up a license plate, I'll buy you a Coke."

"So I guess he's a little freaked out," said Heather.

Mahoney pulled up one of the rolling stools. "Looks that way. He hasn't really said much yet. Hope his brain hasn't spun a bearing."

Scheer appeared at the side door of the garage. Petkau helped him inside, going slow. Diana took his other arm.

Diana took a stab at clarifying the whole mess. "Okay, let [m]e get this straight. Heather's banging this Scrap guy, and [sh]e's doing his books for the dealership. Scrapman —"

"Scrapneck," Heather corrected her.

"Right. Scrapneck is bringing in coke in the used cars." [Sh]e turned to Mahoney. "Your buddy at work is mixed up [in] it."

"He's not my buddy," said Mahoney. "But that means [W]allbanger has got something to do with the selling."

"Why's that?"

Mahoney continued. "Because Wallbanger is already [se]lling drugs for the HRs. Crack would have been big news [do]wn at Hook Me Up. Hell, they probably would've tried to [m]ake it part of my job description. If the HRs had crack, I'd [ha]ve heard something by now."

"I have a question," said Scheer, who was still a little pale. [H]e had his hand raised like a well-behaved grade schooler.

"What is it?" said Mahoney.

"How did drugs, tow trucks, used cars, and sketchy [ac]counting put Heather in the river?"

Heather corrected him. "I prefer *creative* accounting."

"Wait," said Mahoney. "He's got a point. Maybe it's just . . ."

"Just what?" said Diana.

Mahoney looked at Heather. "Heather, you used for a [w]hile, right?"

"So what?"

"So, you know your way around this shit, right?"

"Yeah, pretty much."

"Then why did you OD?"

Heather went to answer, then stopped. Mahoney pressed [h]er.

"This was new stuff. Stuff you'd never done before."

"Feeling better, Rickles?" She guided him to the comfiest of the fold-out chairs.

Scheer nodded, slow and careful as he sat. "Do you got any 7Up?"

"I'll check the fridge." Diana was halfway there when Scheer spoke.

"Not cold, warm. That's what my mom used to give me when I threw up."

"Just like mine," Petkau said. He went over to the side of the fridge, retrieving a can from a shelf of warm soda mixes. He handed the open can to Scheer. He sipped it like soup.

"Can I get a cold one too?"

Diana looked at him, confused. "I thought you wanted it warm?"

"The cold one's for my forehead."

Diana rolled her eyes. "Men. They all turn into boys when they're sick."

Mahoney rolled his stool over to Scheer. "Rickles, I'm guessing from the yack-fest, you had a chat with the bus guy. I know you're freaked out. I *still* get freaked out every time I talk to *her*." He pointed at Heather to drive the point home.

"That's 'cause you're a pussy," said Heather.

Mahoney didn't acknowledge the dig. He continued. "We gotta know what he told you. Anything and everything."

Scheer sipped his 7Up. "He said he saw you tow his car."

"Which car? When?"

"Mercury. No, wait! The one that's not a Mercury, sounds like it."

"That's a Merkur," said Petkau. "They got one in the other day at Bridgeway. It's like a German Ford or something. Double rear spoiler. Ugly fucker."

Mahoney pressed Scheer. "What about the Merkur? Is there something in it?"

"The key," said Scheer. "He said there's one in back, under the spare tire."

"Is there anything else in the car?"

"No, I don't think so."

Mahoney paused. The car that belonged to the would-be thief of his Hot Rod was sitting in the compound at Hook Me Up. He was formulating his next question when Scheer remembered something.

"He said he tried to buy the Camaro at the auction."

"He was bidding against me at Autopac?"

"Yeah, he was . . . he was buying it for Scrap."

"Scrap? He was going to scrap it?"

"No, the guy he was buying it for. Scrap, Scrap . . ."

Heather unexpectedly broke in. "Scrapheap . . ."

They all turned to look at her. She was looking at Scheer. "Scrapheap. It's Scrapheap."

Mahoney turned to Scheer. "Rickles, who the hell is Scrapheap?"

Scheer struggled to remember. "It wasn't Scrapheap. It was Scrap-something. Scrap…"

"Neck."

Mahoney looked at Heather. "Scrapneck? Is it Scrapneck?"

Heather nodded. "I called him Scrapheap."

Mahoney had heard the name but couldn't place it. "Who is he?"

Scheer suddenly remembered. "No Dicker–Sticker!"

Fiddler leaned in. "The late-night used-car guy?"

Petkau laughed. "He's always wearing a different rug, right?"

"That guy's hilarious," said Diana. "He's gotta be on coke."

The group at large continued its surface conversation of the known facts. Mahoney zeroed in on Heather. He rolled closer to her. Even in her otherworldly form, he could tell that whatever remained of her once-beating heart was in distress. He touched her hand. It felt as real as any he had ever touched. She raised her head to look at him. He pushed some stray hair away from her face.

"Heather, you knew him, didn't you? Who was he to you?"

"He was just somebody."

"Somebody who?"

"Somebody I knew." She leaned back in the driver's sea[t] She massaged her face with her hands as she processed th[e] information.

Mahoney figured there had to be more to it. He went [?] broke. "Heather, how did you know this guy? Was he y[our] boyfriend?"

Heather started to laugh beneath her hands. "Fuck no[,] was like a, like a . . . you know."

Diana finished the thought. "A fuck buddy?"

"Yeah, a fuck buddy."

Mahoney pressed. "How did you meet him?"

"He was the go-to at the dealership. He was bring[ing] the coke in the used cars."

Mahoney took a think break, a short one, cons[idering] everyone, including the recently departed, was wai[ting] him to put it all together. He said the first thing that[?] into his head.

"Fucking Wallbanger!"

"What? A Harvey Wallbanger?" asked Scheer.

"Wallbanger. Jerry Waller. He works at Hook M[e] and pimps. I saw him at Commonwealth. He was[?] that Scraphe — I mean, Scrapneck guy!"

"Yeah, I guess so."

"Who gave it to you?"

On this point, Heather was certain. "It was Scrap. *Fucking Scrap!*" She slammed her hand on the Camaro's steering wheel.

Scheer raised his hand again. Mahoney acknowledged it.

"Yes, Rickles."

Scheer lowered his hand. "So, who's the bad guys in all this?"

"I'm not really sure," said Mahoney. "But I know where to start looking."

CHAPTER
FORTY-
TWO

JUNE 26, 1985
8:07 A.M.

Steve Mahoney didn't know what he would
say to Jerry Waller. He knew he couldn't
strong-arm him into a confession; Wallbanger
could snap Mahoney's bones like twigs. He
thought about feigning interest in joining the
seedier side of Hook Me Up, but he had no
idea how to do it. Undercover wasn't his style.
Maybe I should talk to that cop. He also wasn't
convinced that telling the detective-sergeant
what he knew was a good idea. He remembered Milroy saying he talked to the ghosts of

the victims he'd investigated, *every goddamn night*. It had to be just a figure of speech, right?

Mahoney made a right turn onto Bowman. Something was definitely up at the entrance to the industrial park. There were three black-and-whites parked outside of the main gate and a uniform cop motioning him forward.

"Morning, constable."

The uniform leaned down to the window. "Morning." He pointed inside the compound. "You work at one of these places?"

"Yeah, Hook Me Up. What's going on?"

The uniform looked at Mahoney, deadpan, but with a little something extra. *Oh, great. They found the stash.* Mahoney did his best not to reveal a tell, but judging by the simmering grin on the uniform, he was failing miserably.

The uniform pointed inside again. "You better park and go inside the office. One of the investigators will want to talk to you."

Shit. They found the stash. Mahoney decided to play it as cool as he could. He parked next to the compound. The guard dogs wagged their tails as he headed towards the office.

The overhead buzzer sounded more like a bullhorn when Mahoney entered the office. He wasn't expecting any of what was in front of him. Larry Ballendine was blubbering like a five-year-old who had dropped his ice cream cone. Dolores Favel was snivelling just as Ballendine was, but still managed to have two cigarettes on the go in her ashtray. Two of the Hook Me Up drivers that Mahoney only knew in passing were giving statements to the plainclothes officers. One of them turned to look at Mahoney. It was Detective-Sergeant Milroy.

"Hey, Tow-Job," Milroy said. "Might as well wait outside for a couple of minutes. I'll come out there to talk to you."

Mahoney did as he was told. He pulled out a Colt from the pack in his pocket. As he lit it, he noticed that Wallbanger's Corvette was still in the parking lot, wearing a coat of dust from the police car traffic. He probably wasn't back yet from his shift; Unit 32 was nowhere to be seen on the Bowman lot. Mahoney looked down the street, hopeful that Waller was just running late. Maybe he could talk to him before he was questioned by the cops.

The Colt was about half finished when Milroy came out of the office. "Let's go for a walk," he said, motioning towards the compound. *They probably want me to snitch.* Mahoney had already decided that he would tell Milroy what he needed to know. *Fuck Hook Me Up.* Working for shit money in some shit garage for a shit boss was looking more sensible by the minute.

Milroy walked into the compound, probably the only spot at the Bowman that would provide something resembling privacy. The guard dogs must have sensed something alpha approaching; they trotted back towards their milk truck apartment instead of trying for their usual ear scratch from Mahoney. The detective-sergeant paced among the varied selection of vehicles in the Hook Me Up compound. He stopped at an early '60s Pontiac that was missing all of its glass, the word SCAB spray-painted on every available panel. Milroy nodded towards it. "Looks like somebody got mad."

Mahoney wasn't interested in small talk. "So, what the fuck is going on?"

Milroy turned. He smiled at Mahoney. He reached into his pocket, retrieving a small plastic baggie. He tossed the baggie at Mahoney. He caught it, a much easier catch than the key tosses of Dolores Favel. Mahoney looked at the bag. It looked like some kind of pellet.

"What is it?"

Milroy chuckled. "Don't give me that."

"Don't give you what?"

Milroy reached into his pocket. He had a handful of the mystery bags. He started walking towards Mahoney, pelting him with the bags as he went. "You know exactly what this fucking shit is!"

Mahoney tried to protect himself the best he could. "Hey, knock it off!"

Milroy pointed to the bags. "Now pick that shit up."

"Why? It's not mine."

"Once you pick it up, it will be. Possession with intent to distribute. Pick it up."

"Hey, fuck you, cop. I'm not into this shit."

Milroy kicked out the only headlamp on the Pontiac that hadn't been smashed. "I said pick it the fuck up!"

Mahoney did as he was told. He held the bags aloft in his left hand. "There! Now put the fucking cuffs on me and arrest me, asshole!"

It happened fast. The next thing Mahoney knew, his face was resting against the hot hood of the Pontiac, warmed by the morning sun. His right arm was locked behind him by Milroy. The Detective-Sergeant leaned in close.

"You know, it's one thing to sell this shit to junkies, but when you start trading it for a kid's paper-route money, I get a little pissed."

"What the fuck are you talking about?"

Milroy placed the handcuffs on Mahoney's wrists. He made sure they were uncomfortably tight. He flipped him around fast to answer the question.

"You read the paper, Tow-Job?"

"Maybe."

"You hear about that kid at the Ex? The one in the hospital?"

"What about him?"

Milroy grabbed Mahoney by his shirt and pulled him so close that Mahoney could smell the Player's that Milroy must have smoked that morning.

"He died this morning. He OD'd on that crack you and that piece-of-shit Waller have been selling."

"I'm not selling shit!" said Mahoney. "Ask Ballendine! He'll tell you!"

"Don't worry, he's getting asked. He looks like a real throw-you-under-the-bus kinda guy." Milroy chuckled to himself. Mahoney had no idea why.

"What's so funny?"

"The bus," Milroy said. "I thought that was what ran over your partner last night, until we found the Buick. We found his stash in the tow truck when they were scraping his brains off the pavement."

Wallbanger's dead? "What partner? What Buick? I'm telling you, *I don't deal!*"

"Let's go downtown and talk about it." Milroy led Mahoney to his unmarked LTD. He made sure to whack Mahoney's head hard on the door frame when he shoved him in the back seat.

"Please watch your head, sir."

CHAPTER
FORTY-
THREE

Mahoney's head was smarting. He couldn't
rub it, thanks to the handcuffs that were still
digging into his wrists. At the Public Safety
Building, Milroy had put him into an interroga-
tion room that seemed more like a repurposed
broom closet. It couldn't have measured more
than five-foot-square, covered floor to ceiling in
small acoustic tiles. There were no windows, no
one-way mirrors. There wasn't a new-fangled
video camera on the wall. It stank of cigarettes,
piss, and desperation. This room was for the
interrogations no one got to see.

The way out, or in, was the doorknob on the wall facing him. Whoever had attached the tiles had done such a good job that it was hard to make out the outline of the door. When it finally opened. Milroy came into the room with a large file folder. Sticking out from the folder were large photographs, a size that wasn't available at any of the one-hour photo shops Mahoney knew about. Underneath the folder was something he did know about: the White Pages. Mahoney had heard stories about the White Pages at the PSB, how they were seldom used for looking up a phone number. The Yellow Pages directory had become much too large for any of Winnipeg's finest to use in interrogations. The White Pages had been allegedly used by certain patrol car teams, not that you would ever find a copy of it in the trunk or under the front seat. Mahoney remembered a story by a kid he went to high school with, a Marcel Something-or-other. He had lipped off at a couple of uniform cops at a Pic-a-Pop store in East Kildonan, which had earned him a "ride-along" to discuss the distributors of illicit drugs in the neighbour-hood. While he was sitting in the back of the cruiser waiting for the ride to commence, the rookie in the passenger seat got out, went over to the bank of pay phones on the wall, and ripped a White Pages directory from its holder. Marcel returned about an hour later, his face swollen, absent of the marks associated with fists or nightsticks. He didn't lip off to the cops after that.

Milroy didn't open with any pleasantries or phone books. He removed the photos from the file folder and placed them, one at a time, in front of Mahoney. The first photo was from inside the cab of Unit 32. It was littered with fast food bags, clipboards, and the repurposed night deposit satchels used to hold the cash. There was another bag, a zippered pouch that had been opened. Inside it were the smaller pouches of the mystery drug that Milroy had made Mahoney pick up, a drug that must have been the crack cocaine.

The next picture was the exterior of Unit 32. It needed some serious detailing. The driver's door had seen some form of collision, judging by the mangled mess of the exterior mirror and the buckled door skin. It was more than just body work that was needed: something large and dark red had stained the white paint on the door, enough of a stain that the Hook Me Up lettering was almost completely obscured. *Something happened to Waller,* Mahoney thought. *But what?*

The next picture took in a larger scene. A red Mustang II was parked at the side of the road, with Unit 32 parked behind it. Beneath the mangled door was something covered with a white sheet, a sheet that Mahoney had also seen before while waiting to pick up the wrecks from fatal accidents. *Waller . . .*

The next picture was Waller up close. Mahoney couldn't be 100 percent sure, as the head of the victim had been reduced to a mash of hair, blood, and something greyish in colour. *Waller's brains.* There were wounds on his back, most likely from the mangled remnants of the exterior mirror supports. Mahoney had a feeling that if he looked away from the picture, Milroy would tell him to look at it, maybe jam it in his face to make sure. He put as many cuddly puppy thoughts in his head as he could, to keep from throwing up his morning Pop-Tart.

The next picture was of a car that was more Milroy's style than Mahoney's. It was a large dark green Buick coupe, definitely a '71, as the rear shot of the car showed the trunk-mounted louvres that almost every GM car had in '71. A second picture of the car showed collision damage on the passenger side, damage that must have occurred when the

Buick slammed Waller into Unit 32. The third picture of the Buick showed the point of impact for Waller's head, the inside of the fender. *Nice cuddly puppies! Nice cuddly puppies! Nice cuddly puppies!*

The last batch of pictures must have been inside the morgue at the Health Sciences Centre. There were five shots in total, all head shots of the recently departed. The first four looked like they had all endured hard miles on the road of life. Two of them had the jailhouse teardrop tattoos under their eyes. The last one was a fresh-faced kid who Milroy seemed to be the angriest about; the kid Mahoney had seen having a seizure at the Ex.

Milroy put the pictures back in the file. He placed them underneath his well-used copy of the White Pages. He put his elbows on the table, folding his hands in front of Mahoney. He wasn't looking directly at Mahoney; he was looking at the folder of pictures and the phone book. Probably the phone book.

"That kid was only fifteen."

Mahoney didn't know what to say.

"You know, I've seen a lot of horrible things that people can do to other people," Milroy continued. "Knives. Guns. Baseball bats. Hammers, from claw to sledge. There's usually a pretty good story behind it. It may still send somebody to Stony Mountain for twenty-five years, but there's always a story. Some are better than others. I've seen rooms that ended up looking like blood-filled wading pools because of a dime bag."

Milroy moved his hand closer to the spine of the White Pages. Mahoney tensed himself for what was coming.

"It's one thing when we're pulling a body out of a rooming house on Redwood, or the Savoy, or the Sutherland. It's not like it's a big surprise to the family, even the neighbourhood. It's just . . . *the way it is*. I can handle that. Doesn't even make me reach for a Labatt's Lite anymore." His fingers curled tighter around the spine of the directory. "It's when I've got to drive into the cul-de-sacs. The fucking suburbs. It's the last place you expect to see a police car, even an unmarked one. And yet, everybody knows what it is. *Everybody* knows what it means. Do *you* know what it means, Tow-Job?"

"Uhm . . . no. No, I don't."

Milroy jumped up from his chair and swatted Mahoney with the White Pages, knocking him out of the chair. Mahoney's head hit the opposite wall on the way down, adding a new blemish to the already damaged acoustic tile. He could hardly move with the handcuffs on. He felt something on his upper lip, perhaps blood from his nose.

Milroy squeezed around the table. He got down on his knees, grabbing Mahoney by his shirt. "It means I've got to tell somebody that they have to bury a kid who has no right to be buried, you drug-dealing piece of shit!"

"I'm not a dealer! I've never dealt anything!"

"Sure, you're not! If it ain't drugs, you must be pimping those underage girls in the back of the office. Your boss Ballendine is going away for a long time."

"I'm not a pimp!" said Mahoney, snorting up the blood the best he could. "Wallbanger was the pimp. I'd pick up the girl if they asked, but I never dropped off! Ever!"

"Get up." Milroy had moved back from Mahoney. He made him stand against the wall as he moved the chair back into position. "Sit the fuck down, Tow-Job."

Mahoney did as he was told. Milroy continued.

"I hope you've got your resume up to date, 'cause Hooker-Me-Up Towing is dead as disco. Then again, where you're going, I'd get your pretty-boy lips ready. Maybe you'll play some football for the prison team. They'll start you out as a tight end, then move you to wide receiver."

Mahoney knew he had to spill something that would at least temper the next round of beatings from the detective-sergeant. Something that would get him to back off. Something that would change the conversation. "The Buick . . ."

Milroy leaned in. "The what?"

"The Buick, the one in the picture."

"The Centurion? What about it?"

Milroy's definitely a car guy. "It was stolen, right?"

That got Milroy's attention, not enough to change his opinion of Mahoney. "Yeah, so it was stolen, so what? You're the one who stole it."

"I was with people last night. They'll tell you."

Milroy leaned back in his chair. "*Sure* you were, Tow-Job, and they probably crawled out from under the same rock you crawled out from."

"The car was stolen from a dealership, wasn't it?"

Milroy leaned closer. "So, you stole it from a dealership?"

"I didn't steal it."

"You keep saying that."

"Was it Commonwealth?"

Milroy looked at Mahoney. "Yeah, so what? You oughta know if you stole it."

Mahoney knew he'd found his opening. "Look it up. You tell me when it was reported missing."

Milroy was starting to look puzzled. He wondered why Mahoney was digging his own hole. He pulled a small coiled notebook out of his front pocket. He flipped to his most recent notations. "Communications logged a call at 8:15 this morning from Commonwealth, said they saw the car was missing this morning. We actually had a call at just before 8 from the garage where you dumped it."

Mahoney decided not to argue Milroy's guilt brush for the moment. "Who made the call? From the dealership?"

"What does that got to do with anything?"

Mahoney pressed. "What's the name of the guy who made the call?"

Milroy checked his notebook. He looked at Mahoney. "What makes you so sure it was a guy?"

Mahoney went for broke. "It was Scrapneck, wasn't it? Peter Scrapneck."

Milroy still wasn't giving in. He checked his notebook. He flipped it shut, stuffing it back in his pocket. "Okay, Tow-Job, tell me more. How do you know this Scrapneck?"

"I don't. Wallbanger did."

"You mean Waller, right?"

"Right. I saw Scrapneck at Commonwealth with Waller."

Milroy looked at him for a long time. He reached into his pocket for the notebook. He pulled a pen from the same pocket. "Keep talking, Tow-Job."

Mahoney explained how he had seen the exchange between Jerry Waller and Scrapneck at the dealership. He told him about the Toronado, the one with the mashed-in trunk lid, and how it was already repaired for its TV close-up that evening on CKND.

Milroy scribbled furiously. "So, there's coke in the trunk lid, right?"

"Not now, it's already been moved," said Mahoney.

"Moved where?"

"Wherever Scrapneck was turning it into crack."

Milroy stopped writing. He put the pen down on the table. He looked at Mahoney.

"How can you possibly know all of this and not be involved?"

Mahoney thought about what to say next. He looked over at the phone book. He went for broke.

"Scrapneck killed Wallbanger."

"How do you know for sure?"

"I don't. And I'm pretty sure he had something to do with the girl in my car. The one you said offed herself."

Milroy looked at Mahoney, hard, waiting for a guilty tell. It didn't come. "You sure know a lot for someone who isn't part of this."

Mahoney agreed. "You're right, I can't prove it, at least not the way you or any cop wants to prove it. But I think I can help." Mahoney went for the heart strings, knowing that doing so could mean a second reading of the White Pages, the close and personal kind. "I can help you get the guy before he kills another kid."

Mahoney braced himself. The phone book swat didn't come. Milroy looked down at his notebook. He flipped through the file folder of pictures, stopping at the picture of the late Braeden Westmacott. He put the file folder on top of the phone book. He looked at Mahoney.

"So, what's the plan here, Tow-Job?"

"We need drivers," said Mahoney. "And keys. And a phone call."

"A phone call? To who?"

Mahoney smiled at Milroy. "Channel nine, cable twelve."

Peter Scrapneck was wiping his nose clean from his bathroom bump when he heard the overhead page at Commonwealth Motors. He nodded at Lisa Bentley to send the call through to his desk. Dick Loeb had left for an early lunch. Scrapneck was hoping he could fire through a few bigger discounts on deals that were close to being written before Loeb got back.

Scrapneck pressed the flashing line two. "Sales, Peter Scrapneck speaking."

"Hi, Mr. Scrapneck? It's Andrew Bradley

down at CKND. I'm the cameraman who does the commercials for you."

Scrapneck had no idea why an Andrew Bradley would be calling him. "Uhm, okay. Something I can help you with?"

"Yeah, sorry about this. We had a problem with the master for the last commercial we shot."

"What's a master?"

"The tape. I'm afraid it got erased."

Scrapneck wasn't pleased. He said as much. "How the fuck did that happen?"

Bradley apologized. "I'm really sorry about it, but we've had a slow day so far, so I could bring one of the trucks down in a half-hour, re-shoot the spot for you. No charge, of course."

"Damn fucking right it's no charge!" Scrapneck felt a headache coming on — the headache of having to pull the cars off the line for the spot and getting the wash bay to move at something faster than the speed of smell. He stood up from his half-walled office. He quickly got the attention of one of the senior salesmen, Donny Fischer, as he held the phone to his chest.

"Hey, Fish! Over here!"

The salesman ambled over, a pair of reading glasses perched precariously on the tip of his nose. Scrapneck made gestures to him that could only mean to pick up the pace.

"What's up, boss?"

"How many of the cars got sold from the commercial we just ran on CKND?"

Fischer gave a sly grin. "None of them. They're all turds."

Scrapneck pointed to the key cabinet. "Give the keys to the wash bay. CKND is coming down to re-shoot."

"Fuuuuuuuuck." Fischer headed towards the cabinet. Scrapneck continued his call. "Hey, hello? Bradley? Still there?"

"Yes, sir, I'm still here. Are we good to go?"

"Yeah, we'll have the cars ready." Scrapneck reached for his script from the last commercial. "It'll be the same cars we did on Monday."

"Got it. See you in a bit."

Scrapneck hung up without any additional pleasantries.

Andrew Bradley hung up the phone in the production suite at CKND. He pressed the line that was flashing on hold.

"Okay, Mr. Milroy?"

"Yes, go ahead. Did you talk to Commonwealth?"

"Yes. I'm going to head there now."

"Don't go right there," said Milroy. "Meet us at the Shell station at Portage and Maryland."

"How will I know it's you?"

There was a pause. Then Milroy answered.

"I'll be next to a purple Camaro."

JUNE 26, 1985
12:09 P.M.

Steve Mahoney's wrists were still stinging from his morning in handcuffs. The Coke Slurpee and Hot Rod meat stick that Detective-Sergeant Milroy bought him as a peace offering were going down quickly, maybe too quickly, if the grumbles from his stomach were any indication. He was still a little queasy from Milroy's lights-and-siren ride to McTavish Street to pick up the Hot Rod. Mahoney thoroughly enjoyed the police escort to the rendezvous. He would have never dared to drive that fast in the city for kicks. Heather had yet to appear in the shotgun seat. He had a feeling that she would soon.

The four keys that Mahoney had requested from the detective-sergeant were lined up in their respective lock cylinders. The first set dangled in a dark green Buick Centurion, the one that had turned Jerry Waller into hamburger. The next was in Unit 32, its driver door still stained with the blood of the former Hook Me Up driver. The third set was in the lock cylinder of Jerry Waller's Corvette, its top down as if ready for a sunny Wednesday drive. The fourth key was the spare, the one that the late Guy Clairmont had told Rick Scheer about for his Merkur that had been towed to the Hook Me Up lot. The final key was Mahoney's. The rabbit's foot swayed in the dash-mounted lock cylinder of his Hot Rod, the engine still giving of its heat ticks from the recent run. If good luck truly existed, he hoped it was in that bunny's paw.

Mahoney looked over at Milroy. He was busy talking to the cameraman from CKND. An introduction was being made with a plainclothes officer that would accompany the cameraman as his assistant, in case Scrapneck made a break for it. Milroy made the necessary final nods with the cameraman and his new assistant. He walked over to Mahoney, pointing at the icy drink in his hand.

"Coke, right? I hear that shit will dissolve a nail."

Mahoney looked at the Slurpee. "If it hasn't eaten through the cup yet, I think I'm okay."

Milroy smiled. He pulled his pack of Player's out of his pocket and grabbed the last soldier inside. His Bic had died. He reached into the Merkur to punch in the cigarette lighter. He scanned the car's interior.

"What the fuck is a Merkur, anyway?

"German Ford," Mahoney explained. "I think it's the same guts as a T-Bird Turbo."

Milroy kept scanning. "Sure is an ugly fucker, or should I say fuck-*ur*," said Milroy. He turned to Mahoney. "So, you think this stunt is going to make this Scrapheap guy spill?"

Mahoney smiled. "That's what *she* called him."

"That's what who called him?"

"Never mind," said Mahoney. He didn't have time to explain, especially since an explanation might immediately put the brakes on the whole operation.

Milroy turned to the rest of the plainclothes officers. They were actually uniformed rookies who had changed into T-shirts, shorts, and ball caps, trying their best to look like the typical dealership lot boys. "Everybody get in your cars and start 'em up. Remember, we've got a civilian cameraman and Mr. Mahoney here in his car. We'll roll up the side street, come into the lot from the rear. I'll badge the lot guys at the rear of the shop once I get confirmation that Scrapneck is out front for the TV. I'll drive the first car in. It's uh, it's uh . . . hey, Tow-Job, what's the first car for the commercial?"

"Should be a silver Concord."

"Okay, silver Concord. As long as the guy doesn't make me for a cop, we should be good. Everybody clear?"

The nods and hand gestures from the task force said that they were. Milroy got into his LTD and led the convoy.

CHAPTER
FORTY-
FIVE

Peter Scrapneck was in front of the dealership, having a smoke. He was taking a closer look at one of the new Cherokee models that had just arrived, a red Chief trim with black accents and white-lettered, off-road Michelin tires. It was a two-door, which would move slower off the lot than a four-door model, even more so with the stick shift that rose up from the floorboards. *Somebody fucked up on this order.* It was time for a new demonstrator. Scrapneck figured that he might even be able to buy it outright.

The flapping of the overhead pennants were interrupted by the quick chirp of a horn. It was the mobile production unit from CKND television, a Ford Econoline, with the extended body and raised roof to house its television tools. The station identification was accompanied by a large ellipse-shaped logo beneath it, the numbers nine and 12 on each side.

Scrapneck walked over to the passenger side of the van. He didn't know who the passenger was. He made it known that he didn't care.

"I thought you were going to fucking be here by noon!"

The passenger did his best to calm the man in charge. "Sorry about that. We had to clean the heads on the camera before we came out."

"Whatever," said Scrapneck. "I've got the script, same shit as last time." He looked towards the spot where the first car would come from. The nose of the silver Concord was at the far end of the lot, waiting for its cue. Scrapneck held up two fingers to advise the driver to wait. The cameraman readied his equipment. The man that Scrapneck didn't know readied the boom mic. Scrapneck checked his rug in the mirror of a nearby Renault. He was ready.

"Okay, we're rolling," said the cameraman. He mimed the numbers as he spoke. "In three, two . . ." Scrapneck turned to wave at the Concord. He always wondered why the cameraman never said "one." *Must be a TV thing.*

Scrapneck jumped into high speed. "Hi, folks, Peter Scrapneck down here at Commonwealth Motors, the home of the No Dicker–Sticker on the Portage Avenue Strip . . ."

The Concord rolled to a stop. Scrapneck provided the details as best as he could remember.

" . . . a rare Concord hatchback coupe with deluxe trim,

whitewall tires and AM-FM radio, No Dicker priced at *twen-ty*-seven-*ninety*-five."

The Concord pulled away. Scrapneck heard the next car come forward. The script said it was a Colony Park station wagon. He started with that.

". . . and what better way to get to the lake this summer than a Colony Park station . . ."

Scrapneck caught himself. The car next to him wasn't a Colony Park. It didn't have woodgrain panelling. It was black. He quickly glanced at the badge on the rear deck. He gave the car a bullshit name.

"No folks, it's a, it's a late-model Mercury XR4! Yes! The *baby brother* of the XR7, fully loaded, and a price so special you've got to *see it to believe it!*"

Scrapneck made a mental note to fire whoever was driving it. He heard the third car pull up behind him. A big V8. It had to be the Toronado. *It damn well better be.*

"And cruise out to Falcon, uhm, I mean Grand Beach in *big* car style, in this beautiful green Oldsmobile Toro—"

Scrapneck saw the green car pull up next to him. The passenger side mirror had been broken off. It was still attached by its adjustment cable. Scrapneck reached for the mirror instinctively, trying to somehow re-attach it with a hope and a prayer. It dangled as the Buick Centurion that killed Jerry Waller started pulling away. Scrapneck knew the car. He started to falter.

"And, and we've . . . got . . . uhh . . . a great selection of . . . *scratch and dent* cars here at Commonwealth Motors . . ."

The Buick pulled out of the camera frame. Waller's Corvette pulled up in its place.

"That's uh, that's uh . . . a Sting . . . a Sting . . ." *What the hell was happening?*

The Corvette pulled ahead. Unit 32 from Hook Me Up Towing was next. At least it was the passenger side. Scrapneck fumbled his way through.

"And . . . and we've got, uh . . . used, uh . . . *commercial vehicles* at Commonwealth Motors . . ."

Unit 32 pulled ahead. Scrapneck had yet to turn to see the car that replaced it. The driver revved the car's powerful engine to get his attention. Scrapneck was falling apart. He was shaking. He dropped the clipboard that held the script. He turned his head slightly to see. It was a car that Scrapneck knew all too well.

". . . And our, our . . . last . . . special No . . . Dicker . . . Sticker. A classic nine . . . nineteen . . . sixty, nineteen sixty . . ."

A woman's voice corrected him. "Seven!"

The "seven" snapped Scrapneck back into character. "A classic 1967 Chevrolet Camaro coupe, performance-modified, ready for Sunday cruising for only, just —"

"One million dollars, you fucking asshole!"

Scrapneck froze. *Heather!* He turned to look at the passenger seat of the Camaro. Heather Price was looking back at him, wearing her green sweater and his acid-washed jeans. He looked back at the camera for the sign-off in absolute fear.

"AT COMMONWEALTH MOTORS, HOME OF THE NO-DICKER-FUCKING STICKER ON THE PORTAGE AVENUE STRIP!"

Scrapneck ran for the front door of the dealership. The mic operator dropped the boom pole and grabbed a two-way radio on the front seat of the van.

"Suspect has entered dealership! REPEAT! Suspect has entered dealership!"

Scrapneck ran into the showroom. It took him a moment to get his bearings. The rest of the staff and customers were looking at him as though he was a rabid dog from a nearby back lane. He ran through the service door to the shop. He bolted the door behind him. He looked for a point of exit. The overhead door at the rear of the shop was wide open. Scrapneck looked to the left. The Toronado that held the last shipment of the cocaine was getting towelled off. He ran to the driver's door, pushing the lot boy to the rear. The Toronado started without protest. He slammed the car into drive and hit the gas.

The path to freedom had obstacles. Scrapneck saw someone pointing a gun at the Toronado as he picked up speed. A bullet shattered the driver's side glass of the Toronado, a second bullet shattered the strange wraparound rear window. *Almost there!* Scrapneck heard a third bullet hit the sheet metal of the Toronado. He was wondering where the fourth one would hit when the purple Camaro screeched to a halt outside, passenger-side facing the opening to the shop. Scrapneck hit the gas for his escape. He knew his mass would easily win.

Scrapneck was almost on top of the Camaro when Heather Price decided to say hello. The Camaro's passenger door flung open to its widest detent. It was the ball of fiery red light that came from her eyes, mouth, and the rest of her body that first got his attention, followed by a scream that came from a place he never wanted to visit. He hit the brakes hard. The Toronado skidded into the floor hoist at the last stall on the right, narrowly missing the mechanic who was working on the car above. Scrapneck's head slammed into the steering wheel on impact. He was dazed, bloodied, and still trying to escape. He pushed with all his might against the jammed driver door. That's when he heard the groan.

The groan came from the undercarriage of a midnight blue '79 Lincoln Continental. It teetered on the top of the hoist that he had just slammed into. Scrapneck watched as the rear arms of the hoist buckled. The last thing he saw was the Continental logo coming straight for his head.

JUNE 26, 1985
1:15 P.M.

Dick Loeb wondered what all the fuss was about. The front of the Commonwealth lot was packed with police cars, a tow truck, and even a beat-up Buick that must have been from the wholesale row. There was even a CKND van parked in the mix. *Shit, that's almost a Sandra Lewis.* He parked his Grand Wagoneer on Portage Avenue. He walked around the police cars into the showroom.

The scene inside was anything but car dealer. There were plenty of people in the various cubicles and offices, though few of them were employees. Some of the cops were using the hood of a Cherokee in the showroom as an impromptu desk. Paper coffee cups were leaving rings on the paintwork. He was going to say something when Lisa Bentley grabbed him. She had been crying so hard, it looked like her face had melted.

"Oh my god! Mr. Loeb! Oh my god! It's *terrible!*"

Loeb stared blankly. "Yes, Lisa. What's, what's going on?"

"I don't know, Mr. Loeb. All I know for sure is Mr. Scrapneck is dead!"

"Dead? *What?* Peter is *dead?*"

"Yes sir, he's in the shop. Oh my god. It's horrible!"

Loeb pushed past her. He swung open the door to the shop and saw the massive blue Lincoln, its nose pointing at the ceiling. The rear of the car had landed on the front seat portion of a green Toronado. The Toronado must have been supporting most of the Lincoln's weight; its front suspension looked like it had completely collapsed. Loeb's entire contingent of mechanics, lot boys, and dealership staff were standing about 20 feet back from the accident, a buffer that was being enforced with yellow police tape. Loeb assumed that the man taking flash pictures of the aftermath had to be with the police. He didn't think the press would be allowed in that close.

Loeb ducked under the police tape and headed towards the scene. One of the uniform cops tried to stop him. His weight propelled him towards the scene. He was almost there when another police officer stepped in front of him. He was in plainclothes, a badge on his belt, and had salt-and-pepper hair.

"I'm sorry, sir, I can't let you back there."

"You sure as hell can! I'm Dick Loeb! I own the place! What the hell happened? Who are you?"

"Sir, I'm Detective-Sergeant Milroy. Peter Scrapneck is your sales manager, right? I regret to inform you that he's deceased. He's in that green car over there. Mr. Scrapneck was also under investigation."

"Investigation? For what?"

"I'm not at liberty to say, sir. However, I do need to speak with you. Can I talk to you in your office when we're done here?"

"But, but, my, my dealership . . ."

"I'm sorry, sir. If you could, please . . ."

Loeb allowed Detective-Sergeant Milroy to manoeuvre him to the crime-scene tape, lifting it over their heads as they went. Once Loeb was out of the crime-scene area, the Detective-Sergeant returned to the scene. Loeb kept watching the going's-on. He sensed that someone was looking at him. He looked towards the open door of the shop. He had to keep looking, making sure his eyes weren't playing tricks on him. As the various tiers of public service moved back and forth in front of the door, he saw a woman sitting in the passenger seat of a two-door coupe, a car that Loeb couldn't place as to make or model. She looked familiar. There was one thing he couldn't understand. As he stared at her, it seemed as though her hair was floating, the way that hair floats in water.

Loeb backed up through the crowd of assembled staff. He made his way back to his office. He shimmied around his desk. He didn't know what had been said, understood, or discovered by the police. He did know that they would be looking closely, at Commonwealth, at Scrapneck, and at him. Definitely at him.

Loeb looked up at the buzzing Nash clock. He was still staring at it when the detective-sergeant tapped on the glass.

"Mr. Loeb? I'm ready for you now."

Loeb motioned him into the office.

CHAPTER FORTY-SEVEN

JUNE 30TH, 1985
5:45 P.M.

Steve Mahoney was wondering where it had gone. It wasn't the burgers that Diana was cooking on the Hibachi for the Canada Day long weekend. It wasn't the fresh Biddy bannock that Fiddler had brought. It certainly wasn't the over-the-top splashes of Drakkar Noir on Rick Scheer's person. The Saint Bee stink. It had taken the night off on McTavish Street.

Mahoney flipped through the pages of the story that he had been immersed in over the last few weeks. The *Sentinel's* lead story was about the mess at Commonwealth Motors, the untimely demise of Peter Scrapneck, and the arrest of Richard Loeb on multiple charges, thanks to a truckful of files found at Scrapneck's house in Southdale. Mahoney didn't understand much of the white-collar crime charges that Loeb had copped to, charges that apparently were pending for other Winnipeg businesses. There was a story about some guy named Ted Rogers, who was trying to renege on arrangements that he had made for acquiring rooftop leases from one of Loeb's shell companies. There was only one story that Mahoney was interested in. It was buried on page nine: "Death of accountant in Commonwealth Motors scandal probed."

Mahoney had just popped off the cap of a Black Label with his Bic lighter when he saw the red Wildcat pull into the driveway. He had told Detective-Sergeant Milroy about the little get-together, one that wouldn't be in a five-by-five closet with a telephone book. Milroy greeted the rest of the crew as he made his way to the open garage door. He had a bottle in his hand. It looked like scotch, the good kind that Mahoney never bought. He placed it on the workbench. He looked around the rest of the garage.

"So, I'm guessing that the only cups you got out here are Styrofoam or plastic."

"You guessed right," said Mahoney, as he looked at the bottle. It was a Glen-something. "What do you recommend?"

"I recommend fine crystal for this nectar. But, when in Rome . . ." Milroy chose the plastic. He poured healthy doubles into the cups. He raised his inferior vessel. "Here's looking at you, Tow-Job."

Mahoney gulped more than he should have. The burn was intense, but a better burn than any bottle of Silk Tassel. He coughed before he spoke. "Uh . . . yeah. Smooth."

"It is if you sip it, Tow-Job. If you sip it."

"Are you ever going to stop calling me that?"

Milroy took a healthy pull of the whisky, a burn he clearly was used to and enjoyed. "I guess I should, you being out of a job and all. Any feelers out there?"

"Nothing yet," said Mahoney. "That Terry Balkan bullshit is still haunting me."

"That's too bad. Of course, if you were working for the city . . ."

Mahoney's ears perked up. "Say again?"

"I talked to my buddy at the police garage. You've got your Red Seal, right?"

"Since 1975."

Milroy took another sip. "Then you should go talk to him Tuesday. Name's Oystreck. He's a good guy. Do the work, he leaves you alone. I think you get cost-plus-ten on parts too."

Mahoney smiled. "That'll come in handy."

"And I think we can prove that this Scraphead had something to do with that Price girl."

You mean woman. "Yeah, what you find?"

"Went and checked the clothes she was wearing," said Milroy. "Didn't think we'd find any fibres or anything after the river, but we did find something."

Mahoney took a sip from his cup. "What?"

Milroy gulped the last of the pour from his cup. "Her jeans were men's, a 36 waist. Same as Scrapyard."

Mahoney grinned. "Shit. She'd have to hold those up with one hand to keep them from falling off." He glanced at the Camaro to see if Heather was listening in. He couldn't see her, but he knew that she was. He hoped that she was smiling.

Milroy snapped his fingers. "Shit, I almost forgot. I got something in the car for you." He walked back to his Buick

311

with his cup. He came back to the garage with something in a brown paper bag. "You got a VCR, right?"

"Yeah. Why, is that an Electric Blue?"

"I wish," said Milroy. "No porno, but still an interesting watch. It's the video that the CKND guy shot. I didn't even know he was actually recording."

Mahoney peeked in the bag. "I'll take a look at it. Thanks. And thanks for the job tip."

"You're welcome. Now, *Steve*. Whose dick do I gotta suck to get a hamburger in this joint?"

"Follow me," said Mahoney. He brought him over to the Hibachi for more formal introductions.

JULY 1, 1985
12:22 A.M.

Mahoney couldn't sleep. Diana had turned in around 11:30, right after the rest of the group had left. He slowly lifted her arm off as he left the bed. He headed for the living room.

The VCR needed a good cleaning; it took a good 20 seconds for the tracking fuzz to even itself out. The tape was the last commercial that Peter Scrapneck would ever do for Commonwealth Motors, a commercial that would never air. Mahoney turned the volume down to nothing. What he needed to see wasn't in need of a soundtrack.

Mahoney fast-forwarded through most of the commercial, past the flustered reactions of Scrapneck as the cars rolled past. Then it was time for the Hot Rod. Mahoney could see that Scrapneck was looking at someone — someone who was sitting in the passenger seat of the Camaro. Mahoney knew who it was; he had seen and heard the whole thing, including the fiery explosion that had given Scrapneck a 5,000-pound headache. He watched. He rewound. He used the slow-motion function. Heather Price was nowhere to be seen, or heard. She wasn't on the videotape, just like the audio cassette from Diana's mini blaster. When they had played back the cassette from the garage interview, the only voices heard were those of the living.

Mahoney scooped up his clothes from the living room couch and got dressed. He headed outside to the garage. The fluorescent light tubes did their weird warmup over the Hot Rod. Heather Price was waiting for him.

"Hey," she said. She was sitting in the driver's seat, her arms crossed and resting on the top of the driver's side door.

"Hey." Mahoney didn't know exactly what to say. For some reason, he didn't think there was much left to say at all.

"You want to go for a ride?"

"I'd love to."

Ten minutes later, Mahoney, Heather, and the Hot Rod were heading north on Main Street. He didn't have to ask her where to go. He just knew. He slowed for the exit to the North Main boat launch. The place was quiet. There were no fire engines, no police cruisers, no weeping grads watching them from the *Paddlewheel Queen*. It was just Mahoney and Heather.

She opened her door. She held up Peter Scrapneck's acid-washed jeans as she exited the Camaro. There was a sliver of moon out that night. Mahoney didn't know what kind.

Heather looked at Mahoney. "Thank you, Steve. I couldn't have gotten here without you."

Mahoney walked around the car to her. He knew this was goodbye. He fumbled his words like a high-school junior. "So, umm . . . do you like, know where you're umm . . ."

"Going? No, but something tells me it's going to be okay."

"That's good."

"Steve?"

"Yes."

"There is one more thing."

"What's that?"

Heather snapped her fingers. The Supertuner in the Hot Rod came to life, playing Diana's mix tape. A Corey Hart song was just ending. A silent pause. A new song began, one that both of them had heard before. She looked at Mahoney with her otherworldly greens.

"Will you dance with me?"

Mahoney moved in to meet her. She placed his hands on her hips and whispered in his ear.

"Dance like we're in grade nine, so you can hold my pants up."

"No problem." He put his hands around her, gripping the fabric over her hips.

The song was "Cry" by Godley and Creme. There was the synthesized organ, the strong guitar riff, and the substantial bass. Mahoney had to admit, it sounded pretty great.

MAHONEY'S CAMARO MIXED TAPE

Songs from the book, and the background
Volume setting: Eleven

"Hollywood" — Streetheart

"Back in the Saddle" — Aerosmith

"Bust the TV" — The Pumps

"Strange Animal" — Gowan

"Sunglasses at Night" — Corey Hart

"Never Surrender" — Corey Hart

"I Want to Know What Love Is" — Foreigner

"Dirty White Boy" — Foreigner

"Cry" — Godley and Crème

"I'm on Fire" — Bruce Springsteen

"Girls Just Want to Have Fun" — Cyndi Lauper

"Doesn't Really Matter" — Platinum Blonde

"Can't You Hear Me Knocking" — The Rolling Stones

"Curried Soul" — Moe Koffman

"Time Has Come Today" — The Chambers Brothers

"In-A-Gadda-Da-Vida" — Iron Butterfly

"Legend of the U.S.S. Titanic" — Jaime Brockett

"30 Days in The Hole" — Humble Pie

"Mama Let Him Play" — Doucette

"For Those About to Rock (We Salute You)" — AC/DC

"Red Barchetta" — Rush

"Good Girls Don't" — The Knack

"Let It Go" — Def Leppard

"Everybody Wants You" — Billy Squier

"Action" — Streetheart

"Turn It Loud" — Headpins

"Blackout" — Scorpions

"When I'm With You" — Sheriff

"Follow Your Heart" — Triumph

"Rainy Day People" — Gordon Lightfoot

"Carefree Highway" — Gordon Lightfoot

"Blinded by The Light" — Manfred Mann's Earth Band

"Breaking the Law" — Judas Priest